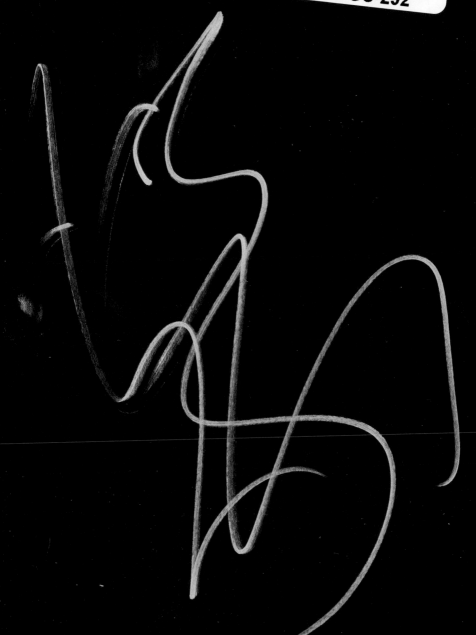

CATHERINE CAVENDISH

DARK OBSERVATION

This is a **FLAME TREE PRESS** book

Text copyright © 2022 Catherine Cavendish

FLAME TREE PRESS
6 Melbray Mews, London, SW6 3NS, UK
flametreepress.com

US sales, distribution and warehouse:
Simon & Schuster
simonandschuster.biz

UK distribution and warehouse:
Marston Book Services Ltd
marston.co.uk

Publisher's Note: This is a work of fiction. Names, characters, places, and
incidents are a product of the author's imagination. Locales and public names
are sometimes used for atmospheric purposes. Any resemblance to actual
people, living or dead, or to businesses, companies, events, institutions, or
locales is completely coincidental.

Thanks to the Flame Tree Press team.

The cover is created by Flame Tree Studio with
thanks to Nik Keevil and Shutterstock.com.
The font families used are Avenir and Bembo.

Flame Tree Press is an imprint of Flame Tree Publishing Ltd

flametreepublishing.com

A copy of the CIP data for this book is available from the British Library
and the Library of Congress.

HB ISBN: 978-1-78758-683-3
PB ISBN: 978-1-78758-681-9
ebook ISBN: 978-1-78758-684-0

Printed and bound in Great Britain by Clays Ltd, Elcograf S.p.A

CATHERINE CAVENDISH

DARK OBSERVATION

FLAME TREE PRESS
London & New York

For Colin, as always,
and in loving memory of
Doris May Buttery
(October 23rd 1920–March 13th 2018)
who served as a Staff Sergeant in the ATS 1939–1945
There's a lot of you in Vi, Mum.

PART ONE
HEATHER
PRESENT DAY

CHAPTER ONE

The house hadn't changed. But then I suppose five years isn't long in the scheme of things. The city hadn't either. Salisbury. Such a historic place, with its iconic cathedral, picture-postcard river and uncanny ability to lead you into believing you had walked miles, only to discover you were back where you started. Wonder if Lewis Carroll ever drew inspiration from it.

As for me, I had moved away from my home city of Birmingham and spent the intervening years working in Vienna for NATO until my contract finished. Now I was back, but wished it wasn't for this reason.

I was still gazing vacantly up at the windows when the front door opened and my mother, dressed in a smart black skirt suit, emerged into the spring sunlight.

"Come on in, Heather. It's too chilly to be standing outside."

"I was just remembering."

"Yes, I expect we'll do quite a lot of that in the days to come."

She descended the shallow step and, as if I was still her little six-year-old girl, took my hand and led me over the threshold into the familiar lavender-and-polish warmth of my grandmother's small house. Mum closed the door behind me, and its lock engaged with a small but decisive click.

The place felt empty and I shivered.

"It *is* a bit chilly in here. The heating's been off since they took your gran into hospital."

I didn't tell Mum that it wasn't that kind of chill. Gran would have understood. She would have got it. The coldness in her house at that moment wasn't anything to do with temperature. In fact, I knew if there had been a thermometer handy, it would in all probability have registered a pleasant ambient sixty-five or seventy plus on the Fahrenheit scale. This was a different kind of cold entirely. One born of emptiness and darkness. Out of the corner of my eye, I saw shapes move. Shadows where there were no dark corners. A feeling of being watched, but by something that wasn't there.

I couldn't explain it. Mum wouldn't understand. But Gran would have.

At that moment, I missed her more than ever. I wasn't ready for her to die.

Mum disappeared off to the kitchen, muttering something about making a cup of tea. I sat back in a comfy chair and tried to ignore the distractions that vied for my attention. I closed my eyes against them and let my mind drift back. To the time I first realized my gran understood far more than I could ever imagine.

* * *

It had happened a few years earlier – before my move to Vienna – on the morning of our full day in London. As we set off on our first exploration, Gran was unusually hesitant.

"I don't think this is such a good idea, Heather."

Her tone worried me. I had never known my gran to be so disconcerted. She was always such a strong woman. Even then, in her nineties, she might walk with the aid of a stick, but you always got the impression she could manage perfectly well without it and only used it to placate her daughter and me.

The trip to London had been my idea. A birthday present for Gran. Mum and I had been squirreling money away for a few years so that we could do something really special for her one day. If ever we were going to do it – and she was to be in a fit state to enjoy it – now was the time. A special long weekend in London, staying at Claridge's for three nights in a gloriously luxurious suite. A show in the West End, dinner in Michelin-starred restaurants, trips to some of my gran's old haunts from her childhood and during the war.

Today was no exception.

We had climbed out of the black taxicab outside the entrance to the Churchill War Rooms. As time had gone by, more and more secrets of those war years had gradually emerged, and we were surprised to learn how close Gran had actually been to the man himself. When I was a child, she had always described her war effort as being a typist, a lowly civil servant who happened to work in the Treasury. Then, one day, when she was satisfied she wouldn't be prosecuted under the Official Secrets Act, she got Mum and me together and told us what she really did. I always felt she was keeping something to herself though and now, as she hung back, staring around her, eyes wide and fearful, I felt I had almost caught a glimpse of what was scaring her.

I touched her arm, surprised to find she was trembling. "What is it, Gran? Did something awful happen here? We don't have to go in if you don't want to. I just – *we* thought that you might like to see where you used to work. The powerhouse where the big decisions were made and where you used to have your meetings with Churchill."

"I didn't have meetings with the PM. He summoned me from time to time and dictated letters to me. We chatted a little, that's all. I don't know where you got the idea we had meetings."

"Well, not meetings, then. But you did get to know him rather better than most people in this country."

"He was a great statesman and underneath all the bluster and bravado, a kind and thoughtful man. He was the greatest wartime leader this country has ever had. Oh, I know, some of his beliefs and ideas are anathema these days, but those were different times. People weren't as enlightened. It was a different world then and, without Winston, who knows where we would all be today."

"No one's arguing with you here, Mum," my mother said. "Come on, let's find a café and have a cup of tea. You'll feel better then."

"Don't treat me like a child, Constance."

Both Mum and I recoiled. I had never heard Gran speak like that. The angry woman in front of me was not the gran I had known all my life; the comforting presence who had cuddled me when my beloved cat died, who kissed away the pain when I fell over in the playground and who stoically stood by me when I announced to her and my mother that I thought I was gay. Mum had experienced real difficulty with that. She had always wanted to see me trot up the aisle, wearing a white floaty confection and trailing a long veil, dutifully carried by a couple of cherubic page boys. Me, of all people! I barely remember ever wearing a dress. As it happened, my attraction to my then-best friend turned out to be a one-off thing. We experimented and decided we both felt there was something missing on the physical side of things and went back to being just good friends. Even that petered out after we went our separate ways to universities at opposite ends of the country. I found a boyfriend, nothing serious, then another and that *was* serious. Serious enough to send me trotting up that aisle, albeit in a short oyster-colored dress with no veil and no trace of tulle.

Two years went by and it became clear that Jason wanted children. I discovered I didn't. And that was that. He is now happily married to wife number two, with three kids, two dogs and a hamster called Marigold. We send virtual Christmas cards each year.

Through this and all of life's ups and downs, Gran had been there for me. She had intervened whenever Mum and I had a row. She was the peacemaker. So to see her like this....

Gran must have seen the shock in our eyes. Her features softened. "I'm sorry, girls. Come on, let's go inside and see what they've done with the old place." She threaded her hands through Mum's and my arms, and I carried her walking stick. Old Gran was back.

"This entrance wasn't here in my day," Gran said as we made our way carefully down a flight of steps. "You had to go into the Treasury Building and make your way down from there. All very hush-hush and every door manned by an armed soldier or a marine."

We reached the bottom and Mum bought tickets. Then came the usual security processes of having our bags searched.

"Goodness," said Gran, "You'd think there was a war on." The security guard winked, and Mum and I exchanged smiles.

We followed a steady stream of people along a narrow corridor with cream-colored walls and a ceiling festooned with boxed-in pipework.

"Air-conditioning," Gran said, pointing upward. "I remember the noise from that. Awful. Used to keep us awake at night if we were sleeping in the Dock."

"The Dock?" I queried.

"It was below this level. When there was a real flap on, we sometimes had to work extra shifts and it was easier to keep us here, so we slept, ate and worked for days on end, barely seeing the daylight. That's why this was quite useful." She pointed up at a wall-mounted box containing a sign that read, *Fair*. "At least you could imagine what the weather was doing even if you couldn't see it. It gave you some sort of perspective."

The crowd was quite thick as we approached some of the key rooms. *There is to be no whistling or unnecessary noise in this passage,* proclaimed a notice stuck to a wall.

Gran paused, looked up at it and smiled. "The PM hated noise. He said it disturbed his concentration."

"I can understand that," I said. "When I'm working, I can't stand all the chatter around me in the office. I have to block it off or I make mistakes."

"That would never do," Gran said. "That's international security you're dealing with."

"And she's very good at it too, Mum." My mother was always my greatest fan.

Gran smiled at me and winked. "I know she is, Connie. I know she is."

Hearing Gran call Mum 'Connie' again reassured me. Her use of Mum's full name, Constance, had been bad news.

We peered in room after room. The displays had been recreated to give a real feel of what it must have looked like at the time. Even down to tiny details. Ashtrays. A half-smoked cigar (guess whose?). A wax model of Churchill on the telephone to the White House. Every room a revelation.

"Does it bring back memories, Gran?" I asked, noting a stray tear brimming over Gran's right eye and threatening to spill down her cheek.

She said nothing, merely nodded. We carried on, past more rooms, some numbered, others with names above the doors. From time to time, Gran stopped, and it was as if a film was replaying in her mind. She said little but it was clear she found the experience moving and, in some way, it transported her back over the years to the faraway days of World War II when she was just a young girl, barely out of her teens.

We turned a corner – and that's when everything changed.

She held me back. "It was down here. I remember. Down here and to the right."

"What was, Gran?"

She seemed not to hear me. Then, as if in a dream, she put one foot in front of the other and began to walk slowly down the corridor.

Mum and I followed a few steps behind. I whispered to my mother. "What is it? Did something happen here?"

My mother whispered back. "I have no idea."

The crowd had thinned out considerably. There really wasn't much of obvious interest down here and no signs had pointed to any room of note.

On and on we went until we were the only ones left, our footsteps echoing and the thrum of the other visitors fading into the background until we hit silence. A weird silence that felt heavy and unnatural, as if all the sound had somehow been sucked out of the atmosphere.

Gran stopped and faced the space between two doors. We caught up with her in a second and followed her gaze. There was nothing there.

She pointed a shaking finger at the wall. "It was here."

"What was?" Mum asked.

"The room. The room I met them in. At least – it was a difficult time and these people…. Sometimes you didn't know what was real and what they had put in your head. Especially…." Gran looked from one to the other of us and our expressions must have deterred her from carrying on. I'm guessing we looked as confused and disturbed as we felt.

"But sometimes it was here and sometimes it wasn't." Gran didn't seem to be talking to us anymore but to someone behind us. I even turned to see who it was, but there was no one there.

My mother tried again. "What was sometimes there, Mum?"

There was a hint of desperation in the look Gran gave us. "How can I ever explain it? You had to be there. You had to see what I saw…." Her voice faded and she lowered her hand. She continued to stare at the empty space as if doing so would somehow change it. I continued to stare too and, for a second, I fancied I saw something. A door. A number, but it was gone before I could fully register it. Gran stiffened. Maybe she saw it too.

She shook her head and rested both hands on her stick. "Come on, let's go. It was all so long ago. Maybe I've remembered it all wrong. I haven't thought about it for years."

The way she said it sounded as if she wished she hadn't thought about it now either. I began to regret, with all my heart, bringing her here. The silence seemed to settle all around us as if we were wearing it, like a cloak. I wondered if Mum felt it as I did.

I took Gran's free arm and she patted my hand. "Ignore me, Heather. Just the ramblings of an old woman with a faulty memory. Heavens, in those days, I was younger than you are now."

At that moment, she stiffened. Her cheeks blanched as she stared straight ahead. I followed her gaze. Mum stopped, turned and looked at us, bemused, but I swear I saw it too. Two figures, shadowy, indistinct, but distinctly human. One male and one female. They were both tall and, as they moved away from us, they left an invisible trail, an atmosphere of pure evil. I could taste it. A foulness, like some rancid meat. I shivered. Gran staggered. Mum and I caught her seconds before she fainted.

People parted to let us through. Murmurs of concern, whispers, fingers pointing, some clearly relishing the spectacle of a middle-aged woman and a younger version half-carrying a much older woman along the corridor. No one offered to help.

We made it to the café, which was heaving, but, mercifully, two good Samaritans, in the form of a couple of young women who looked and sounded as if they might be foreign students, immediately vacated a table so we could steer Gran into a seat. One offered to fetch her a glass of water and I nodded my thanks.

A security guard came over at that point, offering to call an ambulance. Mum declined, saying she was sure Gran simply needed a few moments – that she was probably dehydrated from not drinking enough water that day.

The guard moved off, after extracting a promise from us that we would call on him if Gran didn't rally in the next five minutes.

My heart went out to her as she sat there, slumped over, floppy as a rag doll, disoriented, not knowing where she was and probably not caring. The water arrived. I thanked the girl, who smiled and murmured her best wishes for Gran's speedy recovery. Gran managed to sip some water, coughed, drank some more and gradually the roses began to bloom once more in her cheeks.

Conversation returned to a more normal pitch as people got back on with their own lives, the drama from our quarter now safely contained.

"I'm so sorry, dears," Gran said. "I feel much better now. I don't know what came over me. It was as if…as if…." She shook her head and didn't continue.

"When you've drunk your water, I think we'd better head back to the hotel," Mum said, and I agreed.

"What a spectacle I've made of myself," Gran said. "I feel so stupid."

"Don't be daft, Gran. You've probably made their day. Now they have something to tell their kids, boyfriends, husbands, wives or whatever. Don't beat yourself up about it."

Gran smiled at me and the years fell away. She had the smile of a sixteen-year-old, so few wrinkles for someone of her advanced years. The smile faded, but she continued to look at me. Hard. So hard, it became uncomfortable. I wanted to ask her to stop but, after what she had been through, I hadn't the heart.

"You saw them, didn't you?"

I hadn't expected the question and I certainly wasn't prepared enough to lie, even if I wanted to. "I saw...something."

Mum looked from one to the other of us. "What's going on? What did you see? I didn't see anything."

"To be fair," I said, "you weren't looking where we were. Down the corridor. Right before Gran fainted. Two shadowy figures. A man and woman. I'm sure of it. I got the impression they were dressed as they would have been in the 1940s, but there was something wrong about them. Oh, I don't mean the obvious – that they shouldn't have been there – I mean that.... That there was something...." I couldn't put it into words and gave Gran a pleading look.

"It's all right, Heather," she said. "They seemed not of this world, but of one so far removed from us as to be unimaginable."

"Good grief," Mum said. "You're sounding like *The Twilight Zone.*"

"This isn't science fiction, Mum. This was real. I have never felt what I did then. As if I was in the presence of something ancient and evil." *Now*, I had put it into words. And they were well-chosen.

Gran nodded her agreement. "I'm glad you didn't see it, Connie. I truly am. I wish Heather hadn't either. I had hoped she would be spared...."

She wouldn't be drawn on what she meant by that, merely insisting she was tired.

*   *   *

That marked the end of our activities for the day. We caught a cab back to Claridge's, stayed in our suite, ordered up room service and enjoyed the decadence of five-star luxury service and attention. Gran perked up and became her old self. She wallowed in the oversized bath, perfumed with deliciously scented bath oil, and declared it the most exotic experience she could remember.

"So relaxing. I could feel all the aches and pains drifting away from my joints. Of course, as soon as I struggled to my feet again, it all came back but, oh, it was sheer unadulterated self-indulgence. Thank you both so much. This has been the best birthday present I've ever had. Perfect in every way."

The strange experience in the Cabinet War Rooms melted away. Later that evening, we even persuaded Gran to join us for a cocktail down in the Fumoir – the hotel's elegant, bijou bar, dimly lit and offering privacy along with a chance to fully unwind. We drank Brandy Alexanders. Delicious.

"John Lennon's favorite tipple," Mum said.

Strange, I thought, that the self-proclaimed 'Working Class Hero' should enjoy something so lavish and rich, but then he was a millionaire many times over, so why not? "I always imagined him drinking a pint of bitter with his mates down at a pub in Scotland Road in Liverpool, or somewhere," I said.

"That would have been Ringo," Mum said. "He grew up in Scotland Road. With Cilla Black. Of course, she was just plain Priscilla White then."

"I used to love Bing Crosby," Gran said. By now her third Brandy Alexander was taking effect. "He had beautiful blue eyes." She leaned closer to me. "A bit like that waiter over there."

She indicated a young man who had served our latest round of drinks. He was certainly good-looking.

Gran sighed. "Ah, now if I was fifty years younger…."

"I think you mean sixty," Mum said, and we all started giggling like schoolgirls. The waiter must have cottoned on and he smiled over at us. I expect he was used to being admired by female guests – maybe even a few male ones too.

Eventually we made our way, a little unsteadily in Gran's case, to the elevator and back to our suite, where we found the beds turned down and complimentary slippers placed on linen towels on the floor next to each one. Mum and I changed into Claridge's fluffy dressing gowns while Gran declared herself too sleepy to stay up any longer. She retired to her room.

Mum and I sat in the living area and turned on the TV. I cast my eyes around the suite. "I could move in here," I said.

"Me too. Imagine having so much money you could do just that."

"I reckon this suite is as big as my flat anyway," I said.

"At least. Fancy a nightcap?" She opened the drinks fridge and extracted two single-serve bottles of chilled champagne. Goodness alone knew how much our final bill would come to, but who cared? For once, we were living like queens.

"Go on then," I said, and Mum poured.

★　★　★

The next day, Gran needed a couple of aspirin, but armed with those and some strong, delicious coffee, she was ready for another adventure.

"Where to today, Gran?" I asked.

"Well, I would like to go back to Turnham Green, where I grew up. Oh, I know the house isn't there, but they must have redeveloped it all by now. It would be interesting to see what they've done with it."

"Tube or cab?" I asked.

We settled on the Tube. Yesterday's extravagances needed reining in a little today.

Coming out of Turnham Green station, Gran did the full 360-degree scan.

"Well, Gran? Do you recognize it?"

"Yes and no. I would know where I was but…. Let's walk a bit. I'll take you in the direction of the old street and see what we can find."

We spent a pleasant hour in which Gran discovered the park she used to play in and remarked more than once on how much cleaner it all looked. Greener too. "The shops are more colorful, and they sell different things. There are more cafés too. More variety."

"So, do you think you could live here again?" I asked.

Gran shook her head. "Gracious, no. I left London many years ago. I always carry it with me. Here." She touched her chest. "But it's not my home anymore. I've been away far too long. No, I'm perfectly happy in Salisbury. That's where my friends are. And you and your mum come and visit me as often as you can. That's all I need."

There was a wistfulness in her voice which was at odds with the words she spoke. Mum caught it too. I could tell by the way she looked at me and raised her eyebrows slightly.

We went for a coffee so Gran could have a rest before we moved on to our next port of call. Back on the Tube. This time to Westminster and two more of Gran's old stomping grounds.

*　　*　　*

Boscawen Walk was only a twenty-minute stroll away from the Treasury. That's what Gran said anyway. The only problem was we couldn't find it.

"But I know it was down here," she insisted. "I know, except…."

"Except what, Gran?" I asked. She shook her head. "No, go on, you were saying. Except?"

"They must have demolished it completely. It did take quite a hammering in the Blitz. They probably thought it wasn't worth saving and started again. "I remember my last visit…." Her voice tailed off. "I don't remember these houses. They look quite new, don't they?"

The elegant town houses didn't look particularly new to me. They blended in well with all the other Georgian architecture around but, of course, an architect could have designed it that way.

"I expect you're right," my mother said and motioned me not to challenge her.

I shut my mouth.

"What is this street called?" Gran asked and I peered upward, looking for a sign on a wall that might tell us.

I found it. "Bottomley Way."

Gran nodded, a slight smile twitching the corners of her lips. "Ah yes. It would be."

I had no idea what she meant by that, but let it go.

"I'll take you to Quaker Terrace instead," Gran announced and strode off, stick barely needed. Mum and I hurried after her.

She had more luck this time. At least she found the road. We wandered along it while she peered at all the numbers.

"There it is. Number Nineteen." Gran stood, triumphantly smiling. "That's where I used to live after we left Boscawen Walk. Of course, Tilly never remembered...." She appeared to abandon the rest of that memory as she peered at the building in front of her.

The house was neat and trim. Freshly decorated, it looked like the current owners had done their best to preserve the integrity and history of the place while their neighbors had opted for a more modern approach. For them, UPVC double glazing had done away with the need for painted window frames. Neat pocket handkerchief-sized front gardens had given way to tarmac and paving to provide off-road parking. Number Nineteen by contrast looked as if it had escaped from a book on life just after the war. It was, if anything, too authentic.

"Maybe it's one of those National Trust houses," Mum said. "You know, like Forthlin Road in Liverpool. Just a normal house restored to how it used to be. Forthlin Road is restored to how it was when Paul McCartney grew up there in the Forties and Fifties."

Mum could be right, but I had a strange and not particularly comfortable feeling about Nineteen Quaker Terrace. I didn't know why but I would be glad when Gran had had enough of this particular wander down Memory Lane. I had to keep reminding myself that this trip was all about *her* and the places *she* wanted to visit, things *she* wanted to do.

She had a curious look on her face, as if something of what I felt was inside her too. I was about to remark on it when the front door opened.

Gran did a sort of double take. She gave a little cry. The woman on the doorstep stared straight at her but seemed not to see her. I couldn't take my eyes off her. She wore her gray hair in an old-fashioned bun and her skirt reached well below her knees. Plaid slippers shod her feet and her pale blue blouse was fastened at her neck with a plain silver brooch. She would have looked right at home in *Mrs. Miniver*, but certainly not here, in twenty-first-century London.

By my side, I knew Mum was staring as I was. Only Gran seemed capable of speech.

"Mrs. Sinclair. But you can't be."

"Yes?" The woman didn't smile, and her voice seemed to come from far away. All around us, the air stilled, the noise of traffic dulled, and around the woman, a sort of shimmering served to fray the edges of what I was seeing. I was reminded of old televisions I had seen in vintage films, when the reception would suffer from interference and the picture would fade out.

As we stood there, the woman on the doorstep became less and less distinct until she too faded from sight and we were left staring at the closed door of a house that now seemed quite neglected in between its neighbors. A chilly breeze blew across our faces. An unnatural breeze, emanating from the house itself. A distinctive smell of beeswax wafted through it, reminding me of stately homes I had visited.

The noise of the traffic resumed as if someone had turned the volume back up.

Gran stirred. "It isn't. It isn't all right at all." She seemed to be talking to someone neither Mum nor I could see. "No, George. I won't. Not yet. It isn't time."

My mother took hold of Gran's arm. "Come on, Mum. Let's get you back to Claridge's. We'll take a cab."

She signaled to me, forcing me out of my stupor, and I dashed to the end of the terrace to hail a taxi.

★   ★   ★

The journey back to Claridge's was a silent one, each of us buried in our own troubled and confused thoughts. For me, I couldn't explain anything of what I had just witnessed. All I knew was that it had happened.

Gran was quiet for the rest of the day and went to bed early, leaving Mum and me to mull over the woman in Quaker Terrace.

"Mrs. Sinclair," I said. "That's what Gran called her. Does that name mean anything to you?"

Mum shook her head. "I don't remember your gran ever mentioning her. Everything about her was so strange. And that house...."

"As if we were tapping into an old memory," I said.

"That's it exactly. Is that sort of thing possible? I don't think I've ever heard of it."

"Haven't a clue, but whether it is or isn't, it certainly seems it may have happened to us. Either that or some simultaneous hallucination."

We compared notes, going over every detail. There was no doubt we had both seen the exact same phenomenon and we could only assume, from her behavior, that Gran had too. "The person she seemed to be talking to right before we got the taxi," I said. "George. Could that be her brother? The one who died during the war?"

"Could well be," Mum said. "I didn't like the way she seemed to be fending him off. Telling him it wasn't time yet. You hear of people seeing loved ones just before they pass away...."

"Don't get upset, Mum. She could have been saying it wasn't time to leave Quaker Terrace yet or...or it wasn't time to share something with us. There are lots of possibilities."

I could tell by the way Mum looked at me that she wasn't convinced. Neither was I.

★ ★ ★

The following morning, you wouldn't have known anything untoward had happened. Gran was back to her usual self and ready for a trip to Harrods and Liberty's.

"I've never been able to afford to shop there, but I thought I might treat myself. Maybe a nice scarf, or a mug with Harrods' name on it. Your granddad bought me one from there once, but it got broken years ago. I always meant to replace it."

Granddad Scott. I never knew him. He and Gran had met around the time the war ended. He had even helped her get a job at the insurance office where he worked. They had to pretend there was nothing going on as there was a strict policy against employees fraternizing. Calling each other 'Mr. Scott' and 'Miss Harrington' at work must have felt distinctly odd, although Gran always insisted that was just the way things were and she never really thought about it. Calling the boss 'sir' would have stuck in my craw, but again, times were different then. Much more formal.

Of course, the inevitable happened and someone saw them in the queue for the cinema one evening. Their relationship came to the attention of the branch manager, who summoned them into his office and gave them an ultimatum. Either one of them left or they could both go. If Granddad had volunteered to leave, he would almost certainly have been given a transfer to another branch. They weren't so accommodating to their female staff. Gran and Granddad promptly announced they were getting married and Gran left work at the end of the month. Granddad was promoted to branch manager, necessitating a move from Cheltenham to Salisbury. Soon, Mum came along, and Gran became the traditional Fifties housewife and mother – a role she performed successfully until Mum herself left home at the age of eighteen to pursue a life in London.

Granddad – a lifelong heavy smoker – succumbed to lung cancer and passed away in the Seventies. He was only in his mid-fifties. Suddenly, Gran found herself 'financially embarrassed', as she put it. She managed to get a job in a bank, where her secretarial skills were soon polished back up and she fitted right in.

Mum came home from London and lived with Gran in Salisbury. Her salary as an office supervisor and then manager of the general office of a financial services company helped pay the bills until she met Dad, moved to Birmingham and a few years later, I came along. Like her, I was destined to be an only child. That only bothered me for the first sixteen years of my life.

*   *   *

Let loose in Harrods, Gran was like a young girl, marveling at all the ridiculously overpriced clothes and shoes and trying out the perfumes I was quite sure were far cheaper almost anywhere else.

Mum and I followed in her wake, delighted to see her so happy again.

"She seems none the worse for yesterday," I said to Mum as Gran trotted off in search of that replacement mug. She found what she was looking for and brandished it, a smile lighting up her face from ear to ear. I waved back.

"You'd think it had never happened, wouldn't you?" Mum said. "I asked her about it this morning and she changed the subject. But...."

"But what, Mum?"

Mum blinked a couple of times. She seemed to be unsure whether to tell me any more and it reminded me of so many half-started conversations over the years.

"It's just that...I've always felt your gran was keeping something from me. Something that happened during the war. Oh, I know that's not so unusual. Lots of people prefer not to recall those years, but with your gran, I feel it's because she doesn't trust her own memories, however crazy that must sound. Like yesterday. She can chatter away quite happily, remembering this and that and then, all of a sudden it's as if she has a mental block, or isn't sure whether what she's saying actually happened or if she imagined it. I've tried probing her for more information, but she clams up, changes the subject and that's that."

"Best let it lie then," I said, hoping I sounded more convinced than I felt.

"I suppose we must."

Gran finished paying for her mug and rejoined us. "Goodness, *that* was expensive. I think I'll forget about buying a scarf. I'll probably need to take out a bank loan."

"That's Harrods for you, Mum. Ready for lunch at Fortnum and Mason now?"

It was our last day and our final splurge. The fact we would both be paying for this for the next year didn't matter. Gran was enjoying herself. My new job at the UN would help. It was a massive step up for me. The only drawback was having to leave Mum and Gran, but I would only be a few hours away by plane and Vienna was hardly the back of beyond.

★   ★   ★

Gran enjoyed her lunch, then declared she needed to have a lie down to sleep it off, so we went back to the hotel. Mum was also feeling tired, so I took myself off for a walk around Mayfair's exclusive streets. The early autumn weather was still warm, sunny and bright, and I enjoyed mooching around, pleasing myself.

A few streets from Claridge's, I came across a couple who did what no one ever does in London. I had never met them, but they deliberately made eye contact with me. I gave them a half smile, which I regretted immediately. That was even more un-London-like and marked me out as a tourist for sure. Probably one who didn't belong in Mayfair.

There was something about this couple that raised the hairs on the back of my neck. If *I* didn't belong there, *they* certainly didn't. Once again, I was reminded of the woman at Nineteen Quaker Terrace. These two seemed cut out of her mold. Out of time.

I quickened my step and crossed over the street. When I looked back, they were gone. Goose bumps rose on my arms and I hurried on, anxious to put as much distance as possible between me and any possibility of bumping into them again.

Galleries and fashion houses vied for my attention. I looked in their windows at the fabulous displays of items I could never afford, and which had no prices on them. I tried to concentrate on what I was seeing but, all the time, kept casting quick glances over my shoulder, to make sure the strange couple weren't following me. In the end I gave up and returned to Claridge's, where the uniformed porters welcomed me, and life seemed reassuringly normal again.

I never told Gran or Mum what had happened and put it down to an overactive imagination. Looking back now, I wished I had mentioned it because, as it turned out, that would be the last holiday Mum and I took with Gran.

★   ★   ★

The last time I saw Gran was a couple of months before she passed away. We had such a strange conversation. By now, she was in a care home, following a stroke, which had left her paralyzed down her right side. She could still speak, but you had to listen carefully as she spoke out of one side of her mouth and what she said didn't always make total sense.

I remember our last conversation. I arrived in the afternoon, armed with a bunch of her favorite red carnations. She smiled her lopsided smile and I sat on a chair next to her bed.

As always, I took her left hand in mine.

"How are you, Gran?"

"Not too bad, dear. George came to see me today."

"You mean Uncle George? Your brother?"

"Yes. He *was* shot down. He told me. They lied you see. Another of their lies."

"I thought he was killed in a motorcycle accident and...Gran, who lied to you?"

"Those...people. George wasn't killed on that road. Someone else. Not him. His body. Crushed. We never saw him after.... He showed me. He was shot down. I saw his plane."

She was becoming agitated and her speech was more difficult. Certain letters – like 'p' – were hard for her to form. I wanted her to stop, but what she was saying had me gripped.

"Keep away from them, Heather. Promise me. Promise me."

"I will. But who are *they*, Gran?"

Her eyes had closed, and she had fallen asleep. It happened a lot in those days. One day, I reckoned, she would close her eyes and never awaken. I stayed another half hour but she slept on, her breathing steady and rhythmical. Her pulse strong.

CHAPTER TWO

Gran passed away at the age of ninety-nine. She never spoke to me about the strange things that had happened to her on our trip to London, and I didn't know whether to ask her about any of it. I came close many a time but couldn't find the right words somehow. In the end, as the months went by and I became absorbed in my new job, it seemed less and less important, especially as nothing else occurred. At least, not that I was aware of.

Until her stroke necessitated the move to a care home, everyone remarked on how well she looked, how fit and healthy, and they were right. Every day she would take herself off for her daily walk around the neighborhood, stopping to talk to people she knew, learning all the news and gossip. Every week, she and one or more of her friends would have lunch out, and she looked forward to those trips, refusing to be 'fetched and carried' by any of them, as she called it. She called the local taxi firm and they ferried her wherever she needed to go.

The lunches lessened as, inevitably, old age, infirmity and death took one friend after another away from her with increasing rapidity. Still she remained bright as a woman half her age – until the last of her contemporaries died. Then she seemed to not so much slide as hurtle downward, living in her memories. Not demented as such. She could still function perfectly well with everyday life, but she stopped wanting to leave the house, and the increasing likelihood that she might not be able to stay in her own home for much longer took its toll on Mum. She knew how much it would hurt Gran to leave the house she had lived in for fifty years. It was a blessing that, in the end, Gran's stroke took matters pretty much out of her hands.

We gave her a good send-off and there were far more people at her funeral than Gran had anticipated.

"There's no one left," she would say. "You'll not need caterers, that's for sure."

Well, she was wrong there. Thirty or more people crowded into Violet Scott's front room, noshing happily away on sausage rolls, pork pies, sandwiches with all manner of tempting fillings and an irresistible trifle so loaded with sherry, I hoped no one who ate it was planning to drive home.

One guest I was especially glad to see. Gran's wartime friend, Tilly. The old woman was wheeled in by a woman of similar age to Mum.

Mum was almost beside herself as she bent to take the older woman's wrinkled hand in hers. "Oh, my goodness, it's so wonderful you could come. It would have meant so much to my mother."

Bright eyes blinked behind metal-rimmed spectacles. "Lovely to see you too, Connie. I haven't seen you since...my goodness, your christening I believe."

"Well, if you will go off and live in Canada...." Mum laughed. "Heather, this is Tilly Layton. Oh no, I'm sorry, you *were* Layton."

Tilly's companion chimed in. "Montgomery. I'm her daughter, Sara. Dad passed away ten years ago." The woman's friendly smile and soft Canadian accent endeared her to me, and we exchanged greetings.

I took Tilly's proffered hand and she clasped mine, her grip tightening. The bright smile vanished and I was astonished to read fear in her eyes. "Heather. You look so much like her. Be careful. They *will* find you. They can twist reality until you don't know what to believe. They did it to me and they did far worse to your grandmother."

"Mom. Stop it!" Sara prized her mother's hands off mine. Tilly seemed to shrink in her wheelchair. She cast her eyes down. "I am so sorry about that," Sara said to Mum and me. "I'm afraid this journey has been a bit too much for her, but she insisted on coming. Her mind wanders a little these days. She's always talking about the war and her accounts are becoming more and more bizarre. I suppose we must accept it now she's getting so old and frail."

"I think it's amazing you've come all this way," I said to Tilly, and smiled at Sara. "Don't worry," I mouthed.

"Thank you," Sara whispered. They left a short while after. Tilly had fallen asleep.

The wake was a happy affair. Lots of sentences beginning, "Remember when..." followed by laughter at some long-forgotten event or chance remark of Gran's.

"I could never understand why she hated Clark Gable so much," Mum said. "If ever he came up on television, she would switch channels or leave the room. She positively detested him. I was nearly thirty before I saw *Gone with the Wind*. Mind you, I can't say I was all that impressed. It was pretty dated even then."

"Yes, that Clark Gable aversion of hers was odd," I added. "Most women of her generation used to swoon over him."

"She was loyal to Bing Crosby," one of her younger friends said. "I was a Sinatra girl, myself. A real bobby-soxer in my day."

After a couple of hours, they started to drift home. Mum and I cleared up and finished the wine with a toast.

"To Gran," I said. "The best."

Mum sighed and raised her glass. "One of a kind."

★　　★　　★

Tilly never made it back to Canada. She passed away in her sleep that night.

We helped Sara with her arrangements for shipping her mother's body back home. After we saw them off at the airport, it was time to help Mum clear out a lifetime's treasures. Every so often she would let out a little cry. "I haven't seen that in years. Who would have known she kept it?" This one punctuated by the vigorous waving of an old school photograph. Mum in old-fashioned National Health wire-framed glasses peering out somewhat disconsolately at the world, her school uniform slightly awry. "I must have been...seven or so at the time. Goodness."

A little later…. "Oh look at this, Heather." I set down the pile of old Christmas cards I was flicking through and wandered over to Mum, who looked up at me, tears brimming her eyes. A pair of small pink leather baby shoes lay in the palms of her hands. "They were mine." Her voice cracked and I put my arms around her.

"Then you must keep them, Mum."

She hesitated. "Perhaps for a little while."

She placed the little shoes carefully on top of her 'To be kept' pile and I knew that when it was my time to turn out my mother's belongings, there they would be, and I would probably do exactly as she had just done.

I returned to the settee opposite Mum and carried on going through the pile of stuff I had found at the back of the loft that morning. Here were old books, souvenirs of royal weddings, going back to that of Queen Elizabeth II and the suave and handsome Prince Philip, magazines celebrating the Coronation, births of the Queen's four children, a booklet anticipating the coronation that never happened – Edward VIII's. Fascinating stuff I had never seen before and which must have been languishing in the loft since she moved into that house all those years earlier when Granddad was still alive.

My 'To be kept' pile was fast growing out of control – all that historical memorabilia I simply couldn't throw out. Then I came to a worn and somewhat battered old photograph album. Others of Gran's had been bulging, photos slipping out from their moorings where once they had been tucked securely into photo corners, but this one might even be empty. How odd she would keep a tatty old album that had seen far better days, when it didn't contain anything. Except, it wasn't empty.

I opened the cover and the unfamiliar face commanded my attention.

Shot in monochrome, a striking woman stared out at me – her expression one of defiance. Her cheekbones were high and so pronounced they looked as if they could cut through paper. From what I could tell, her make-up was flawless, her lips probably a deep red, her eyebrows perfectly sculpted. Her eyes were striking; they seemed to bore into the viewer. Unusual eyes, dark, from what I could gauge, with large irises. Hers would have been a gaze that made you uncomfortable. Taken together, here was a glamorous – exotic even – woman, maybe of Mediterranean origin. The photograph showed head and shoulders only and her dress was up to her neck. It looked expensive – like something the Duchess of Windsor would have worn. There was a firm line to her jaw that spoke of a woman who knew her own mind. The whole impression was of timeless beauty but there was a cruelty to the set of her lips.

She reminded me of someone, and it took me a few minutes to realize who. My mind cast me back to the street in Mayfair and the couple who had unnerved me so much. This woman had the same look as the female. Hairs prickled the back of my neck. I read the inscription below out loud.

"Sandrine Maupas di Santiago."

Out of the corner of my eye I saw my mother jump. In a second, she crossed the floor and looked over my shoulder.

"Wherever did you find that?" Her voice was no more than a whisper, as if she was frightened of being heard. I dismissed the thought. Crazy.

"Upstairs, along with all this other stuff. Back of the loft." I flicked through the pages of the album. There was nothing else there. Hers was the only photograph. "Who is she...*was* she?" After all, the woman was unlikely to be alive now. She must have been older than Gran when this photograph was taken.

Mum snatched the album out of my hand and threw it into a black plastic sack, destined to be thrown out. She wiped her hands on her trousers, almost as if she was scrubbing them free of contamination. Her eyes were wild.

"What on earth's the matter, Mum?"

"She's no one you would ever want to meet, that's for sure. Your gran said she was the most evil woman she had ever encountered."

"If that was the case, why on earth would she have her photograph?"

Mum shook her head. "I have no idea. I've never seen that

before. But she told me about her once. It was back in the war."
She shuddered.

"What happened?"

"You really don't want to know."

"Oh, I really do. Especially now."

But Mum shook her head again and charged out of the room. I
heard the door of the cocktail cabinet in the dining room open and a
clink of bottles. Mum rarely drank. Only on social occasions. To be
indulging in a drop of the hard stuff in the middle of the day signified
a great deal. And I had to find out what.

I reached into the black bag, retrieved the album, and hid it inside
the Royal Wedding supplement published by *Picture Post*. As I touched
it, a shock tickled my fingers as if a posse of green ants had decided
to bite. I hesitated. Perhaps I should replace the album in the bag?
Mum would be back soon. I must decide. I grabbed the magazine and
concealed album, and raced upstairs to the room I was sleeping in. I
threw open my suitcase and dumped the lot in there, then returned the
case to the mostly empty wardrobe.

Mum had recovered herself a little by the time I came back
downstairs, but she seemed nervous.

"Sit down, Heather. I need to tell you something you didn't know
about your gran."

I sat like an obedient child, fearful of what was to come. Surely I
knew all there was to know about Gran. We had always been so close,
the three of us.

Mum moistened her lips. "You know, of course, that your gran
worked in the Cabinet War Rooms, handling all sorts of top-secret
documents. She couldn't even tell us that until a few years ago, but
while she was there, stuff happened. I mean, some seriously odd stuff
that she was never able to explain, and I certainly can't. One day, not
long after we came back from our London trip, she sat me down as I
am doing with you now, and she told me about it. I was waiting for
the right time to tell you, because I think you need to know. Maybe
you can fathom it out better than we could. Perhaps you can even find

some answers to all the conundrums that still remain. Now you've found that photograph – and God knows why she kept it – I can't keep this from you any longer. Be prepared, this is a strange story, and remember that this was wartime. The Blitz was at its height and London was being bombed relentlessly night after night. Your gran was younger than you are now and that's when she met Sandrine Maupas di Santiago."

PART TWO
VIOLET
CHISWICK, LONDON, 1941

CHAPTER THREE

Vi wrinkled her nose against the smell of human waste, concrete and brick dust and the stinging after-effects of the smoke that made her eyes water and burned the back of her throat. She coughed. All around her, rubble, smashed glass, people clambering over destroyed buildings in their desperate search for missing relatives, friends, neighbors and pets. Towering above her, half-ruined walls pointed jagged fingers toward the gray-shrouded March sky. Great cracks scythed their way haphazardly across the exposed masonry of any building left standing. Some looked like they could topple at any moment.

She stepped awkwardly over piles of smashed bricks. Here, somewhere, the ruins of her childhood home lay buried under the remains of its adjoining terrace. A piece of red cotton cloth fluttered as if trying to escape. It looked familiar and Vi bent carefully down, stretching her fingers toward it. She made a grab. A tearing sound and it ripped free. She clasped it in her hand, straightened herself and recognized it immediately. A fragment of bathroom curtain from the upper story of her home. She clutched it for a few moments, tears welling up in her eyes. Memories of a happy childhood in that now-devastated home flitted through her mind like a cinema news reel. She chided herself for her self-pity. It was only a bit of old curtain. She let it drop and it fluttered to the ground. At least she wasn't among the scared white faces, calling endlessly.

"Fred, where are you?"

"Marj! Marj. Are you there?"

"Smoky? Where are you, little cat? The bombs have gone now. It's safe to come out...."

A voice at her elbow made her jump. She turned to see Mrs. Johnson from Number Five, three doors down, dressed in her best Sunday coat, its navy blue wool streaked with dust.

"Terrible business, isn't it?"

"Dreadful," Vi replied, shoving her hands deep in the pockets of her dark gray coat.

"It's all gone. Everything. At least your parents were spared this." Her neighbor spread her hands. Tears fell from her eyes, but she didn't seem to notice. Her expression was bland, as if she no longer fully inhabited her body. She was speaking, but the words appeared to come from far away, somewhere disconnected from the rest of her. "They're staying with your sister, aren't they?"

Vi nodded. "In Cheltenham. Jerry's not interested in bombing there. At least not now anyway."

"He's got too much to do here in London first, hasn't he?" Mrs. Johnson gave a mirthless laugh and put her head in her hands. Vi settled her arm around the now-sobbing woman, who managed to find a mostly clean handkerchief in a pocket of her coat. She blew her nose and when she finally emerged from behind the white cloth her face was streaked. Vi realized she must look like that too. So much dust and ash flying around. The stench was growing worse too.

"One of the bombs must have fractured the sewer," she said.

Mrs. Johnson blew her nose again and heaved a sigh that seemed to emanate from the pit of her stomach. "Bound to happen. There'll be cholera next. Or typhoid, I daresay."

"Oh, surely not. Not in this day and age."

Mrs. Johnson gave her a disbelieving look and shrugged her shoulders. "I've heard it's broken out in other places. Coventry for one. Those poor blighters really got it. Razed to the ground, it is. There's nothing left of the city. Except the rats and cockroaches."

"Don't believe all you read, Mrs. Johnson. They say truth is the first casualty of war."

"Oh, I didn't get that from a newspaper. I heard it from Mr. Groves, the butcher, when I went for my meat ration.... Oh Gawd, *his* shop's gone now. Where am I going to get our meat from?"

"They'll make other arrangements. Don't worry about that."

"Course *you're* all right, aren't you?" The bitter tone in her voice wasn't characteristic of the woman who had babysat for her when she was much younger. Vi let it drop. Who wouldn't feel bitter in these circumstances? God knows, *she* certainly did. How her mother would take the news of this, she had no idea, and she would have to tell her today. Mother would be bound to hear of the latest night raid. Cheltenham was hardly the other end of the earth.

Mrs. Johnson wandered away, muttering to herself, leaving Vi alone once more with her thoughts and memories.

Presently she couldn't bear to stay there a moment longer. What was the point? A lifetime of memories gone in a barrage of bombs dropped by strangers. Little treasures stored up, old dolls she had played with and put away, forgotten, in the attic. All buried deep in the rubble beneath her feet, mangled, melted in the heat from flames that seemed to be still smoldering not far from where she stood. At least there was no smell of gas. Police, ARP wardens and soldiers mingled with the distraught former residents, sweeping up piles of window glass that glittered fleetingly as an uncertain sun attempted to peek from behind the cloud, only to deem it not worth the effort and disappear moments later.

Her heart full, Vi turned away and stepped carefully back onto the mangled street. In five minutes, she was back on the main road. Here too, buildings had been hit, rubble strewn over the road. Firemen directed a few hoses onto a former fashion store she used to shop in before the war and rationing meant that 'Make Do and Mend' became the order of the day. Nowadays, Vi wore her sensible suits for work. Her mother had employed her best needlework skills to convert pre-war dresses and coats into serviceable, even fashionable, day wear suitable for a shorthand typist working in the Treasury where the girls were expected to 'blend in'. Vi did as the others did. She alternated two matching jackets and skirts – one in gray and the other in navy – and wore plain white or cream blouses. Her hair was shorter than it had been before the war, styled professionally, and rested on her collar. Her shoes were hardwearing, comfortable black leather with low heels. Stockings presented their own challenges. More than once she had resorted to the now-popular trick of imitation. Gravy browning painted on the legs gave the impression of tan stockings, and using eyeliner to paint a line down the back of each leg created the illusion of a fashionable seam. Today, though, her legs were bare, and the cold draft of an early spring afternoon made her shiver. At least she wouldn't have too far to walk. The Underground was still running. She would take the Tube from Turnham Green station to St. James's Park and walk from there to the New Public Offices at Westminster. On the way, she could stop at a call box and telephone her parents. At least she would get *that* ordeal over with.

⋆   ⋆   ⋆

Vi found a seat on the train and let her mind drift.

She had taken digs nearer to work when the bombing started in earnest. Some nights it had been impossible to get home and sleeping in the air raid shelter near her office was an experience she grew to dread. Dark, musty, cold and damp, full of crying children and sobbing mothers. The communal buckets placed as discreetly as possible – surrounded by thin curtaining designed to protect the user's dignity but doing nothing to conceal the stench of their contents.

Tilly Layton had thrown her a lifeline. "Come and live at Mrs. Harris's. Twenty minutes' walk from work, your own room and she keeps a lovely, tidy house. One of the girls moved out last week and I know she'd be more than happy for you to take her place. Not too many rules, thank goodness. No men allowed, of course, and she serves tea at six thirty prompt. Breakfast is at eight, so if you're working through the night here, you'll have breakfast when your body thinks it's suppertime – or is it the other way around? But she's not a bad old stick. Kind-hearted. The rent's cheap too."

"How many lodgers does she have?"

"There should be three of us. It's a four-bedroomed terraced house. Quite smart and she has a girl who comes in to help with cleaning, washing and such like."

Vi counted the stations as they stopped at each. Only two more to go. She crossed her ankles. That damned draft was really cutting on her bare legs. They felt quite numb. Her mind drifted once more, back to Tilly's strange expression when she said, "To be honest, I'd appreciate you being there. The other girl's a bit...well...odd, I suppose. She has a fancy name. Sandrine Maupas di Santiago."

"Good grief! Not British, then?"

"I'm not sure where she comes from but, no, her accent sounds Spanish or Italian. Maybe Portuguese. Oh, I don't know, but I've written in my MO diary about her."

"MO?"

"Mass Observation. It's a nationwide project, started a few years back. It's for national archives so that people in the future will know how their ancestors really lived. The organizers send us questionnaires – things we're supposed to focus on in our observations. We then report what we see, hear and so on. Our impressions of what's going on. And we have to be really detailed. It's not enough to say you took a picnic to Regent's Park, for example. No, you must say exactly what went into the picnic. Right down to the flavor of jam in your sandwiches – and whether you used white or brown bread, butter or margarine."

"Sounds interesting."

"Oh, it is. You should volunteer. It's all confidential. *They* know your real name of course but you submit your reports under an alias. Mine's Dolly, 21."

Vi found herself smiling. 'Dolly' suited the lively blonde with the bouncing curls, bright blue eyes and permanent happy smile. Nothing seemed to faze Tilly.

So, Vi had moved in. Just a week earlier. Mrs. Harris showed her into a room with chintzy wallpaper, a serviceable Edwardian dressing table with matching wardrobe and bed and the obligatory heavy blackout curtains which served to dampen any illusion of femininity. A ewer and washbasin stood on a stand in a corner of the room. "It's lovely, thank you, Mrs. Harris."

Her new landlady had beamed at her. She must have been quite a good-looking girl in her day and was now, Vi gauged, somewhere in her sixties.

"You get yourself settled in and pop downstairs when you're ready. Tea's at six thirty." The implied 'don't be late' never left her lips and she shut the door behind her, leaving Vi to unpack.

Now, as Vi reflected on the contents of that small suitcase, she felt a sharp pang of regret. She had brought so little with her. Clothes mostly. There had always been the knowledge that she could go home at any time. That's why she had left so much behind and only taken what she needed to her former digs. If only she had packed the large trunk full of her stuff, but that, along with the rest of her belongings, lay strewn all over Durrington Terrace, destined to be bulldozed away when they finally managed to clear the street.

★   ★   ★

The train arrived at her stop and Vi left the station to begin her walk to the New Public Offices, passing piles of sandbags protecting elegant buildings, housing an array of government functions.

She paused at a telephone box, dialed the operator and asked to be put through to her sister's number. The phone rang out. No reply.

Well, her bad news would have to wait. If Vi delayed any longer, she would be late, and that would never do.

Climbing the flight of stairs to the office she shared with the other typists, Vi prayed the fearsome Miss Ogilvy would be kind to her today. Or at least not draconian. The last thing Vi wanted was to dissolve into a sobbing mess in front of the tall, imposing woman with the tight lips and even tighter hair bun.

"There you are at last, Miss Harrington." Miss Ogilvy's lips were fixed in a thin, unyielding line and her bun wound so taut, it seemed to stretch her face out of proportion.

"I'm sorry, Miss Ogilvy. The Tube…."

"In the circumstances, I'll overlook it this time. Now, hurry up. Get to your desk and on with your work. Your in-tray is about to spill its contents onto the floor."

"Yes, Miss Ogilvy," Vi said to her retreating back.

Tilly looked up as Vi rushed in and draped her coat and hat loosely onto the coat stand.

"How was it? Really awful?"

Vi pulled a face. "Pretty bad. The house is all gone. The whole street, actually. I'm so glad Mother and Dad were up at Lilian's. I haven't been able to get hold of them yet, but I shall have to try again when I've finished here."

Vi pulled the cloth cover off her typewriter and sat down.

Tilly stood and came over to her. "I'll get you a cup of tea. Bet you could do with one."

Vi touched her hand lightly. "Thanks, Tilly. But please don't be too nice to me. The waterworks will start, and I really don't want to smudge my mascara. It's hard enough to get any these days."

Tilly smiled and winked at her. "Don't worry, I'll be back to my usual nasty self when I come back with our tea."

Vi sighed and picked up the first paper from the pile. Miss Ogilvy had exaggerated a little. The tray was only half-full, but it would still all have to be typed up, with no errors, and put on her desk before home time. Vi picked up a sheet of top paper and six sheets of flimsy, which she interwove with crackly sheets of carbon paper. She made sure all the sheets were neatly aligned before winding them carefully onto the roller of her machine. Miss Ogilvy was a stickler for precision. No wonky lines or running off the page.

Tilly returned with the tea and set a cup and saucer next to Vi's typewriter.

"Thanks."

Tilly returned to her own desk. "You'll meet Sandrine this evening. She's back off leave today."

"I'm looking forward to that. She sounds so mysterious."

"Strange, more like. I have no idea where she lives, where she went to on leave, or where she works."

"Well, *that's* not unusual. The work thing I mean. 'Careless talk' and all that."

"'Keep Mum, She's Not So Dumb' is my favorite," Tilly said.

"Good posters those, but it's a shame not more people take notice of them. The things you hear bandied about on the Tube. Jerry only needs to send a couple of spies to travel up and down the Circle Line for a day or two and I reckon he'll know all the Allied maneuvers planned for the duration."

"Maybe Hitler's already thought of that and Sandrine is his secret weapon."

Vi stared at Tilly, who nodded and took a sip of her tea. "You're not serious."

Tilly shrugged. "See what you think when you meet her. There's something going on there, but I can't put my finger on it."

"But if you think she's a...Quisling...some sort of Nazi collaborator...or a spy, shouldn't you tell someone? I mean, look where we work. They would listen to you."

"And what would I tell them? That an exotic-looking woman with a foreign accent lives in the same boarding house as me and keeps herself to herself? That pretty much describes half the women we come into contact with."

"Except the exotic bit."

"Anyway, if she was an enemy alien she would be interned by now, not living in plain sight in Westminster."

"Nevertheless...."

Tilly put her empty cup back on her saucer. "See what you think this evening. We'll have a chat after dinner. My room. I wangled a small bottle of something resembling sherry. We can share it."

"Gracious! How did you manage that?"

Tilly tapped the side of her nose. "Don't worry. I didn't sell my body – or any state secrets."

The sound of heels tapping purposefully up the wooden floor of the corridor outside their office shut the girls up. Miss Ogilvy did not approve of chattering. By the time she entered, the only noise was the clatter of typewriter keys.

Miss Ogilvy moved silently from Vi's desk to Tilly's, picking up completed work from the latter's out-tray. Vi could feel her presence close behind her, could smell the faint aroma of lemon verbena that always accompanied her, and sensed her eyes occasionally straying to her bowed neck. She carried on typing. Why was the supervisor still standing there? If only she had eyes in the back of her head.

She finished transcribing the first set of notes and carefully unwound the papers from her machine, then removed the carbons ready for reuse in the next batch. She extracted a paper clip from a small tin in front of her, clipped the sheets together and placed them face up in her out-tray. Instantly, Miss Ogilvy retrieved them and began to read.

Vi picked out the next stapled set of handwritten notes. She frequently didn't know who had written them, but she had become accustomed to the different styles and qualities of handwriting. This latest one was written in pencil, as usual for this author – Sir Hugo Ponsonby. His script was poor and difficult to make out. As if to add insult to injury, punctuation appeared to elude him, making her job even more difficult. Not that she would complain. It wasn't her place to complain, merely to get on with it. She assembled her sheets of paper and carbon and wound them into her typewriter.

Miss Ogilvy left without a word.

CHAPTER FOUR

Vi sat opposite Tilly at Mrs. Harris's dining table. As always, it was covered in a pure white, immaculate ironed tablecloth. In front of the four place settings was the usual array of silverware, plus a water glass. A tall jug of tap water had been paced in the center, along with condiments – salt, pepper and mustard. On the back wall a large Victorian wall clock with Roman numerals and a pendulum ticked away the seconds. At precisely six thirty, the clock chimed the half hour as the door opened and a tall, slender woman entered. She was immaculately made up, with black glossy hair that looked as if it had been polished before being wound into a soft bun at the nape of her neck. Her lips were stained a deep red and she was dressed entirely in black – an elegant, tailored dress with long sleeves and a high neck. Timeless in style, it suited her. The woman's dark brown eyes caught Vi's mesmerized gaze and a small smile played around the corners of her lips. This woman liked being the center of attention. Vi could sense the feeling of power it gave her to know that, once she entered a room, everyone else ceased to exist.

Immediately behind her, bearing a soup tureen, came Mrs. Harris, who laid her burden down in front of her own place setting before beginning to ladle liquid into bowls.

"I'm afraid it's Brown Windsor again. I can't get the ingredients, you see. Oh, of course, Vi and Sandrine, you haven't met yet."

Sandrine smiled at Vi. "We have now," she said and accepted a steaming bowl of soup from her landlady.

Vi could see what Tilly meant about the accent. Surely all Italians were interned, so that left Portuguese, Spanish or maybe somewhere much farther afield?

"I'm Vi – Violet – Harrington." She put out her own hand and met Mrs. Harris's proffered soup bowl. Sandrine made no effort to shake her hand so Vi settled for accepting the food and smiling at her landlady. She inhaled the aroma of watery gravy, and suspected her nose was fairly accurate. These days it was better never to enquire what was in the soup – even when purchased at a restaurant or café. Today, there was no bread either.

Everyone was now seated and sipping the soup. Vi and Tilly made appreciative noises, but Vi thought Tilly's exclamation of "Delicious!" a little too effusive. She settled for a nod of thanks. Sandrine said nothing, merely dabbing her lips with her napkin after each spoonful. No lipstick stained the white linen table napkin so perhaps hers was the indelible sort. Or maybe her lips were always that color. Vi dismissed the fleeting thought. No one's lips could be that shade of red naturally. Could they?

Main course consisted of stew made from some kind of meat. Mrs. Harris had done her best, but it remained gray, gristly and unappetizing. A couple of chunks, bathed in a thin gravy with some lumps of potato, turnip and carrot. Vi was now certain the soup had come from this stewpot.

Salt, pepper and mustard helped, and Mrs. Harris apologized more than once. "The butcher said it was mutton. He swore to me it was mutton. It was on the ration too."

"Maybe it's just old mutton," Vi said. "You know, an older-than-usual sheep."

Tilly grinned. "Maybe it got lost on the moors and wandered into the abattoir before dropping dead of old age."

Vi set down her fork and laughed. It lifted the atmosphere. Mrs. Harris seemed relieved.

Once again, Sandrine said nothing. She ate her meal in silence.

Dessert consisted of tinned pears and condensed milk. At least that was palatable, and Vi had to restrain herself from licking the bowl clean. *Whatever would Mother say?*

When they were all finished, Sandrine stood up, smoothed down her dress with a light pat, and thanked Mrs. Harris. She nodded at the other two and left the room, closing the door behind her. Vi and Tilly helped their landlady with the dishes.

Vi whispered to Tilly as they cleared the table, Mrs. Harris having left with a pile of pudding dishes. "Is Sandrine always like that? Doesn't she ever lift a finger?"

"No. That's typical. You won't see her now until breakfast, but that doesn't mean you won't be aware of her."

"What do you mean?"

"I'll tell you when we've helped with the washing up. I've got that sherry, remember."

"I'm looking forward to that," Vi said.

Twenty minutes later, they were up in Tilly's room, sitting on her bed, tooth mugs at the ready. Tilly poured out from a lemonade bottle.

"Are you sure that's sherry?" Vi stared at the reddish-brown liquid. She sniffed it. It certainly smelled like sherry. A little like the Harvey's Bristol Cream her father used to buy at Christmas. Only not as rich.

"My brother got it from a mate of his when he was on leave recently. They keep an off-license, but this stuff may be brewed at home. Best not to ask these days, isn't it?"

That was a lesson they'd all had to learn. Vi prepared herself for her first taste of…whatever it was. "Here goes, then."

"Mud in your eye," Tilly said, and they raised their mugs in a toast to each other.

The drink hit the back of Vi's throat with a stinging wallop. "Whoa! That's strong."

Tilly coughed. "Not unpleasant though. And it warms you as it goes down."

Vi took another sip. This time, she got more of the flavor and less of the hit. "It certainly tastes like sherry. Thanks, Tilly. This is going down a treat."

The tapping sound, when it came, took Vi by surprise. Tilly merely shrugged.

"Is that…Sandrine?" Vi whispered.

Tilly drew closer to her. Vi could smell the sherry on her breath. "It always starts this way. Light rapping and then it…well, wait and see."

"Is she signaling to someone?"

"Listen really carefully and you'll get it in a minute."

Vi listened to the rhythmic thud…thud…thud. "It's a drum. Like a child's drum. I used to have one. Maybe she's rehearsing to play in some sort of jazz band. It sounds rhythmical. Or maybe a signal code of some sort."

"I think so too. It's not Morse code because I learned that. Went on a course when I thought I wanted to be a spy, back in '39, right at the beginning of the war. I think she's performing some kind of ritual, but I've no idea what kind."

"She's stopped now," Vi said and the two women listened in silence for a minute.

"It's the same every night," Tilly said.

A sudden commotion outside sent them dashing for the light switch. Tilly snapped it off and the two of them crept over to the window. Vi inched the blackout aside.

Down below, an ARP warden, wearing his siren suit and tin hat, was gesticulating wildly up in their general direction. Tilly raised the sash window sufficiently to speak to him.

"It wasn't us, sir. I'm sure it wasn't."

"No, not you. The one next to you. Any Jerries coming over could have seen it a mile away. More probably. Bloody great flash lit up half the street. Tell whoever it is to get that blackout fixed or there will be consequences. There's a war on, you know."

"Yes, sir. We'll tell her."

The warden scribbled something in his book, using a small flashlight to illuminate the page.

A knock sounded at Tilly's door.

Vi replaced the blackout, making sure not the smallest sliver of light could escape, while Tilly crossed the room, careful not to trip in the darkness.

"All right, you can switch on now," Vi called.

The sudden brightness made Vi blink. Tilly opened the door to reveal a flustered Mrs. Harris in her pink candlewick dressing gown.

"Whatever's going on? Was that the warden?"

"Yes," Tilly said and then raised her voice. "*Someone* let some light out."

"Oh no." Mrs. Harris's eyes opened wide. "I don't want any trouble."

"It's all right, Mrs. H.," Tilly said, touching her arm lightly. "I'll sort this out."

Vi came to stand by Mrs. Harris, surprised to find the woman was trembling. Sandrine's door remained firmly shut. Surely she must have heard the commotion.

Tilly rapped smartly on her door. "Sandrine. We need to speak to you. The ARP's on the warpath." Silence. "Sandrine. Open this door, please." Tilly rapped again, so hard she cradled her knuckles afterward. Still no response. She put her ear to the door, then frowned and made an expansive gesture with her hands. She rattled the handle.

"It's locked."

"Do you have a key, Mrs. Harris?" Vi asked.

"Why, yes. Yes, I do. But I don't like…."

"It seems to me," Vi said, "you have two choices. Either we open the door, or you let things lie and end up in trouble with the authorities. It'll mean a heavy fine. Maybe even a court appearance."

"Oh dear. Oh, what do you think the silly girl's doing?"

"Come on, Mrs. H.," Tilly said, steering the poor woman back down the landing. "Let's get that key. Vi, wait here and see if she comes out."

Vi nodded and, as the two made their way down the stairs, took Tilly's place at Sandrine's door, knocking and listening.

A couple of minutes later, Tilly was back with a bunch of keys on a ring. "Mrs. H. is making a cup of much-needed tea," she said. "I told her we could take care of this." She gesticulated with her thumb at Sandrine's door. Selecting from the small collection, Tilly inserted a key in the lock and tried to turn it, wiggling it from left to right. It didn't move. She repeated the gesture with all six keys. Same result.

"There must be some mistake," Vi said. "Maybe Mrs. Harris gave you the wrong keys."

Tilly shook her head. "These are the only keys. One for each bedroom, one for the back door and one for the front. There's only one other key and that's for the outside lavvy. She keeps that on a hook by the back door in case of emergencies."

"So that means Sandrine must have changed the lock," Vi said. "But why would she do that? And how? Without Mrs. Harris knowing?"

Tilly motioned Vi to go back to her room. Once inside, Tilly closed the door. The girls sat down on her bed. "I don't think we can let this pass, can we?" she said. "I mean, do I settle for just reporting it in my MO diary? Or should I take more drastic action?"

"There could be a perfectly innocent explanation. But...I mean, she *has* to be in there, doesn't she? Neither of us heard her leave and the ARP man must have been onto that flash of light in an instant. You know what they're like. There's no way she could have got out of her room and down the stairs without Mrs. Harris seeing her, or us hearing her."

Both girls sat in silence for a few moments, deep in their own thoughts.

Tilly broke it. "It's no good. I can't think of one good reason why Sandrine would barricade herself in like that."

"Or why she would change her lock without at least discussing it with Mrs. Harris first."

"Let's face it, why would she change her lock if she didn't have something to hide?"

"So, what should we do? Tell the police? Report her as a possible spy? We have no evidence."

"Her behavior is evidence enough. And she's definitely not British."

That remark of Tilly's sat uncomfortably with Vi. "But is that reason enough? I mean, that doesn't make us much better than the Nazis with their obsessive nationalism."

Tilly blinked at her. "Are you calling me a Nazi?"

"Good grief. No, Tilly. I'm just saying that simply because she clearly wasn't born here, doesn't automatically make her a spy or a fifth columnist or whatever. What about your MO diary? Where does that go? Who sees it?"

Tilly calmed down, but her lips were still set in a fine line and her voice was more clipped; it had lost its usual friendly tone. "I'm not exactly sure. Some government department. They send us directives too. Those are subjects they especially want us to focus on and report separately about. This month, it's all about changing attitudes to society. What do we think have been the major changes to the way we live in the last hundred years and how do we think that's affected our attitudes toward each other. I have to send that in within the next week. Haven't even started it yet."

"Presumably, someone reads those surveys and reports on them to someone higher up?"

"Presumably, else why get us to report?"

"Why doesn't 'Dolly, 21' report that, as an example of changing current attitudes, behavior which might have been considered merely eccentric before the war, is now viewed as highly suspicious. You could then report everything about Sandrine so far and how your suspicions have been aroused. They know who you are, and where to get hold of you, so if they feel there is something worth following up, surely they'll come knocking on your door."

Tilly's face brightened. "At least then I couldn't be accused of a witch hunt."

"Exactly."

"And if they pursue it and find there's a perfectly innocent explanation, they could merely put it down to me reporting in answer to their directive."

"And no harm done on either side. Plus, if it got that far, maybe Sandrine would feel better if she moved out and that would remove the last trace of the problem once and for all. At least for us anyway."

"Then that's what I'll do." Tilly stood up. She pulled a drawer of her nightstand open and withdrew a lined notepad and fountain pen.

"No time like the present." She grinned at Vi, all trace of her previous annoyance gone.

"I'll take the keys back down to Mrs. Harris and tell her what happened," Vi said.

Tilly made a slight grunt in acknowledgment. She was already scribbling away furiously.

★   ★   ★

Downstairs, Mrs. Harris was clutching a cup of steaming tea, rocking slightly back and forth. She looked up when Vi entered the kitchen.

"Want a cup, dear? I think the pot's still warm." She indicated the dark brown ceramic teapot on a stand in front of her on the oilskin cloth.

"Thanks." Vi set the keys on the table, pulled a chair back and sat while Mrs. Harris poured the deep golden liquid through a strainer into a cup, added a drop of milk and stirred with a small silver teaspoon. She then offered it to Vi, who accepted it gratefully. A reviving cup of tea was exactly what she needed at that moment.

"How did you get on?" Mrs. Harris asked. "What did she say?"

Vi took a sip and laid her cup down carefully on its saucer. *Here goes.* "None of the keys worked."

The landlady nearly dropped her cup. "But that's not possible."

"We tried all of them. None of them worked. Unless you have another key somewhere, it looks like Sandrine has changed the lock. It doesn't look any different from the others, but the fact remains. None of the keys would work. Unless...." Vi had a sudden thought. "Is it possible the lock could be seized up? Maybe it needs a drop of oil."

"I don't think so," Mrs. Harris said. "I saw Sandrine come out of her room yesterday. She locked her door behind her and the key turned, sweet as a nut. I noticed especially because mine had been a bit stiff and I put some oil in a few days ago...." Her voice tailed off.

Vi wondered whether to tell Mrs. Harris what Tilly was planning to do but decided against it. The woman was het up enough already.

Mrs. Harris poured out more tea, her hand shaking so much she could barely hold the teapot. Vi gently took it off her and topped up the landlady's cup.

Mrs. Harris drew her hands through her gray hair. "Oh, Vi, whatever am I to do about her? Why won't she come out of her room? It was only a chink of light, for mercy's sake. We've all had our accidents."

"Neither Tilly nor I could hear anything," Vi said. "But she'll have to come out sooner or later. I mean, she'll need the bathroom for a start."

"I don't like this. I don't like it at all. I want her out of here. I don't want trouble under my roof. I'm too old for this. I've got enough with the war on. And every night the bombs coming over...." She dissolved into floods of tears and Vi cradled her until the crisis subsided, or Mrs. Harris ran out of tears.

Outside, the noise of a siren started up its dreaded wail. "Come on, Mrs. H.," Vi said. "Let's get down to the shelter."

Tilly appeared in the doorway, carrying gas masks in their cardboard boxes, and coats for herself and Vi, plus small overnight bags they kept permanently at the ready. Mrs. Harris reluctantly hauled herself out of her chair and swapped her dressing gown for a more practical overcoat, which she retrieved from a coat stand in the hall, along with a pair of sensible shoes, her hat, gas mask and her own small bag and handbag.

Tilly opened the door.

"No sign of Sandrine?" Vi asked. Tilly shook her head.

"The devil take her, then," Mrs. Harris said and stormed out into the night.

CHAPTER FIVE

Dawn cast a hazy pink glow over the shadowy gloom as Vi, Tilly and Mrs. Harris, along with their neighbors, emerged from the dank, smelly, communal air raid shelter at the end of the street. It had been a long night of seemingly endless bombardment. Vi breathed a sigh of relief as she saw they had escaped the Luftwaffe's attention. She had heard the distant sound of explosions and the returning antiaircraft fire, which seemed far enough away, but, even still, it was always a huge relief to see the house standing, especially after what had happened to her own home a few short miles away.

"Some other poor blighters' turn," Tilly murmured.

Vi nodded, feeling guilty.

Back at Mrs. Harris's house, they all trooped into the kitchen and the landlady made straight for the kettle. "Let's all have a nice cup of tea," she said, as if that one beverage could set the world to rights.

A scrape at the front door. It opened to reveal Sandrine, poised and elegant as ever, dressed in an impeccable black suit and high heels, her hair coiffed and makeup perfect.

"Where the hell have you been?" Tilly advanced toward her. "And what do you mean by sneaking off like that?"

Sandrine looked her up and down as if she was something nasty she would like to scrape off her shoe. "Who exactly do you think you are speaking to? What business is it of yours where I go or what I do?"

"Oh, excuse me, madam, but it is very much our business when you bring the ARP to our house because you light up the entire street and then refuse to answer your door. And then we find you've even changed the bloody lock."

Sandrine blinked once and moved to go up the stairs. Tilly blocked her way. "Oh no, you don't. Not until you answer my questions."

"I am not answerable to you. Get out of my way."

"I'm not shifting one inch. I presume you waited until we had left for the shelter before you let yourself out."

"I don't know what you're talking about. I have been out since shortly after dinner."

Tilly's voice rose. "That's a lie."

"You couldn't have," Vi said. "The ARP warden said there was a flash of light coming from your room. This was around the time we heard a noise from there."

"What sort of noise?" Sandrine's face was expressionless.

"Like drumming."

"Impossible. I told you, I went out a few minutes after dinner."

"How come we never heard you leave?" Tilly said.

"I don't thump around as you two like to do."

"Come on, Sandrine, you know you were there." Vi was becoming exasperated by the woman's barefaced lies.

"And what about the lock, then?" Tilly said. "You're not allowed to go round changing the lock on your door. This is Mrs. Harris's house, not yours."

"Why did you do it?" Mrs. Harris's voice startled Vi. She had never heard the older woman sound so angry before. "And when? I'm here most of the time and you certainly didn't have it changed when I was in the house."

"I don't know what you're talking about. I haven't had the lock changed."

"Then why wouldn't Mrs. Harris's key work?" Tilly asked.

"I have no idea. Maybe you used the wrong key."

"Let's find out, shall we?" Tilly turned to Mrs. Harris. "May I?"

"Of course, dear." The landlady grabbed the bunch of keys and the four of them trooped up the stairs. Mrs. Harris selected a key, inserted it in the lock, turned it and the door clicked open.

Tilly and Vi exchanged glances. Vi stared at the partially open door in disbelief. Sandrine pushed past her, into her room.

"Satisfied?" She slammed the door shut, and immediately locked it.

Tilly looked helplessly at their landlady, whose expression was one of disappointment. "I swear I tried all the keys. Twice. None of them worked.

"I can vouch for that," Vi said.

"You saw her do it?" Mrs. Harris asked.

"Yes."

The landlady said nothing. She made her way back down the stairs. Tilly motioned Vi to follow her into her room.

Vi sat on Tilly's bed as the other girl shut the door before coming over to join her.

"What do you make of that?" she asked.

Vi shrugged. "I definitely didn't hear her go out last evening. The ARP man couldn't be wrong, and you tried the key and it didn't work. But now.... Something peculiar's going on, but I haven't a clue what. Have you written up that directive yet?"

Tilly nodded. "I'll finish it later when I write my diary entry for today. I'm going to write about what happened last night there too. In detail."

★   ★   ★

Bleary-eyed from not enough sleep, the two girls made their way to work. There seemed to be even more sandbags today, stacked up one story high, leaving only a narrow gap for people to enter and leave the building. It was only eight thirty, but Miss Ogilvy looked as if she had been on duty for hours. She was there to greet them when they walked into their office.

"Ah, there you both are. Busy day today. Plenty of work to keep you out of mischief."

"Yes, Miss Ogilvy," they replied. Vi had a memory of being in school, standing up when a member of staff walked in, speaking in unison to return the teacher's formal "Good morning" or "Good afternoon."

Miss Ogilvy nodded. "Miss Harrington? You are to report to Miss

Brayshaw's office on the second floor at precisely eleven o'clock. You are to be interviewed for a position downstairs. Don't be late; Miss Brayshaw hates to be kept waiting and there will be an official from the Civil Service with her."

Vi blinked hard. "But I haven't applied for another position."

"I didn't say you had. Your work has been noted and they wish to see you. It's quite an honor to be chosen. If you are successful, this will mean a considerable rise in your wages."

"May I ask what the position is?"

"You may not. They will tell you all you need to know when you get there. Now, get on with your work, girls."

Miss Ogilvy swept out of the office, her heels tapping down the corridor.

Tilly hung up her hat and coat. Vi joined her.

"Well, Miss Harrington. You're going up in the world." Was Tilly jealous? Maybe a little, but she was doing a good job hiding it in her voice.

Vi meanwhile found it hard to concentrate on the letters she was typing. Why had she been chosen? Tilly had been here longer. Six whole months longer. And what did go on downstairs? With the war on, she knew better than to ask too many questions. She had seen people coming in and out of a door on the ground floor, which was permanently guarded by a uniformed soldier. It had to be something important and probably top secret, but more than that? She hadn't a clue.

★　　★　　★

Her mouth dry, Vi moistened her lips as best she could and tapped on Miss Brayshaw's door.

"Come in."

Miss Brayshaw adjusted the spectacles she was wearing and stood as Vi entered. Next to the dark-haired woman, a middle-aged man in a navy pinstripe suit puffed at a pipe.

"Miss Harrington, this is Mr. Glennister." She gathered a sheaf of papers together and moved away from the desk. "I will leave you to it."

The man lowered his pipe. "Thank you, Miss Brayshaw. Please take a seat, Miss Harrington."

Vi did as she was bid, and Miss Brayshaw closed the door quietly behind her.

The man screwed the cap back onto his pen and laid it down precisely in front of him. Dead center.

He fingered his moustache, which, like his hair, was black, flecked with gray. He wore his navy pinstripe suit like a uniform. It had been immaculately pressed and there was not a speck of fluff or a fleck of dandruff that Vi could see. To add to the traditional look, he wore an old-fashioned detachable wing collar. Just like her father's when he went to work.

"Sorry for all the cloak-and-dagger stuff, Miss Harrington. But careless talk and all that." He spoke like an ex-Eton or Harrow boy and he sported what looked like a typical old school tie – navy with a diagonal pale blue stripe. His neatly trimmed moustache harked back to a military career at some stage, probably during the last conflict. He seemed to be the right age. Late forties, fifty maybe, certainly no older.

"I quite understand, Mr. Glennister."

"Now, I expect you're wondering why I asked to see you."

"Yes, I am actually." So, he had specifically requested to see her? But why?

"What I am about to tell you is strictly for consumption within these four walls. Is that clear?"

"Of course, sir. There's a war on."

A smile twitched the corners of the man's mouth. "Precisely. I see we are going to get on famously. Miss Harrington, do you have any idea of the nature of the work being carried out in the basement of this building?"

Vi shook her head.

"I should have been most disturbed if you had. You will learn more in due course but, for now, suffice it to say that it is work of the highest importance and the greatest level of secrecy. You have already signed the Official Secrets Act, of course, but this goes far and beyond that. You will be unable to tell anyone what you do. And by anyone, I mean precisely that. Not your parents, friends, current colleagues, boyfriend. Do you have a boyfriend, Miss Harrington?"

"Not at present, sir. There was someone...." Why was she babbling? She shut her mouth.

"Good. Good. Should that situation change, however, you would not be able to tell him. And that embargo will not end on cessation of this war. You will be bound by this potentially for the rest of your life, or at least until such information is no longer prejudicial to national security. As far as anyone will be concerned, your war work was a simple office job within the Civil Service as a shorthand typist, rattling out boring old letters of no interest to anyone. Is that understood?"

"Perfectly."

"The reality will be far different. Your wages will increase to two pounds ten shillings per week to reflect the importance of your work, but I should keep that under your hat. Now, I understand you are friendly with a Miss Matilda Layton. You work together and also share digs. Is that correct?"

"Tilly? Yes, that's correct."

Mr. Glennister looked down at a sheet of typed paper. Vi could see a photograph was attached to it. Tilly's photograph.

"Yes, yes. She is of good character. I shouldn't think she'll try and press you for answers so I don't anticipate any trouble on that score but, remember, you cannot tell her anything either. You can tell her you are working downstairs but nothing more."

"I understand. Tilly knows the score. She won't ask awkward questions."

"She's one of our Mass Observation diarists, I believe. Quite a regular contributor by all accounts and a pretty thorough one too."

"Oh, I didn't realize their reports were of interest outside the project itself. Tilly did tell me about it and suggested I might like to give it a go."

"Occasionally something is mentioned which flags up a note for our attention. As for you becoming a Mass Observationist, I shouldn't if I were you. You wouldn't be able to report much, would you? Make no mistake, Miss Harrington, your hours are going to increase. There may indeed be days when you don't make it home at all. Naturally, should that happen, a bed would be made available to you. Here. Downstairs, that is."

Vi nodded, her mind a turmoil of mixed emotions. On the one hand, a thrill of excitement coursed up and down her spine, while, on the other, a fear of the unknown. Just what was going to be expected of her in this new, shadowy role? Would she be up to it?

"May I ask a question, sir?"

Mr. Glennister relit his pipe with a match and puffed out a cloud of aromatic smoke. He blew the match out and dropped it in the ashtray. "You may indeed ask. Whether or not I shall be able to answer depends on *what* you ask."

"Of course. It's just...I wondered why you had chosen me for this job? I mean Tilly...Miss Layton...has been here much longer than I have and...."

"There are other factors to be taken into consideration, over and above length of service, Miss Harrington. I am quite sure Miss Layton would have done an admirable job, but it was felt that, from the point of view of character and certain other factors, you were the best choice. Your father has been a career civil servant, I understand."

"Yes, that's correct."

"Thirty-three years' service so far and not one blemish. You may not realize but he is highly thought of among his peers. Your brother too has already distinguished himself in the RAF."

Vi felt a swelling of pride. "He was shot down over enemy territory and made it back over the line. He was mentioned in dispatches for his bravery in the face of extreme enemy action."

Mr. Glennister puffed at his pipe. "Narrowly missed getting a gong, I believe. His commanding officer was most put out. He said if anyone deserved a medal it was George Harrington."

"He came home safely. That's all we cared about," Vi said.

"Of course, Miss Harrington. That's all any of us can hope for."

A brief wistful expression, a frown. Had he lost a son, perhaps? As quickly as the frown had appeared, the man's face resumed its former serious mask. He stood, pipe in hand. "I think we are finished here. All that is left to do is for me to wish you well in your new position."

"Thank you, sir. I shall do my best."

"I'm certain of it. Ask Miss Brayshaw to show you downstairs. Someone will have collected your things from your old office so you can go straight down and start work."

"Thank you, sir. Goodbye."

"Goodbye, Miss Harrington. And good luck."

Miss Brayshaw smiled as Vi emerged. "Gracious, you look as if you've seen a ghost."

"I can't believe what just happened. I'm to work downstairs. I always wondered what went on down there."

"Well, now you're about to find out. And you will never have guessed. Not in a thousand years. Come along, then."

They made their way down the single flight of stairs to the ground floor and Miss Brayshaw led them to a strong metal door that reminded Vi of the kind of doors she had seen on the ferry to the Isle of Wight. To the right of this was a much grander wooden door guarded by a soldier, rifle in hand, his face expressionless, staring straight forward.

"Come along now, don't dawdle."

Vi quickened her pace and followed her new supervisor through the metal door, which clanged shut behind them. A marine stood like a waxwork, but Vi was sure that rifle he held was loaded and ready to fire at a moment's notice. Security was certainly tight here, with identity checks at every manned post. Ahead, a long, winding staircase stretched seemingly endlessly. Where was 'downstairs' exactly? In the bowels of the earth?

They finally arrived at the bottom and Vi took in her surroundings. They were at one end of a long, dimly lit corridor. Nearby, another soldier was guarding what appeared to be a small kitchen. Maybe they were afraid someone might steal the rations? Around her, the walls were painted a pale cream and closed doors were numbered. Here and there a nameplate indicated the presence of a senior personage although Vi didn't recognize any of the names. In the distance, phones rang and voices clamored to be heard.

Tall cupboards stretched along one wall. Alcoves housed typists working at makeshift desks, so despite the impression of plenty of office space, there clearly wasn't enough to go round.

Fire buckets, asbestos fire blankets and chemical extinguishers were positioned at regular intervals. At least their safety was being considered, even if, so far, she had seen no sign of any toilets.

As they turned a corner, the volume increased. A smell of cooking – maybe a beef stew or something similar – wafted toward them, along with laughter and the clatter of plates and cups.

"Officers' mess," Miss Brayshaw said, indicating an open door through which Vi glimpsed rows of uniformed men sitting at long tables. Farther on, a nameplate proclaimed *General Ismay*. The name rang a vague bell and Vi remembered typing his name on various documents she had been given when she worked upstairs.

They passed a door painted bright red. It looked heavy, made of iron probably, certainly substantial. A little farther and, over a door, she saw a nameplate that made her stop.

The Prime Minister.

"Ah, yes," Miss Brayshaw said. "That is indeed the Old Man's office when he's down here, which is quite regularly. And when he is, we signal to each other. You'll hear a tapping on the pipes. That tells us he's around and about and we need to be quiet. He hates noise. You'll be using a noiseless typewriter for that very reason. He cannot stand the clatter of typewriter keys. Drives him insane. For a man of his age, Mr. Churchill has excellent hearing."

"But…but…." Vi hadn't stuttered like that since she was an awkward teenager.

"Now you see the reason for all the secrecy. This is where the war is really conducted – along these corridors, with tons of cement between us and anything Hitler chooses to throw at us. Welcome to the Cabinet War Rooms."

CHAPTER SIX

"So, you've been posted downstairs then?" Tilly's voice made Vi jump as she wandered home in the early evening sunshine. "Don't worry. I know you can't tell me anything, so I won't ask. Is it fun though?"

"I don't really know yet. It's all too new, but I'm sure I'll get used to it."

"They're sending us someone to replace you but, in the meantime, we all have to do your work between us. They've given me old Ponsonby's stuff. How do you manage to decipher his scrawl?"

Vi grinned. "Practice. And it usually pans out when you look at the context of the sentence."

"It's his *f*'s and *s*'s I have so much trouble with. Yesterday, I hit the *f* key before I realized that what he meant was '*suck* the life out of' whatever it was. Imagine if I'd let that go. As it is, I didn't dare merely correct it. I played safe and typed the page again. It doesn't help that his letters and documents are so flowery in the first place, and he wouldn't know a comma if it flew up and hit him in the face."

Vi laughed. "You'll get used to it. You're a good typist."

"Thanks. Oh, I sent in my report and diary entry to MO today. Let's see if it drums up any interest. Not that I suppose it'll go anywhere outside of the project's office."

Vi bit her tongue. She had almost told Tilly about Mr. Glennister's comments. No harm done, thank goodness, but it served as a warning to be on her guard at all times. It was all too easy for something to slip out.

★   ★   ★

At home, Mrs. Harris was putting the final touches to a pie crust. "Good evening, girls. How was your day?"

"Fine thanks, Mrs. H.," Tilly said. She indicated the pie. "That looks good. What's in it?"

"A bit of chicken and some veg. I managed to pep it up a bit with stock and herbs. Should go down nicely with boiled potatoes and gravy."

Tilly smacked her lips. "Sounds delish."

"Any sign of her ladyship?" Vi asked, her foot on the first stair.

"Apparently she won't be joining us tonight," Mrs. Harris said, her mouth set in a disapproving line. "She has a prior engagement."

Tilly followed Vi up the stairs. "Are you thinking what I'm thinking?"

"That maybe now is the ideal time to investigate her room?"

"Straight after dinner?"

They had reached the top of the stairs.

"Let's check if it's locked now." Vi turned the handle. "Nothing doing."

"She wouldn't make it that easy for us."

"It was worth a try. Anyway, when we've helped Mrs. Harris with the washing up, you grab the keys while I distract her. No reason she has to be a party to this."

"Good thinking. Let's hope the blasted key works this time."

"And that Jerry doesn't decide to pay us a visit."

"See you downstairs."

Vi unlocked her door and realized. When she turned the handle of Sandrine's room, she had heard a sigh. Her instant thought had been that it had come from Tilly. *But it couldn't have. Tilly was behind me. The noise came from in front of me. On the other side of the door.*

Without thinking, Vi sped out into the hall again and leaned right up against Sandrine's door. She held her breath and listened. Not a sound. She must have imagined it. She moved away and a thump came from behind the door.

"Sandrine? Is that you?" Vi knocked sharply on the door.

Tilly appeared from her room. "What's going on? I thought she was out."

"Something hit the door. From inside. I heard it."

"I know. So did I. That's it. I'm getting the key from Mrs. H." Tilly was off down the stairs before Vi could respond. She carried on knocking and rattling Sandrine's door handle, to no avail.

Tilly dashed back upstairs followed at some distance by Mrs. Harris, who was wiping her hands on her apron.

"She's not here, I tell you," the landlady said. "She went out this morning and isn't coming back until sometime later tonight. She told me herself."

"Well, something made the noise we just heard," Vi said, taking the key from Tilly. She inserted it in the lock and turned. The lock clicked open and Vi pushed the door ajar. "Is that the same key you used yesterday?"

Tilly nodded. "It's got a little white paint mark on it."

Vi looked down at the key in the door. A tiny speck of white gloss paint had caught the edge of the key.

Mrs. Harris kept her distance, clinging on to the banister at the top of the stairs while Vi and Tilly stepped in.

"What *is* that smell?" Tilly wrinkled her nose.

"Some sort of aromatic oil, I suppose," Vi said. "Can't say I care for it much."

"It stinks like a cheap brothel."

"I wouldn't know. I've never been in one."

"Neither have I, but…. Oh, you know what I mean."

Standing in the center of the tidy room, Vi took in her surroundings. The bed and table were covered in fringed silk shawls, black in color but embroidered with exotic floral patterns in bright shades of blue, green, red, yellow and purple. A small drum stood on the table with a child-size drumstick. Vi picked it up. "That explains one thing, then," she said, examining the skin stretched taut across the surface. It was darker than usual, maybe through age or wear. She touched it and recoiled. It had felt like…. Vi had never touched a dead body; had never even seen one, but the feel of that...whatever it was.... The closest she could come was the sensation of touching the skin on a joint of pork, right before you rubbed salt in to make crackling. It had never been one of her favorite chores.

"What's the matter?" Tilly took the drum off her. "Oh my God." She threw it down onto Sandrine's bed and wiped her hands on her skirt. "There's something not right about that. If I didn't know better, I'd say that was human skin."

"I hoped I was wrong, but it felt so much like.... It couldn't be, surely? I mean it's a drum, for heaven's sake. An old drum. We're letting our imaginations run away with us."

"So what made that noise we heard? I can't see any sign of anything having fallen over."

"No, neither can I." Vi swallowed. "I can't believe I'm going to say this because all I want to do is get out of here, but this may be our only chance to find out who Sandrine really is."

Tilly nodded. "You're right." She made for the wardrobe, opened the double doors and whistled.

Vi crept up behind her, scared to speak above a whisper. "What is it?"

"Her clothes. I mean, look at them." Tilly was removing hanger after hanger, checking the labels. "These are serious designers. Worth, Chanel...Schiaparelli. Wallis Simpson wears her clothes." Tilly laid the beautiful gowns on the bed, turned back to the wardrobe and bent down. "Good grief. The woman has even got Ferragamo shoes."

"Who?"

"He's an Italian shoe designer." Tilly held out a pair of oddly shaped shoes with thick wedge soles and high heels, layered in different colors – blue, pink, purple, green, salmon and white, with gold buckle straps.

"How on earth would you even wear something like that?" Vi asked, examining them before handing them back to Tilly.

"Let's see, shall we?" Tilly kicked off her own shoes and slipped one of the uncomfortable-looking sandals onto her foot. "Bit small for me," she said, pushing her foot firmly in. She repeated the action with the other foot and attempted to buckle the straps, unsuccessfully. "These feel really odd. I mean, I know they're two sizes too small but even so, I wouldn't dare wear them even if they were my size. I'd be too afraid of falling off them and breaking my ankle."

Vi wrinkled her nose. "I think they're ugly."

"I'll bet they cost more than you and I earn in a month, probably three months."

Mrs. Harris called from the stairway. "Girls. Are you nearly finished in there? I really don't like this. It's Sandrine's room. Her personal things."

"Won't be long, Mrs. H. Just making sure you don't have a fifth columnist under your roof." Tilly removed the shoes and tidied them away where she had found them. She stroked the beautiful silks and chiffons and replaced the designer wear.

Vi fetched down a couple of hatboxes only to find they contained what their labels proclaimed – expensive, exquisitely created concoctions adorned with net, taffeta and feathers. Purely decorative and not suitable even for a gentle summer breeze.

"Nothing here," Tilly said, as she rummaged in the bedside cabinet. "Just a couple of paperbacks. I don't even think they're hers. I mean, Ethel M. Dell? I don't think so." She flicked through the pages and shook the books in case something was lodged. Nothing.

Vi rifled through the drawers of a small chest. Underwear, some with designer labels, most – if not all – silk. Lace handkerchiefs, elegant scarves and three pairs of soft kid gloves. The bottom drawer was empty. "Nothing here either," she said.

Tilly lifted the bedspread and peered under the bed. Apart from the regulation chamber pot....."Nothing."

A small bookcase on the windowsill proved to contain copies of works by Dickens, Conan Doyle and Wilkie Collins, along with a well-worn copy of Palgrave's *Golden Treasury*, a collection of poetry Vi remembered from her schooldays – except this was a first edition, published in 1861. This was much more the sort of reading material she would have expected to find in Sandrine's collection. Next to it,

Vi picked out a small, leather-bound book and stared at the cover. A bizarre etching of a creature with an upper human male torso and a goat's head stared out at her. Its right hand was raised in a parody of Christ pardoning sins. Its lower body was swathed in some loose, flowing material, leaving only its cloven hooves visible. But it was the eyes that captured Vi. Too large for its face, they seemed to be sentient, delving into the furthest reaches of Vi's mind. She could feel something digging, searching.... She threw the book down on the table.

Tilly called over from the other side of the room where she had clambered up on a chair to examine the top of the wardrobe. "Anything?"

"Only...that." Vi pointed at the book. Her fingers shook.

Tilly slid off the chair and replaced it at the table. She picked up the slim volume and Vi winced.

Tilly whistled through her teeth. "This is old." She carefully opened the cover. A strong smell of some bitter herb wafted into Vi's nostrils. "Rue," Tilly said. "My gran used to grow it. She said it repelled insects and drove off evil spirits. Horrible stink. Mind you, she didn't have any sense of smell."

The room had grown darker and was closing in on her. In the distance, the sound of Sandrine's drum and voices, chanting.

"Can you hear that?"

Tilly looked up from the book.

"Hear what?"

Vi staggered and leaned against the wall for support. She recoiled at the sight of tendrils – like black ivy – sprouting from the pages of the book, winding themselves around Tilly's fingers. Squeezing. Yet her friend seemed impervious to it.

"Look at your hands, Tilly. *Look*. Can't you feel it? Can't you see what's happening?"

Tilly looked down at her fingers, turned first one hand and then the other. "What am I supposed to be seeing?"

"That book. It's trying to...I don't know what it's trying to do but

I can see it. It's alive, Tilly. Put it away, for God's sake. While you still can." Her voice seemed to come from far away.

"What? Hey, are you all right?"

Vi could barely breathe. The air was stifling, as if all the oxygen was being sucked out of the room. "I'm fine, but I'm serious, Tilly. There's something wrong with that book. Put it away. Please, and let's get out of here."

"It's just an old book."

"No, it's not. There's something…. Something evil."

Tilly laughed. "Don't be daft. It can't hurt you. It's just paper and writing. Look."

Vi winced as Tilly flicked the pages. The paper gave off an odd, hollow sound. Not like any paper she had ever come across. No gentle rustling, nor crackling. This was more like an echo, a remembrance of a sound that had long ago finished resonating. Her heart thumped faster and the air was growing thicker, making it harder to breathe. "Tilly. *Please*."

Tilly calmly replaced the book on the shelf. "You're really shaken up, aren't you? What was it about that book anyway?"

"You saw the etching on the front? The eyes. It was as if the thing was alive. And that star on its forehead. What is that thing? It looks like something that belongs in hell. Then when those tendrils started to attach themselves to your fingers—"

"What?"

"Please, Tilly, let's put everything back and get out of here. I can hardly breathe."

"Not yet. Look, you're letting your imagination run away with you. Sit down and pull yourself together. I'll only be a few minutes but we have to find out what's going on with Sandrine."

"I think I've had a pretty good dose of it – whatever it is." Vi sank down onto Sandrine's bed.

Vi watched in horror as Tilly retrieved the demonic book and examined the cover. "The star is a pentagram, which is an ancient religious symbol – more pagan than Christian. As for the creature….

It does look like a demon of some kind. The book's in some foreign language, but, really, it's only an old book. Sandrine probably picked it up at some flea market." She put it back on the shelf and moved on, much to Vi's relief.

"Are you all right now?" Tilly asked.

Vi nodded. Her breathing was finally returning to normal and the air had cleared. "I'm fine as long as I don't have to look at that thing."

Tilly turned back to the bookshelf. "Madam certainly has a wide taste in literature. There's a book here by that Aleister Crowley chap. He's a devil worshipper. I read about him in one of the papers. And this looks interesting." Tilly removed yet another ancient volume off the shelf.

"I wish you wouldn't." Vi felt her fear mounting afresh. The air had grown dense around them once again and, this time, when she exhaled, her breath misted.

"Hang on a second." Tilly flipped open the cardboard cover. "He's a nifty-looking beast."

She held up the book and Vi caught a glimpse of a demon with huge pointed ears and a beard, mounted on a mighty winged horse with flaring nostrils, frozen in the act of galloping through the air. "Oh Tilly, please. Enough is enough. Sandrine clearly has strange reading habits and this bloody room of hers is getting to me. Can we just get out of here?"

Tilly was reading. "There's too many *hath*s and *thee*s and *thou*s for me, but this would appear to be some bloke called Eligos, or sometimes he's known as Abigor, and he's a Great Duke. He carries a lance, an ensign and a scepter or a serpent. His horse is born of hell itself. Eligos knows secrets, finds hidden things and can predict the outcome of wars." She shut the book and replaced it on the shelf. "Seems like a handy person to know if you're a spy in wartime."

Vi hugged herself against the increasing cold. "Don't you feel it? It's freezing in here now."

At last, Tilly seemed to have sensed something of what Vi was experiencing, and shivered. "You're right. It has gone cold in here.

Let's go before Mrs. H. has apoplexy or a heart attack. She's huffing and puffing out there like an angry bull." Tilly opened the door.

"She *is* making a lot of noise out there. It's all right, Mrs. Harris. We—"

The corridor was empty.

Vi locked the door. "But we both heard her."

"We both heard *something*. I must admit, the breathing was a bit heavy for Mrs. Harris, but...."

"Come on." Tilly was already halfway down the stairs.

Vi felt another chill crawl like fingers down her body. She shivered as she reached the bottom step.

"Mrs. H.?" Tilly stood at the kitchen door and peered in. Vi stood next to her. Mrs. Harris was peeling potatoes.

"I'm sorry. Dinner will be a little late this evening."

"Oh, don't worry about that," Tilly said. "When did you come back down here?"

"A few minutes ago. Just after I asked if you were nearly finished. Did you find anything?"

"No, no. Not a thing," Vi said. No way could she tell the landlady about the book, or the demon Eligos.

Mrs. Harris nodded and went back to her potato peeling.

Tilly backed away and motioned Vi into the hall. "Tell me I'm not going mad. You *did* hear someone outside Sandrine's door, didn't you?"

"Yes, of course. I heard heavy breathing. I don't understand how it couldn't have been her."

"Except she was already down here."

"We were the only two people up there." But even as Vi uttered the words, she knew they hadn't been. They might have been the only two *humans* up there, but they had been far from alone. Another cold shiver raised goose bumps along her arms. "There's something not right about any of this. I can't explain it but I'm sure there's someone – or something – else in this house."

"I'm so glad you said that, Vi, because at least now I know I'm not the only one. I don't know what you experienced in Sandrine's room. All I felt was a sudden chill right before we came out. I'm sorry I was hard on you in there, but I had to be sure I wasn't imagining things about that woman. I have had the distinct impression there was something evil about her since the first time I met her." Tilly's expression changed. She stared hard at Vi and backed away. "Oh my God. Your face…." She backed away toward the front door, pointing at Vi. Her eyes had grown huge and her face white. Her hand shook.

Vi touched her own face and felt her skin, clammy, cold, but…. "What's the matter with my face?"

"It's…it's not your face…it's distorted. Your eyes…they're hollow." Tilly swayed and Vi moved to reach out to her. "Don't touch me. Don't come near me!"

Mrs. Harris dashed into the hall. "Whatever's going on out here?" Tilly collapsed in a crumpled heap.

Vi rushed to help her. She and Mrs. Harris hauled the unconscious girl to her feet and carried her between them into the living room, laying her gently down on the settee.

Tilly murmured and her eyelids fluttered. She opened them, saw Vi and gave a little whimper before calming herself. "Oh, thank God. You look yourself now." She struggled to sit up, swayed and lay back down again. "I don't feel right. It's as if everything's tilted somehow."

"I'll get a glass of water," Mrs. Harris said.

"What happened, Tilly?"

Tilly stared at her, still white-faced, only a little color beginning to trickle back into her cheeks. "Suddenly it seemed like something was over your face. Like a mask or something. I couldn't see *you* anymore. Only this…this thing with round holes where your eyes should have been and the mouth distorted and it seemed to be moving all the time, changing." She put her head in her hands. "It was frightening. Didn't you feel anything?"

"I felt freezing cold. I seemed to be surrounded by a blanket of icy air that was trying to fold me into itself. I know that doesn't make any sense but it's the best way I can explain it. It all started when we went into Sandrine's room. Nothing has felt right since."

Tilly nodded. "There's something in this house and I haven't a clue what it is or how to deal with it."

Their landlady returned with a glass of water. "Are you feeling a little better now, Tilly?"

Tilly nodded, taking the glass from Mrs. Harris. "Yes, thank you. I'll be fine in a minute. I probably should have drunk more of this earlier."

"May I ask you something, Mrs. Harris?" Vi asked.

"Of course, dear."

"How long have you lived in this house?"

"Oh, now…. About forty years, give or take a year or so."

"And has anything strange ever happened here before?"

"No. It's always been a happy house. My husband loved it here and I brought up our children until they were old enough to fly the nest. Now, I'd better get those potatoes on or we'll never get our meal." She left and Tilly took another gulp of water.

★   ★   ★

Dinner was eaten mostly in contemplative silence, certainly as far as Vi and Tilly were concerned. Mrs. Harris seemed quite happy to refrain from dinner conversation. She was of an age when that had probably been part of her upbringing anyway.

Later, Tilly joined Vi in her room. She took out a packet of cigarettes and offered one to Vi.

"No thanks. I don't."

Tilly gave a wry smile, took out a cigarette and tapped it on the side of the pack. "I keep forgetting. Wish I didn't. They're forever putting the price up. I'll have to start rolling my own soon."

Vi smiled back. She had calmed down considerably. Maybe getting a square meal inside her had helped. "I've never seen Sandrine smoke either," she said. "And yet she's just the sort you could imagine, dressed up to the nines, foot-long black cigarette holder, shoulder-length gloves...."

"Marlene Dietrich with black hair."

"Wonder if she knows the words to 'Lili Marlene'?"

They both giggled. Tilly stood, striking a pose, her cigarette in her hand. Keeping her voice as low as possible, she started the first verse, "Underneath the lamplight..." and promptly burst into a fit of coughing.

In the distance, the front door slammed.

Both women froze. The unmistakable sound of Sandrine's high heels climbing up the stairs, pausing on the landing. The scrape of her key in the lock. Her door opened, closed, locked.

Vi realized she had been holding her breath and exhaled.

"Let's hope we put everything back in the right place," Tilly whispered. "I'll bet she'll notice if anything is even an inch out."

Vi nodded. She would bet Sandrine would know they had been there even if everything was exactly how she left it. That knowledge gnawed at her and kept her awake into the small hours and yet she couldn't help feeling they were missing something obvious. Something right under their noses.

CHAPTER SEVEN

"Miss!"

At her desk in the Cabinet War Rooms, Vi froze. Miss Brayshaw had gone to lunch, leaving her in sole charge for half an hour. Just her luck that Mr. Churchill would pick right now to need some assistance. Swallowing hard, she picked up her shorthand notebook and pencil, stood, straightened her skirt and took a deep breath. *Here goes.*

Vi had never entered the Prime Minister's subterranean office before. Once inside, she took in the giant map of Europe stuck on the wall behind a pristinely made-up single bed with a walnut headboard. Close by, a desk with an array of telephones, each color-coded and no doubt providing direct contact with specific people of high importance in the conduct of the war. Two tall microphones stood next to them. She was aware that Churchill made BBC wireless broadcasts from this office on occasion. A half-smoked cigar smoldered in the ashtray within easy reach of the Prime Minister's right hand, as he sat, engrossed in reading a sheaf of unbound papers.

Vi gave the slightest of coughs. Churchill turned his gaze toward her, and she was taken aback. *He has the most perfect skin. So fair, almost like alabaster.* His eyes, she noted, were a pale blue. Intense.

"You're new." He made it sound like an accusation.

Vi had been warned about his tendency to abruptness. "Don't take it personally," Miss Brayshaw had said. "He's like it with all of us. He has a lot on his mind, after all."

"Yes, sir," Vi said. "I'm Violet Harrington."

He made a sound like a cross between a grunt and a 'harrumph'.

"I don't like change." The voice had become a growl. "Are you Miss or Mrs.? Not that it will make any difference. I shall call you Miss.

I call all of you miss. After all, if I used your name and you weren't there, no one would come. If I shout, 'Miss,' someone always comes."

"Yes, sir. I am not married."

The Prime Minister nodded and clamped his lips around his cigar. He took a couple of deep puffs and a cloud of blueish, pleasantly aromatic smoke poured into the room. "Well? Sit down. Sit down. There's work to be done. I need to dictate a letter to the President of the United States and, as you appear to be the only one here, you will have to do."

"Yes, sir." Vi sat, crossed her legs, licked the end of her pencil and waited for Churchill to begin. She didn't have to wait long. He was fluent, spoke quickly and she struggled to keep up. *If only he would pause for breath once in a while.* Miss Brayshaw had warned her that he didn't like to have to repeat himself and had reduced more than one typist to tears for failing to keep up with him. Vi was determined she was not going to fall by the wayside on her first encounter.

Five minutes later, he was finished.

"Got all that?" he asked.

"Yes, sir."

The dour expression softened and his face creased into the smile she had heard described as 'beatific'. They were right. His features transformed into those of a benign cherub.

"Excellent, miss. It seems we shall get along famously if you keep this up. Mind you, the proof of the pudding will be when I read it through. I don't like errors. Can't abide them."

"No, sir."

Churchill stubbed out his cigar. He reached for the sheaf of papers and shook them at her. "Something else I cannot abide." Three or four random sheets fell and floated to the floor. "How am I supposed to read this if I have to keep sweeping up the sheets every five minutes? Not attached properly. Has anyone shown you klop?"

"Klop...? No, sir. I don't believe they have. I only started two days ago."

Churchill's smile was already history and now he harrumphed

again. "Can't abide staples. Always stabbing myself with the damn things. Ask Miss Brayshaw. She will show you. Klop – handy thing. Next time I ask, you'll know what it is, won't you?"

"Yes, sir."

"Take these away, make sure they are in the correct order, and then klop them."

Vi accepted the unwieldy bundle of papers and left his office, closing the door behind her.

Back in the typing pool, she let out a deep sigh and half staggered to her desk, her heart thumping out a tattoo.

She sat down and, fingers trembling, tried to concentrate on slipping carbons between sheets of typing paper. Miss Brayshaw entered, took one look at her and burst out laughing. "Easy to see what's just happened to you. You've had your first encounter with the Old Man, then?"

Vi didn't trust herself to speak and merely nodded.

"Did he shout at you?"

She shook her head.

"Well, you must have done all right, then. What did he want?"

Vi took a deep breath and tried to free her tongue. It seemed pasted to the roof of her mouth. "He…dictated a letter and…." She picked up the untidy sheaf of paper. "He gave me these. He said something about a…a…." The word wouldn't come to her.

"A klop, I expect."

"Yes. That's it."

"The Prime Minister hates staples and finds paper clips far too unreliable. He prefers we use Treasury tags to keep his papers attached and, for those to work, you first need to punch a small hole in the top left-hand corner." She reached behind her and picked up a device that bore a slight resemblance to a nutcracker. At its tip, it had a single round protrusion capable of penetrating a number of sheets of paper. Miss Brayshaw tidied the sheets, lining them up neatly.

"Oh, wait. No…. Mr. Churchill said they might not be in the correct order and I was to sort them first."

Miss Brayshaw handed the sheets and the unusual appliance to Vi. "Well, when you've done so, you will know what to do with them. A klop is simply a single-hole punch. I have no idea whether it's a real word or not, but it's the one Mr. Churchill always uses. You should find some Treasury tags in your top drawer."

Vi slid it open and picked up a short piece of green string. At either end of it, a metal tag had been attached crossways. One end would be threaded through the hole she created with the klop and the other metal tag would keep the papers attached, but with enough flexibility to allow them to be easily read and turned over.

"Miss!" The voice echoed down the corridor.

"I'll go this time," Miss Brayshaw said. "You get on with the work he's given you. You'll gain extra points for speed and accuracy." She gave Vi a friendly wink and, grabbing her shorthand pad, left.

Vi smiled to herself. She had survived her first meeting with one of the most powerful men in the world and he had smiled at her.

It took a few minutes to sort out the papers – made worse by the lack of page numbers. Fortunately, the paragraphs and sub-paragraphs were numbered. She couldn't help but pick up on a few points. The document concerned intelligence on Nazi occultism. The more she read, the more bizarre it all appeared. Spies from the British Secret Service, identified only with code numbers, had reported that senior members of Hitler's staff had been indulging in some odd rituals designed to help Germany win the war. The author of the document was suggesting that, if this circle could be infiltrated, it could be a way of passing on misleading information she kept coming across. Strange words in some language she had never heard of – *vril*, *vrilja* were among the most persistent. They seemed to refer to some kind of mythical, secret underworld where a superrace lived, intent on taking over the world by interbreeding with humans on the surface.

Vi would have loved to read the whole document but time wasn't on her side. She must get these papers attached properly and have that letter perfectly typed. In triplicate.

Reluctantly, she put the – now neatly 'klopped' and attached –

papers aside in her out-tray and carried on loading up her typewriter.

Five minutes later, Miss Brayshaw returned, a beaming smile on her face. "Mr. Churchill is pleased with you. He said he looks forward to signing that letter and to keeping you busy for the duration. How are you getting on?"

"The document is sorted out and ready for him and I'm just finishing off his letter. Another few minutes and I'll be ready to take them in to him."

"Excellent. As you've not been summoned, don't forget to knock first. He won't be having his afternoon nap yet so you should be fine."

Vi nodded, finished typing the letter and unwound it from the typewriter.

"Let me see." Miss Brayshaw leaned over her. "Good work. Nice and neat, exactly how he likes it. I can see why you came so highly recommended."

"Thank you, Miss Brayshaw."

"Right, off you go and then you can get a cup of tea. Bring me one back, would you?"

"I will. Milk and one sugar?"

"That's right."

Vi knocked and waited.

"Enter!"

Mr. Churchill was seated at his desk, fountain pen in hand. He took the papers off her, glanced at them quickly and placed them down beside his blotter. The corners of his lips twitched. "I see you found klop."

Vi handed him the letter. "Yes, sir."

She waited as Mr. Churchill perused it before adding his signature at the bottom. He blotted it and handed it back to her. "Good start, miss."

"Thank you, sir."

The Prime Minister nodded at her and she knew she had been dismissed. She closed the door quietly behind her, remembering that the Old Man detested noise and disturbance.

DARK OBSERVATION • 73

Back in the typing pool, two of the other girls had returned from lunch. Vi entered, carrying a small tray with two cups of tea.

Ethel, the older one of the two, grinned. "Bad timing. We should have got back a bit earlier, then you could have brought us a cuppa too."

"I can go and get you one if you like...."

Miss Brayshaw took one of the cups of tea. "Violet isn't here to wait on you two layabouts," she said. "She has her own work to attend to. As indeed do you, Ethel. And, Nancy, your in-tray is positively teetering."

"Yes, Miss Brayshaw," they said in unison. Behind their supervisor's back, Nancy stuck out her tongue and winked at Vi, who felt awkward and sat down, relieved she didn't have to look at either of them as their desks were behind hers.

★   ★   ★

Back home, her feet aching from a day of traversing the seemingly endless underground corridors of the Cabinet War Rooms, Vi's earlier elation following her encounters with Winston Churchill had given way to an overwhelming fatigue. In her room, she kicked off the offending tight footwear and slid her feet gratefully into her warm slippers. They had been a Christmas present from her mother in 1938 and she took great care of them. With shortages as they were, who knew when she would be able to replace them? As it was, the soles were wearing thin in places.

Even though there were signs of spring in the trees, with leaf buds beginning to show impending life, the weather was chilly, and this old house had drafts everywhere. The slippers kept not only her feet but her ankles protected.

She was reading when a faint knock on the door was immediately followed by the turn of the door handle.

"Only me," Tilly said. "Are you decent?"

"Yes. Come in, Till."

Tilly looked as if she had spent the day doing something leisurely instead of being hard at work banging away at her typewriter, but then she hadn't the corridors to contend with.

"You look done in, my girl," she said. "They working you too hard down there?"

Vi managed a smile, even though the effort made the corners of her mouth ache. "It's a new job. There's a lot to learn."

"Exciting though, I bet."

Vi nodded. "I'm sure it'll have its moments. How was it upstairs?"

"Oh, same as usual, really. Don't like the replacement they've drafted in for you. Sullen type. Olive Grimshaw. Comes from Bolton, 'oop narth'. Has the accent and the gruff attitude to prove it."

Vi laughed. "You'll get used to her, I'm sure."

"Won't make any difference if I don't. I'm stuck with her. Can't imagine inviting *her* to stay here if anyone leaves, though."

"Well, I'm not going anywhere for the foreseeable and neither are you, so that leaves Sandrine. As we haven't a clue what she does every day, we have no way of knowing." Vi checked her watch. "Come on or we'll have Mrs. Harris on our case. It's nearly half past."

★   ★   ★

Dinner consisted of some kind of indeterminate meat stew again. When Mrs. Harris had delivered their plates, she returned briefly to the kitchen for a jug of gravy.

Tilly mouthed at her, "What do you think it is? Mutton?"

Vi sniffed the aroma. "Could be," she mouthed back. "Or maybe rabbit."

"Probably best not to ask," Tilly responded.

Mrs. Harris returned and was sitting herself down when the dining room door opened and an immaculately turned-out Sandrine appeared. She nodded briefly to her fellow dinner guests and took her place.

Vi could tell by Tilly's expression that she was in a mischievous mood. True to form, she didn't disappoint.

"So, how was your day, Sandrine? Vi here is worked off her feet and I have a new colleague who would be more at home on a Lancashire sheep farm."

Sandrine glared at Tilly. "I don't believe we should be discussing our war work with others not involved in it."

"All right, keep your knickers on, I only asked what sort of day you'd had, not what you were doing. It's called making polite dinner conversation."

Sandrine laid down her knife and fork. "First of all, I do not make polite dinner conversation and secondly, I find your tone anything but polite."

Mrs. Harris rapped on the table. "Girls, girls, please. Can we please enjoy our meal in peace? I had to queue for hours for this meat and, before you ask, I don't know what it is either. If the butcher did, he wasn't telling."

Tilly giggled. "I'd bet a bob or two they're missing a couple of old horses at the knacker's yard."

"*Tilly.*"

"Sorry, Mrs. H. Actually, I think you've done a bang-up job with this. The gravy particularly is delicious."

The landlady appeared mollified. She smiled. "Thank you, Tilly."

Vi murmured an appreciative, "Thank you." In fact, it wasn't bad. In common with her own mother, Mrs. Harris had the gift, apparently possessed by so many women of her generation who had gone through the First World War. She could make something tasty out of virtually nothing.

As soon as everyone had laid down their knives and forks, Sandrine dabbed the corners of her mouth with her napkin, pushed her chair back and stood. "Thank you, Mrs. Harris. An excellent meal."

"Oh, aren't you staying for pudding? There's jelly and custard."

"No, thank you. I have some work to do in my room." Without acknowledging Tilly or Vi, she left the room, closing the door behind her.

"That really gets on my tits," Tilly said, out of earshot of Mrs.

Harris, who would have been shocked at such language. "She never even clears up her own stuff, never mind helping out."

Vi helped her stack the plates. "She's probably used to servants." The two took the washing up into the kitchen. "It doesn't occur to Sandrine that we all have to muck in here."

"It's going to be worse now," Mrs. Harris said, dishcloth in hand. "The girl who comes to do the washing and some of the cleaning, Margery, she's been called up. She heard today. She's joining the ATS, so I won't have any help at all, and what with my arthritis playing up..."

"Don't worry, Mrs. H. Vi and I will help where we can. We can do our own washing. I draw the line at Sandrine's, though."

"You don't need to worry about that. She takes hers to be laundered."

Tilly stuck her nose in the air and struck an exaggerated pose. "Oh, how very la-di-da of her."

Vi grinned. "Told you she was used to servants."

Tilly smacked her arm playfully. "What else can we do to help? We clean our own rooms anyway, so how about if I draw up a cleaning rota for the rest of the house? I'll stick Sandrine on it. She can surely wield a duster and polish a bit of furniture without breaking one of her precious nails, can't she?"

★　★　★

Fifteen minutes later, up in Tilly's room, the two of them began drawing up the rota on a sheet of light brown wrapping paper. Like so many things, paper was in short supply and every scrap that could be reused was saved to be pressed into service later. They had been at it for a few minutes when the familiar noise of Sandrine's small drum sounded through the adjoining wall.

Tilly cocked her head toward the source of the sound. "She said she had work to do. If that's work, I'd like to know what it is."

"We could always ask her." But already the beginnings of the fear she had felt previously were starting to re-emerge.

"Good idea." Tilly leapt to her feet. "Come on."

Tilly was already out in the corridor, knocking on Sandrine's door. Vi came out and stood next to her, her heart beating wildly. The sound of drumming stopped. Sandrine opened the door. Vi peered around her. She couldn't see anyone else. Sandrine's ice-cold stare chilled her.

"What are you doing?" Tilly demanded.

"That is none of your business." Sandrine replied, making to close the door.

Tilly wedged her foot in it. "Oh no, you don't. Look, Sandrine, we know you're up to something and if you don't tell us, we may well report you to the authorities as a potential spy."

Sandrine's eyes grew wide before she threw back her head and laughed. Not a pleasant, ringing laugh but a raucous, coarse one at extreme odds with her sophisticated appearance. "That is ridiculous," she said. "A spy? On what grounds? Because I like to practice playing the drum?"

"I think it's code of some sort. I know it's not Morse but, nevertheless, I think you're practicing a code of some kind to transmit information to the enemy. That's treason."

Tilly was in high dudgeon and Vi inwardly cringed. If Sandrine really *was* guilty as charged, she had just put the two of them in considerable danger.

Sandrine's laughter was replaced by an unpleasant sneer. "If you think I am telling you what work I perform, you are wrong. And if you persist with these ridiculous accusations, it is *you* – both of you – who will find yourselves in considerable trouble."

Vi had to speak up. "Could you simply tell us why you're using that drum? We're not asking you to divulge secrets, but surely if it's only a hobby—"

"What I do, where I go, none of these matters are your concern. We have to share this house but let us do our best to stay out of each other's way in future."

The two girls were staring at a closed door.

Vi turned to Tilly. "Not our most successful evening."

Tilly motioned Vi back into her room and closed the door behind her.

"Listen, Vi. I know you're doing top-secret stuff downstairs and I don't want to know anything about it, but is there any chance there's someone you could speak to about Sandrine? Maybe she's already known to MI5. For all we know, she could be under surveillance."

Was there someone? Of course there was, but she could hardly march into the Prime Minister's office and start sharing tittle-tattle about the odd goings-on of someone she shared a house with. But, Miss Brayshaw, on the other hand....

"I can talk to my supervisor. Sound her out and see what she says. May I mention your MO diary and the report you wrote?"

"Of course. Don't forget my nickname, Dolly, 21."

★   ★   ★

Vi had to wait until lunchtime the following day before she could catch Miss Brayshaw on her own. The older woman listened patiently, occasionally frowning, sometimes nodding. Vi finished off with mention of Tilly's Mass Observation work and was relieved when, for the first time, her supervisor picked up her pencil and scribbled down *Dolly, 21.*

"So, what do you think, Miss Brayshaw?"

Her supervisor exhaled deeply. "It's probably nothing to worry about, but you did the right thing to tell me. Anybody behaving in an unusual way, especially one who is clearly not British, should be investigated at this time. What was the young woman's full name?

"Sandrine Maupas di Santiago." She spelled it out for her and then wondered how she knew. If her memory was correct, she had never actually seen the name written down anywhere yet she had rattled it out confidently.

For the second time, Miss Brayshaw scribbled a note. "Leave it with me, Violet. I will look into this and, as soon as I have any news for you, I will let you know. One thing though."

"Yes?"

"I would urge restraint. Your accusations last evening were not wise. If this woman is indeed a spy, she now knows you suspect her. Not only is that dangerous for you both but it could also cause her to go underground. Disappear. Please don't repeat that and, although you won't like what I am going to say, I would advise you both to apologize to her for your behavior. Tell her you were mistaken. That the noise of that drum had got on your nerves and put you on edge. Tell her anything you like but diffuse the situation if you can."

Vi nodded, although how Tilly would react was a different matter.

*　　*　　*

"I am not apologizing to that woman under any circumstances."

"Keep your voice down," Vi whispered. "All right, *I'll* apologize to her. I'll say I had a bad day and goaded you into confronting her. I'll take full responsibility."

"There's no earthly reason why—"

"Tilly. My supervisor urged us to do it, for the reasons I have explained. We want Sandrine to think we no longer suspect her. That we made a mistake. I mean *I* made a mistake."

"Oh, for heaven's sake."

"Look. If we don't do this and we're right, think of the consequences, the damage she could inflict if she really *is* a spy."

Tilly blinked rapidly. She seemed to be having an inner struggle with herself. Surely she could see Vi was right.

Finally, Tilly chewed her lip before replying. "All right. If your supervisor says we should, then I'll do it. We can't run the risk of a spy slipping through the net. But let's do it now before I change my mind and, no, you're not taking the blame for this. I was the one who confronted her. Come on."

Sandrine opened the door a crack and, on seeing the two of them, made to close it. Once again, Tilly's foot came in handy.

"I've come to apologize," she said. "I got it wrong and I'm sorry. No excuses. We're very different people, you and I, and probably should keep out of each other's hair as much as possible, given we're living in the same house."

"I apologize too," Vi said.

Sandrine stared at them both as if they had developed extra heads. "Apology accepted," she said at last. Tilly removed her foot from the door and Sandrine closed it.

A surge of relief flowed through Vi's veins, immediately followed by a wave of exhaustion. "I'm off to bed," she said. "It's been quite a day."

"See you in the morning."

Tilly's voice held a harshness and rancor that grated on Vi. Loss of pride, no doubt.

★ ★ ★

Vi opened her eyes. Something had woken her. She peered through the gloom. In the blackout, with no light seeping in from outside and none within, she could make out nothing. She reached out next to her, to the bedside table, but her fingers met nothing, until they knocked against some smooth and unfamiliar wood. With a rush of surprise, she realized she wasn't in bed. She was sitting on what seemed to be a ledge of some kind.

I'm dreaming. I'll wake up soon.

But something didn't feel right about that either. With her other hand, she felt next to her and her fingers closed on the unmistakable shape of a simple candlestick, but it was more the size of one she would expect to find in a church. As her fingers traveled up its stem, she touched a large wax candle. Where there was a candle, these days, a box of matches was usually not far away. Vi shifted position and her legs swung out. She *was* sitting on some kind of ledge. Taking care not to knock anything off, she heaved the candlestick from her right hand to her left and felt around for the matches. In a second, they were in her grasp. An unusually large box of them. She placed the candle holder carefully down beside her and opened the heavy matchbox, taking care not to spill the contents on the floor. Who knew how high up she was? And she certainly wasn't about to find out by jumping off. She struck a giant-sized match and blinked at the flash of light.

Her hands trembling, she lit the candle and peered out into the gloom. In front of her loomed a giant table and an equally massive chair. Against a wall, an impossibly enormous gas cooker stood four square on its cast-iron legs.

As she moved the candle around, she saw the floor a few feet beneath her. Into her mind flashed a picture from her childhood. John Tenniel's famous illustrations for *Alice in Wonderland*, when Alice took a drink and shrank.

Vi shook her head. *This isn't real. It isn't happening.*

A loud thump set her ears ringing. It was followed by a series of raps and she recognized the sound of heels on linoleum, but magnified ten, twenty times. More, probably. She licked her fingers and snuffed out the flame, stifling a cry from the burn. The sound of the kitchen door opening was almost deafening, as were the voices that spoke. They seemed to be lower and slower than normal, like a record being played at the wrong speed.

An unfamiliar male voice spoke. "Someone has used a candle in here recently. I can smell it. Is the blackout in place?"

A familiar female voice answered, "Yes. Mrs. Harris doesn't really trust electricity. She uses candles frequently. I will turn on the lights."

Vi was nearly blinded by the brightness. Her eyes watered and she shaded them until she could become accustomed. Once everything came into focus, she recognized Mrs. Harris's kitchen, but from the perspective of a mouse. A small mouse, trapped on a shelf. The now-familiar brown-painted shelf unit she saw every day. But never from this angle.

She craned to see who the two people were who had come in. As she suspected, one was Sandrine. The other was a man of around the same age, maybe a little older. With his pencil moustache and slicked-back hair, he resembled Clark Gable in profile. He stood directly in front of her. Vi prayed he wouldn't turn around. She could smell the brilliantine or Brylcreem in his hair and the strong smell of aftershave, which nearly choked her, so that she had to cram her hand over her mouth.

"You are certain no one will disturb us?" the man asked

"They are all in bed. It is safer we talk down here. I share this house with two interfering, silly young girls and an old woman who likes nothing more than to gossip about her neighbors."

The man gave a long, lazy laugh. When he spoke again, Vi couldn't understand what he was saying. He spoke in a language that sounded European. Probably Spanish or Italian. Definitely not French or German. She caught the occasional familiar name. "Churchill", "Hitler", "Mussolini". Surely they shouldn't be discussing them in such a clandestine fashion and Mrs. Harris had strict rules. This man wasn't even supposed to be here. Once or twice, Sandrine addressed him by name. Alex.

She might not understand a word they were saying, but she was still vulnerable. What if they discovered her? They could crush her as easily as a fly. Vi looked anxiously around for something to hide behind and spotted a tin of cocoa. Silently, she edged her way along the shelf, noting she was dressed as she had been before she woke up there – in her nightgown with a pair of her brother's old socks on to keep the chill out. At least she wouldn't freeze to death, until she could find a way of returning to normal. A sudden fear struck her. She had shrunk to this size without warning. She could return to her normal size the same way.

A momentary lapse in concentration saw her hand catch the edge of a piece of paper and the stub of a pencil. The paper floated but the pencil made a sharp rat-tat as it landed on the floor and rolled.

Vi stood and made a dash for the cocoa tin, squeezing behind it a split second before the man spun on his heel and faced directly where she had been mere seconds earlier.

"What was that?" Sandrine asked, looking around her.

The man bent down and picked up the pencil. "Just this." He put it on the scrubbed wooden draining board.

Vi thought she was safe. Only for a second.

"Ah, we have a little visitor," he said. In a second, Vi was staring into two sets of enormous eyes. Both with dark brown, almost black irises. Sandrine and her companion. Their gaze captivated her. She seemed to sink deeper and deeper into those eyes. Within them, something stirred. A winged creature – like a dragon – unfurled its wings and stretched them wide. It kept its head bowed.

"Eligos...." The whisper echoed through her head, repeated itself, layer upon layer of voices chanting again and again, growing louder and louder until Vi clapped her hands over her ears to try to stem the noise. But it came from inside her. Piercing, thrumming, vibrating simultaneously.

Sandrine laughed that grating, harsh laugh.

"Oh, little one," her companion said. "Now perhaps you will know to keep away from matters that don't concern you. Forces you cannot even begin to comprehend. Eligos is waiting. He will not have to wait long." The man extended his hand. Vi squeezed her eyes shut but could sense the whorls and loops and arches of his fingers. "I could crush you like a little gnat. Snap you like a dead twig. Remember that."

His voice faded into the distance, along with Sandrine's hollow cackle.

Exhaustion took hold and Vi's eyes grew heavy.

*   *   *

The knock at her door woke her with a start.

"Vi. Come on. Mrs. Harris has the breakfast on and there's bacon today – and an egg each. You don't want to miss that."

"Coming." Vi shook her head, thoughts swimming like fishes caught in a vat of strong cider. She was back in bed, in her own room and everything was as it should be. So, it had been a dream. *Crazy*.

She dressed hurriedly in a casual skirt and navy blouse, with a warm red cardigan her mother had knitted for her as a birthday present. No stockings today. It was Saturday. Maybe she would go for a walk in the park, or up west. Take in a show. There was a revival of the musical *White Horse Inn* running at the Coliseum. Perhaps Tilly would like to come along too.

Downstairs, Mrs. Harris was already serving breakfast. She looked up as Vi entered. "Hello dear, did you sleep well?"

Tilly was pouring tea from the pot. Sandrine was ignoring everyone as usual and delicately spreading marmalade on a slice of toast.

"I had an odd dream," Vi said.

Sandrine paused and looked directly at her. There was something in that gaze that made Vi decide not to say any more.

"Well, come on," Tilly said, replacing the teapot on its ceramic stand. "Don't keep us in suspense, tell us."

Vi couldn't take her eyes off Sandrine. "It didn't make any sense so I'll never be able to retell it. Just the usual nonsense you get in dreams."

"What a letdown," Tilly said. "I thought you might have had some secret assignation with Errol Flynn."

Vi forced a smile. "As if that's ever going to happen." Sandrine's steady, unflinching gaze was making her uncomfortable.

Mrs. Harris emerged once again from the kitchen. "Have any of you girls seen my shopping list? I seem to have mislaid it. I thought I'd lost my pencil too, but that turned up. It's rather peculiar because I always put it in the same place, next to my shopping list on the middle shelf in the kitchen, but today it turned up on the draining board, of all places."

Vi dropped her table napkin and was glad of the opportunity to bend down and not have to meet Sandrine's eyes for a few moments while she composed herself. She retrieved the cloth and stood. "I'll come and help you look," she said.

"Thank you, dear. I'm sure it can't have gone far. I must be getting forgetful in my old age."

Vi went straight to where she knew the piece of paper must be. It had fluttered off the shelf, right next to where…. There was the cocoa tin and there…. A corner of the paper peeked out from under the unit. Vi stooped, picked it up and handed it to the landlady.

"Thank you, dear. Well spotted. I doubt I would have seen that until I mopped the floor. Why…your hand's trembling. Aren't you feeling well?"

Vi managed a smile, her head dizzy. "I'm fine. Thank you for asking. Just a bit tired, that's all. It's been a busy week."

"I'm sure it has. Never mind, you can take it easy now it's the weekend. That's if Mr. Hitler leaves us alone. I so hate going to that shelter." Mrs. Harris opened the kitchen door and went outside to bring some washing in.

Tilly came in from the dining room. "Madam's gone."

"Thank God for that."

Tilly touched her hand. "What's wrong, Vi? You look awful."

"I don't even know how to explain it. You'll never believe me. I thought it was a dream until…."

Tilly looked at her questioningly. "Now you're definitely going to have to tell me everything. On our walk. And I mean everything. It's that dream, isn't it?"

Vi nodded. "The thing is, I don't believe it was a dream. I believe it actually happened, however incredible that's going to sound."

CHAPTER EIGHT

Sleep came hard that night. An early air raid warning had sent Vi, Tilly and Mrs. Harris scurrying down to the shelter. Sandrine, as usual, was nowhere to be seen.

Neighbors from both sides of the street trooped in until every inch of seating was occupied.

Tilly nudged Vi. "Miss High and Mighty would have had to sit on the floor anyway. I'll bet *that* would have got right up her snooty nose."

Vi giggled, feeling relieved to have unburdened herself to Tilly earlier. "I think I'd have paid good money to see that," she said.

Her laughter was short-lived as the familiar drone of Nazi planes drew closer and passed overhead. One or two of the neighbors crossed themselves, closed their eyes and their lips moved rapidly in prayer. Vi wished she hadn't lost her faith somewhere along the way. Or maybe she had never really had it in the first place. Hers was not the most religious of families. Christmas, Easter, baptisms, weddings and funerals. That was about the sum total of her church attendance.

More planes were approaching. Ever closer. Their menacing droning incessant, like amplified bees. Nervous chatter died down until the shelter was silent. Each person wrapped up in their own fears, thoughts and supplications to the Almighty. Tilly slipped her hand into Vi's and the two held on to each other. Next to her, Vi felt Mrs. Harris tense up.

The antiaircraft guns fired their barrages of artillery, desperately trying to bring the planes down. Some distance away, an explosion, then another. Then an earsplitting, thunderous crash that shook the shelter like an earthquake. Someone screamed. A man yelled.

"That was too bloody close," Tilly said, as the two women clung to each other. Vi felt hot tears stream down her cheeks. She squeezed her eyes shut and waited for the next one.

Another explosion, then another and another. From somewhere the screaming whine of a descending airplane. The *ack-ack* guns had got one at last. But where would it fall? They all heard its final blast. Vi prayed that not more innocent lives had been lost in trying to defend their country. Chaos took over the shelter. Two children burst into hysterical sobs and screams, their frightened mothers seemingly powerless to control them. An old man told them to shut up. Another man threatened him with his fists and had to be hauled off. There was now more noise inside the shelter than outside.

Vi struggled to her feet. "Listen," she said, then repeated herself. Louder. "*Listen.*"

The clamor died down as all eyes turned toward her.

"It's gone quiet."

The man with raised fists lowered them. He ran his hand through his hair and cast his eyes downward. The men who were holding him back let him go and he mumbled an apology. The old man acknowledged him.

"We made it," Mrs. Harris said. "Let's pray our homes did."

"By the sound of it, some poor blighters have copped for it," the old man said.

They waited, mostly in silence, for the all-clear to sound. When, at last, it did, they emerged into the black night, the only light coming from their flashlights.

Mrs. Harris's house had escaped, as had the neighbors'. Silently, they all made their way to their homes.

Once inside, Vi made cocoa, glad when she could replace the tin on the shelf. Had she really hidden behind it last night?

Tilly had listened to Vi's story open-mouthed. She seemed to believe her but, as she added hot water to the cocoa powder, Vi wasn't convinced Tilly hadn't been merely placating a friend. After all, if the positions had been reversed, wouldn't she have done the same?

"Come on, Vi. Has the kettle gone on strike?" Tilly hated to wait for anything, especially her nightly hot drink.

Vi arranged the mugs on a tray. "Coming."

In the dining room, she sat opposite Mrs. Harris. The three of them sipped their drinks for a few moments until they heard the sound of a key in the front door.

"She's back," Tilly said. "Come on, Vi."

The two women left Mrs. Harris staring into her mug of cocoa and made straight for the hall. Sandrine was closing the door but, before it was entirely shut, Vi was sure she made out the silhouette of a man. The same one as last night?

"Where were you tonight, then?" Tilly asked. No, she *demanded*.

Sandrine ignored her and made for the stairs. Tilly sped forward and blocked her way.

"Oh no you don't, missy. This happens every night. You go out before the air raid warning and don't come back until the all-clear, so where do you go?"

"I refuse to be spoken to like this. Get out of my way." Sandrine tried to push Tilly aside but the girl's anger gave her added strength.

Vi thought back over Miss Brayshaw's warning and, seeing the seething rage in Sandrine's eyes, knew she had to try to stop this.

"Tilly, please," she said. "We're all a bit strung up over the raid. Coming on top of night after night of it, none of us have much energy left and our nerves are all on edge. Let's all cool down a bit and get some sleep. Or at least try."

Tilly glared at Vi, but she must have remembered what her friend had said about Sandrine and moved aside. Vi saw her clench her fists until the knuckles blanched.

Sandrine brushed past her, stomped up to her room and slammed her door.

Tilly turned on Vi. "That bloody woman."

"I know, Tilly, I know, but we have to stay in control of our feelings when she's around."

"If only we could find out for sure about her."

"I'll talk to Miss Brayshaw again tomorrow. See if she's found out anything. In the meantime, it's probably best if you don't go near her. I'll certainly be keeping my distance. There are things in her room that...." Vi shivered at the memory of the atmosphere, the strange books. And that drum.

Maybe Tilly was remembering too. She had calmed down and now she nodded, returned to the dining room and finished her cocoa. "Right, I'm off to bed. That's if Jerry will let me, of course."

Vi took their mugs into the kitchen and they bid Mrs. Harris good night.

Now, as she lay in bed, all Vi wanted was to sleep without dreams and wake up refreshed in the morning, but she tossed and turned for what seemed like hours. Finally, right before she dropped off, she had the distinct impression she was no longer alone in her room, and the aroma of a burning cigarette wafted toward her.

★   ★   ★

The following Friday, as soon as she arrived home after work, Tilly grabbed Vi and ushered her into her room, closing the door firmly behind them. Her face was flushed. "I got summoned today."

"What? Who by?"

"Some senior toff in the Civil Service. Didn't give me his name. Spoke like Neville Chamberlain."

That could have described any one of a dozen or more senior civil servants both Vi and Tilly rubbed shoulders with every day. "So? What did he want?" Vi prompted.

"He had read my MO report and was interested in anything else I had to tell him about a certain neighbor of ours."

Vi sat closer to the edge of Tilly's bed. "And?"

Tilly came to sit next to her. "You know what they're like, they don't give anything away, but he took notes, asked loads of questions about her movements and so on. He seemed particularly interested in her comings and goings whenever there's a raid on. I got the distinct impression he knew more than what he'd read in my report, though. For one thing, he slipped up once."

"How?"

"I told him Sandrine's name, but not all of it. In my report I gave her a pseudonym. Well, only an initial actually. It's something we were advised to do in our reports and diaries. It keeps us and them anonymous. When I write about her, she's *S*. Today, when I met him I referred to her as Sandrine di Santiago but when he mentioned her he called her Miss *Maupas* di Santiago. He didn't get the extra bit from me, I can assure you."

"So she's already known to the authorities, then."

"It would seem so. I didn't mention his little *faux pas*. I could kick myself now, of course, but at the time...those Whitehall types faze me. I always think they're looking down their aristocratic noses at me."

"Did he say what was going to happen next?"

Tilly shook her head. "He thanked me and told me he would be in touch again if they needed any more information. Then he extended his hand to shake mine and that's when I saw something a bit odd. He had this tattoo on his inner wrist. It wasn't visible normally, but his shirtsleeve slid up his arm a little and I saw it, clear as anything. I think he caught me looking because that was the briefest handshake I've ever experienced."

"What was it?"

"It's a weird...symbol, I suppose you'd call it. Probably something to do with some secret society he was in when he was at school or university. It's a bit difficult to describe but I could draw it for you. Hang on, I have a bit of paper from my last packet of stockings."

She jumped off the bed and opened her dressing table drawer. She grabbed a scrap of paper, spread it out and picked up a pencil. A minute later she returned and thrust the drawing at Vi.

Vi examined it. It looked familiar. "I've seen this somewhere before," she said. "My brother, George, loves myths and legends and he bought a book once full of Nordic and Viking folklore. I used to love to borrow it and read all about the great goddess Freya. There was a page of runes and George and I used to send notes to each other written in the runic alphabet. If only I could remember.... There's something wrong...something different...."

Vi racked her brains. "Got it. Lend me your pencil a moment." Vi put the paper down on Tilly's dressing table. She drew the symbol as she remembered it.

She showed Tilly. "You see. It doesn't have the...feet, if you like...but, apart from that it's the same. It's an ancient Viking rune, part of their alphabet from hundreds of years ago. It's called the Odal rune, and, among other things, it represents a vowel sound, a sort of mixture of *o* and *e*."

Tilly stared at the two symbols. "It can't be a coincidence, can it? So, what's an ancient Viking symbol doing tattooed onto the arm of a senior British civil servant?"

Vi shrugged. "Haven't a clue but you're probably right. In America they have these fraternities, don't they? They have pins and so on, with symbols. Greek ones mostly, I think. It's probably something like that."

Tilly laid the paper down. "That sounds likely. Ah well, curiouser and curiouser, eh?"

Vi recoiled. "Oh don't. You're reminding me of that awful experience I had. The more time goes by, the more I feel I actually know what it was like to be Alice."

Tilly's face clouded over. "You do know *that* was a children's story."

"Of course I do but...you had to be there, Tilly. It was *so* real.

And if I could only draw better, I reckon I could sketch an accurate depiction of that man Sandrine was with. I'd certainly know him again if I saw him. In fact, I'll never be able to look at Clark Gable again without seeing him in my mind. I'll never go and see *Gone with the Wind* again, that's for sure."

★   ★   ★

Maybe a sound woke her. Vi sat bolt upright in bed, heart pounding. From next door, shuffling sounds. *Sandrine must be moving around.* Vi switched on her bedside lamp and glanced at her clock. Three thirty in the morning.

The room was stifling. A warm night and thick blackout blinds hardly helped air circulation. Beads of sweat had formed on her forehead, and her whole body felt clammy.

She threw off the covers and swung her legs out of bed. The linoleum floor welcomed her feet with its coolness as Vi padded to the door. She leaned hard against it, straining for any sound. Nothing.

Vi stood close up to the dividing wall between her room and Sandrine's.

The faintest knocking seeped through to her ears, as if Sandrine was tapping on that drum. A steady, rhythmic, almost soporific thrum. Vi felt her eyes closing. She swayed, nearly fell, and steadied herself by placing her right palm flat against the wall. It felt unpleasantly clammy and she withdrew her hand. She sniffed at her fingers and a fusty, damp odor penetrated her nostrils.

She made for the ewer and basin and washed her hands, scrubbing at them vigorously with the meager scrap of perfumed toilet soap she normally reserved for special occasions, keen to get rid of the vile smell as soon as possible. It reminded her of a time before the war, when she was a child, visiting an old aunt who lived in two shabby rooms in London's notorious Hoxton. Now, as she scrubbed, she pictured the first cockroaches she had ever witnessed as they scurried out from behind the fireplace. Her mother had bashed them with a coal shovel while little Vi huddled in a corner, clinging on to a tattered, mildewed cushion and bawling her eyes out. Her aunt had railed at her mother, telling her not to make such a fuss; that she was upsetting Vi.

Her mother had shouted back, scooped up the crying child and left, never to return.

As she dried her hands, all these years later, Vi wondered what had happened to Auntie Nellie. Her name had never again been mentioned in her hearing. Why should she think of that now? That bloody smell, damp and…roaches.

Vi snapped on the main light and picked up a broom she used to sweep the floor. She had never seen a cockroach in this house, but that didn't mean they weren't here, lurking somewhere dark, damp and preferably warm. Heedless of Sandrine and whether she might hear her, Vi poked about in the corners, opened the wardrobe, swept under the bed.

Nothing. *Thank God.*

She returned the broom to its corner and made to switch off the light. At that moment, she caught sight of something in the corner of her eye. There. On the wall.

Right where she had touched it, a patch of brown damp had appeared. Maybe twelve inches in diameter. Like a puddle, it fanned out, its edges frayed. As if someone had thrown water on there over a long period of time. The closer she approached it, the more pronounced the smell of damp and decay.

Vi backed away. That stain had not been there when she went to bed. She glanced up at the ceiling. No sign of any leaks. Besides, that wouldn't explain how it could appear in the middle of a wall. Were there any water pipes between them? Hardly likely. One thin wall separated the two rooms. There was no cavity in between.

She stared at it, aware that all was now quiet next door. No doubt Sandrine had heard her and stopped whatever clandestine activity she was indulging in.

The damp patch hadn't spread. If anything, it seemed to be retreating a little.

Vi switched off the main light and settled herself back in bed. By now thoroughly awake, she picked up her book and tried to lose herself in it. Agatha Christie usually never failed to absorb her and this was her latest. *One, Two, Buckle My Shoe* had her Belgian sleuth, Hercule Poirot, once again in the thick of it. But however hard she concentrated, Vi's gaze kept wandering to that single patch of wall. The damp *was* retreating, or drying out. The thought brought her a modicum of comfort and, eventually, she was able to set down her book and switch off her lamp.

★   ★   ★

"Miss!"

Vi was, by now, used to the summons from the Old Man, and usually welcomed it. She was accurate, produced her work in timely fashion and it was always neat and free of errors. Mr. Churchill didn't ask for anything less than perfection, so they maintained a civil working relationship. She had grown accustomed to him snapping at her when something was going particularly wrong or he was especially preoccupied and, these days, she mostly ignored it and got on with her assigned tasks. Today though was a little different. Today, he used her name.

He looked up as she entered, sitting at his desk with the inevitable cigar in his mouth. He removed it and tapped it on his ashtray.

"Ah, Miss Harrington. I'm glad it's you. I wanted a word with you. Sit down." He indicated an office chair a few feet away and she perched on the edge of it.

She opened her shorthand notebook and waited for his instructions, pencil in hand.

He pointed at it. "Never mind that for now. As *you're* here, I want to have a word with you about something else. Something of importance I believe you may be able to help us with."

Vi's heart beat a little louder.

The Prime Minister puffed once more on his cigar. "Miss

Harrington, I understand you are acquainted with a woman who goes by the name of Sandrine Maupas di Santiago." He dragged out the last part of her surname, making it sound like 'Santiarrrgo'.

Vi swallowed, her mouth suddenly dry. "She has a room in the house where I live."

Mr. Churchill glanced down at the foolscap sheets in front of him. "Yes, you and a Miss Matilda Layton, who works upstairs in the Treasury, I believe."

"That's right, sir."

"Miss Layton has expressed some concern about the activities of this woman."

"Yes, sir. Tilly's part of the Mass Observation project and she thought she should report her concerns."

"Quite. She made a statement recently on the subject."

"I believe she did, sir." Was she supposed to know that? Should Tilly have told her? Vi hoped she hadn't got her friend into trouble.

Churchill's fingers tapped the arms of his chair. "Miss Harrington, I shall not insult you by saying, as everyone seems to these days, that there is a war on. You are quite well aware of that, but I will say that this woman, this...." He consulted his notes again. "Miss Santiago is someone in whom we are taking a degree of interest. As a result, if you see or hear anything suspicious, you should report it."

"Yes, sir." Should she tell him about her companion, Alex? Maybe he already knew. But if he didn't.... "Sir?"

"You have something you wish to tell me?"

"Yes, sir." The question was, how much? Certain things would stretch the imagination of any rational human being. "I believe Sandrine has an accomplice...or a friend. I'm not sure which but I've overheard them talking...not in English. I don't know what language. Not French...." *Stop gabbling and get on with it.* The PM was tapping the fingers of his right hand on his desk. "I'm sorry, sir. I'm finding this a bit hard."

"Evidently. Take a deep breath, Miss Harrington. Spit it out."

"She calls him Alex. I've never heard a surname. But he's easy to recognize. He looks almost identical to Clark Gable."

"Clark Gable. The Hollywood actor."

"Yes, sir."

"My wife very much enjoyed *Gone with the Wind*. Didn't care for it, myself."

Vi found she hadn't a clue what to do with her hands. She fiddled with her shorthand pad and then stopped, realizing how irritating that must look.

Churchill had stopped tapping and was now fingering the signet ring he always wore. He stared straight ahead, seeming to have forgotten her existence, deep in his own thoughts.

Vi jumped when he broke the silence. "Thank you for your help. That will be all for now, Miss Harrington."

So, that was to be it? Vi knew better than to question him.

"Very good, sir."

⋆　⋆　⋆

The siren sounded in the early evening, as Vi and Tilly were playing rummy with an old pack of cards in the dining room.

Tilly slammed her cards facedown on the table. "Oh, give it a rest, Adolf."

"Come on, let's go." Vi pushed her chair back. By now the relentless bombing night after night and the ensuing sleep-deprived nights were taking their toll. Tempers were frayed, patience short. Mrs. Harris met them in the hall, her small suitcase in hand. Her face was white and her eyes seemed to have shrunk into her face.

In the distance, the drone of airplanes rolled in like thunder.

"Theirs or ours?" Vi muttered.

"I'm guessing theirs," Tilly said. "Come on, we haven't got much time. They'll be overhead any minute."

"No point in asking where Sandrine is, I suppose," Vi said.

"Oh, bugger her. She won't be around. Come on." Tilly grabbed Mrs. Harris's hand and half dragged her out of the house.

Vi locked the door behind them and looked up. The noise of the engines was far too close for comfort. At this rate, they would be lucky to make it to the shelter. In the distance, she heard the *ack-ack* guns beating out their familiar tattoo. Flashes of orange, bright yellow and white light pierced the darkening sky. Vi raced down the street, catching up with Mrs. Harris and Tilly. They made it into the shelter as the first bomb went off. The noise was deafening. All around her, their neighbors huddled together, terrified. Some crying, one or two almost hysterical.

Another thunderous crash sent them all reeling as the ground shivered and trembled.

And another.

The shelter shook as if an earthquake had erupted beneath them.

Closer. Ever closer.

One of the men spoke. "They're right overhead."

The cacophony in the shelter silenced as everyone looked up. In the dim light, provided by a couple of kerosene lamps, Vi could see a few of the women mouthing prayers. One man crossed himself, as they all waited for whatever would come.

A screaming engine could only mean that its airplane had been hit. The machine was coming down. The only question was where?

They didn't have to wait long.

The explosion shook the shelter so hard, Vi was sure it would collapse on top of them.

Somehow it stood.

But outside, something had fallen. Not only the airplane. It had taken something massive with it. Crammed in next to her, Mrs. Harris wept silently, her shoulders shaking. Vi put her arm around her and held her close.

A few murmurs, but other than that, no one spoke. They were all in shock; all fearing what they would find when they eventually emerged from the place that had somehow withstood the bombardment and saved all their lives.

The all-clear sounded. Instead of the usual rush to get out, everyone seemed reluctant to go first.

Vi got to the door. "Look, we're all here and we're in one piece. Everything else we can deal with. Let's go." She thought she had steeled herself for whatever might await them. She was wrong.

Fires raged – some small, like family bonfires. Down the street, the end house had fallen, and firemen were already aiming hoses at the conflagration. Plumes of water shot upward, waging a seemingly unwinnable war against the shooting flames. Everywhere, people shouted, screamed, called for each other. Whistles blown by ARP wardens and policemen chorused through the air – providing a surreal kind of accompaniment to the apocalypse around them.

The airplane they had heard go down seemed to have broken up. As Vi shone her flashlight around, its narrow, weak beam picked up bits of torn fuselage that had been ripped apart as easily as she might tear a sheet of paper. She could even make out a swastika on part of a wing.

"So that answers that," she said to Tilly. As she spoke, she tasted plaster dust, ash – all mixed together in a foul, dry cocktail that stuck to the roof of her mouth and coated her teeth.

"Thought it was probably one of theirs," Tilly said. "Well at least that's one less to come back tomorrow."

A few yards away, a woman wailed.

Tilly and Vi looked at each other. "Mrs. Harris," Vi said.

They scrambled over bricks, plaster, twisted metal and piles of indeterminate debris. Broken glass cracked under their feet until they reached her.

And they saw what she saw.

Where her house should have been were only bricks and mortar, lying in a heap. Miraculously, there was no smell of gas so the main hadn't been ruptured. And there was no fire.

"Oh, Mrs. Harris. I'm so sorry." Vi once again put her arm around the sobbing landlady's shoulders. Tilly followed suit and the three women, tears falling unheeded down their cheeks, stared at what had once been their home.

Vi felt someone close behind her, glanced over her shoulder and, at first, thought she had imagined it. Then she realized there was someone there. Two people in fact. They were standing in shadow, calmly watching. They didn't even look solid enough for humans, but that was crazy.

"Sandrine."

Tilly tapped her arm. "What was that?"

In the split second she took her eyes off the woman to look at Tilly, she was no longer there. Nor was her male companion. "I thought I saw Sandrine and her accomplice, but I must have been wrong. They're not there now. Probably a trick of the light."

Tilly looked back at the ruins. "We might be able to salvage something. In the morning, when it gets light."

"We'll have to be early though," Vi said. "Before the looters get here."

"You'd think people would show more respect, wouldn't you?" Tilly said. "After all, we're all in this together."

Mrs. Harris made a noise somewhere between a sob and an expression of disgust. "Some people have no morals." She gave a little cry and staggered forward, clutching her chest. Vi caught her just as she fell.

"Oh hell, I think she's having a heart attack. Tilly, call an ambulance."

"With all this going on? It'll never get here on time. I'll find a warden or a policeman."

Vi knew it was already too late. It no longer mattered whether Tilly managed to call an ambulance or not.

Mrs. Harris was dead.

Out of the corner of her eye, Vi caught a movement a few feet away. Expecting it to be a neighbor, she raised herself up from where she had been laying Mrs. Harris gently down on the rubble-strewn road.

But this was no neighbor. Sandrine was suddenly inches from her. How she had made it there without disturbing any of the shattered debris, Vi had no idea. She cleared her throat, trying to swallow down the emotion which had formed itself into a large lump in her throat. "Mrs. Harris has passed away," Vi said.

Sandrine's expression never changed. Her eyes seemed like black holes in her alabaster skin that shone with a translucent glow. "It was her time," she said.

A figure formed out of the shadows and dust. Alex joined Sandrine and smiled at Vi.

Eligos....

She didn't hear it; she felt it. The word came to her and she knew, somehow, that they had put it there, planted it in her brain. She cringed away from them as they melted into the gloom.

For some time after they had gone, she stared after them, wishing she had imagined it but knowing she hadn't.

★　　★　　★

"If I have to spend one more night in that hostel...." Tilly didn't have to finish her sentence. The Salvation Army did their best with their limited and much-stretched resources, but it still felt like living in an unpleasant school dormitory, with the ever-present odor of carbolic soap and disinfectant, the worn and scratchy blanket, and rickety collapsible beds that threatened to trap the unwary sleeper by suddenly closing up, or by simply collapsing and depositing the occupant unceremoniously on the floor.

"One night is quite enough," Vi said. "We need to find somewhere." She glanced at her wristwatch. "Come on, the paper will be out. Better get in quick."

The paper boy on the corner of the street was calling out and the women bought the *Evening Standard*. They went into the nearest Lyons Corner House and perused the *Rooms to Let* section.

"Not much here," Vi said. "Here's one though. 'Suitable for two professional women, sharing.' The rent's reasonable and it's not far. Let's hope by 'professional' they don't mean...."

"What? Oh, Vi." Tilly let out a guffaw that attracted disapproving looks from a couple of respectable-looking older ladies sipping tea at the next table.

Tilly covered her mouth, but the two of them were now trying unsuccessfully to stifle giggles. After the trauma of the previous evening, Vi felt guilty. Poor Mrs. Harris was lying in the hospital morgue while a search was made to trace her relatives. That morning's visit to what was left of Boscawen Walk had been grim. Early daylight revealed that around half the houses had either suffered a direct hit and been demolished when the airplane came down or had suffered catastrophic damage and were unsafe to return to. Even though Vi and Tilly got there shortly after daybreak, the looters were already around. Fortunately, police and the army arrived, and the thieves soon legged it, taking whatever they could carry.

Seeing the state of the house seemed like déjà vu to Vi. "My home looked like this," she said to Tilly. "I doubt we'll find anything worth saving."

Tilly squeezed her arm. "Oh, I don't know. We might strike lucky and find Sandrine's bloody drum. Maybe we can use it to summon up a friendly spirit who'll rebuild the house."

But there had been no drum, no friendly spirit and anything recognizable was either in tatters or smashed beyond repair. The furniture was firewood and even Mrs. Harris's cooker was a mass of twisted metal.

After an hour, they gave up. At least they had their small suitcases with their essential documents – ration books, identity cards, money, and, as they only had the clothes they were wearing, they bought what they could afford from a nearby shop.

"It doesn't go far, does it?" Vi said as she handed over the last few shillings she could reasonably afford. After all, they had rent to pay out on new lodgings yet.

The shop assistant smiled sympathetically. "If you've been bombed out, you can always go to the WVS. You know, the Women's Voluntary Service. They can help you out with essential clothes and so on."

"Thanks," Tilly said and grimaced at Vi. "I don't fancy wearing someone else's knickers, do you?"

Vi screwed up her nose and shook her head. "If we only knew

someone who could get hold of some parachute silk, we could make our own."

That had been their first giggle and it felt good. Now, in the coffee house, their laughter was on the verge of hysteria and the more guilty she felt, the more Vi couldn't help herself.

"Come on," she managed at last. "Let's go before someone else gets our room."

★　　★　　★

At Nineteen Quaker Terrace, the door was answered within seconds. Evidently the owner, Mrs. Sinclair, believed in polishing her brass door knocker within an inch of its life as it nearly blinded Vi and she felt duty bound to give it a little wipe with her glove in case she had smeared it.

A pleasing, homely smell of lavender wax polish wafted through the partially open door.

"We're here about the room," Tilly said.

Mrs. Sinclair looked them up and down. She opened the door wider. "Come in, girls."

"We passed the test," Tilly whispered to Vi, who shushed her.

They followed Mrs. Sinclair down the hallway. Vi noted it appeared recently painted; a pleasant cream color adorned the walls. It struck her as unusual. She was used to wallpaper, usually with little sprigs of flowers on it – her mother's choice, and Mrs. Harris's, come to that.

At the top of a single flight of stairs, Mrs. Sinclair opened a door, revealing a large, airy and light room, this time with the expected wallpaper. On either side, a single bed, neatly made up with matching pink quilts, and small bedside tables with lamps next to each. Two single wardrobes stood side by side. An Art Deco dressing table with long mirrors was positioned in front of a large bay window, which was adorned with net curtains and the regulation blackout.

After determining that they were indeed 'professional' working girls, Mrs. Sinclair delivered her rules. "I won't tolerate any nonsense or hanky-panky. No followers, of course."

Vi couldn't look at Tilly throughout the list of *do*'s and *don't*s.

"Rent is payable one week in advance, with one week's notice on either side should the arrangement not work out. Breakfast is at seven thirty a.m. Monday to Friday and at eight thirty on Saturdays and Sundays. Dinner is at seven p.m. If you should not require any, I should be obliged if you would give me at least twenty-four hours' notice."

"That may not always be possible," Vi said, and noticed Mrs. Sinclair had the ability to raise one eyebrow independently of the other. "It's just… the war work I'm engaged in. The hours aren't always regular. They've warned me I may have to stay overnight at extremely short notice."

The landlady nodded and appeared to consider this for a moment. "I'm not going to ask you what kind of work you're engaged in. Careless talk and all that. I'm assuming, given our location, that you are probably based around the government offices, so I shall be flexible in the circumstances. For your part, please be prepared that your dinner may have been freshly cooked the day before and, by necessity, have been stored until you were in a position to eat it."

"Of course. I quite understand. And I will try and give you as much notice as possible. Do you have a telephone?"

"No, I don't hold with the things."

"Well, I'll do my best anyway."

"So, you will be taking the room, then?"

Vi and Tilly exchanged looks. They nodded.

"Thank you, Mrs. Sinclair," Vi said. "We'll pay you the week's rent now."

They handed over the money and Mrs. Sinclair produced a small rent book from the folds of her pre-war skirt. She handed over a set of keys to each of them and left them to it.

Tilly sank on the bed by the wall. "Can you believe her? What century is she stuck in? The eighteenth?"

"Shhh. She'll hear you." Vi listened at the closed door. From downstairs she heard a door close.

"Not as free and easy as dear old Mrs. Harris, is she?"

Vi sighed.

CHAPTER NINE

Down in the Cabinet War Rooms, Vi passed the familiar sign, *There is to be no whistling or unnecessary noise in this passage.* Farther along, past more offices, she sniffed the air. Masking the familiar stale cigarette smell, a fragrant expensive aroma of good-quality cigars signaled the presence of their most illustrious inhabitant. Mr. Churchill was around. Probably chairing a meeting of his chiefs of staff. Vi had learned he didn't enjoy these meetings and deliberately sat the generals, in all their military splendor, in a line directly in front of him.

"Like naughty boys at school," Ethel had said, after she had taken minutes at one of those meetings. "The Old Man really gave them what for. Tore strips off them. I had to edit my notes really carefully to get rid of all the expletives! Talk about making a general squirm."

The cigar aroma was growing stronger the farther Vi progressed down the corridor. Her sensible shoes made little noise but, as she passed Room 69 – the Cabinet Room – she walked on tiptoe. A sentry with a stern expression stood guard outside the closed door. Vi carried straight on, turning moments later to enter her own office.

Ethel and Nancy were both typing at their noiseless machines, which were not truly silent. Instead of the usual sharp repetitive clack as each key was depressed, a soft, muffled *thwump* punctuated their dexterity and considerable speed.

Nancy looked over at Vi and winked. Vi smiled, closed the door quietly and sat at her desk.

The first few documents were tedious, almost unintelligible and mostly written in some sort of code. Vi concentrated on the task at hand, pushing away all thoughts of the previous day. She typed the reference numbers, copying them carefully. One error here and the document could end up in the wrong hands, or at least be delayed.

Vi centered the carriage, ready to type the document's heading, and stopped. She couldn't have read it incorrectly. There it was, in its author's neat, slightly sloping handwriting.

Sandrine Maupas di Santiago.

There was no salutation. What followed was sheer gobbledygook to Vi. Its addressee would no doubt understand it, but she had to type up the whole thing. A foolscap and a half of meaningless unconnected words and random numbers requiring a code breaker's handbook to decipher. Apart from the heading, there was no clue as to the document's contents.

Of all the work she typed that day, this was the most solidly encrypted, with the exception of its heading.

But why not encrypt that too?

One thing was certain. Whoever Sandrine was, she was certainly attracting significant attention at the highest levels. She had to be an enemy spy, and Vi was sworn to secrecy by the oath she had taken. She couldn't even tell Tilly about this latest discovery. One girl had been fired from her post upstairs only last week when she had been overheard chatting about work with a friend, in a café down the road. Three years' loyal service without a blemish on her record and then, that was it. One mistake. But a fatal one. Out on her ear. She was working in a munitions factory now. What was that Gracie Fields song?

'I'm the girl that makes the thing that drills the hole that holds the ring that drives the rod that turns the knob that works the thing-ummy-bob'

A far cry from the Treasury.

*   *   *

"You're very quiet," Tilly said as the two of them walked home. For once, they both finished on time, although Vi had been told that, from the following week, she could expect to have to work extra shifts, arriving at three p.m. and not leaving until maybe four the following afternoon. Repetitive, relentless typing with scarcely a glimpse of the outside world. How much longer would this dreadful war drag on? But thinking about the future was not advisable. One day at a time was recommended. That's what her mother said, anyway. It had helped her get through the First World War. Hard though when you really didn't know what was going to be left at the end of it. Even harder when your current world had turned strange. Vi felt she was constantly looking over her shoulder. That, at any moment, Sandrine and Alex might appear. Or worse.

Eligos.

★ ★ ★

Vi and Tilly were Mrs. Sinclair's only tenants and they ate alone in the immaculately clean and tidy dining room.

"Bit different to Mrs. Harris's, isn't it?" Tilly whispered as they tucked into an excellent toad in the hole.

"Mrs. Sinclair's a great cook though." Vi couldn't remember when a meal had tasted so good. "This gravy is delicious."

Tinned pears and condensed milk finished off their meal and, as she laid her spoon down in the empty bowl, Vi stretched her arms and legs. "I'm so tired. I think that excellent meal has been such a shock to my insides it's worn me out."

"If we eat like this every night, we'll be the size of houses by the end of the month."

"No such luck for me next week, I'm afraid," Vi said.

"Are they putting you up somewhere or do you have to sleep in the office?"

"They have emergency sleeping quarters down there. It won't be for long anyway. Just the odd night now and again."

"I wouldn't like that. I like to come home to the same bed every night."

"Me too, but there *is* a war on, you know."

They both laughed. Mrs. Sinclair chose that moment to come

in. She gave them a slight smile, which only served to make Vi feel awkward – almost like a naughty schoolgirl. The landlady began to collect up their plates.

"Oh no, that's all right, Mrs. Sinclair," Tilly said, grabbing a dish. "Vi and I will do that. We used to at our other place."

Mrs. Sinclair grabbed at the dish, like a child scared of losing a favorite toy. Her eyes held an almost rabid quality, although why she should react in that way to a simple offer of help was beyond Vi. When the landlady spoke, her tone was clipped and curt. "That's quite all right, Tilly. I'll do it. I'm sure you could both do with putting your feet up."

Tilly let her take the dish from her and the two girls watched as Mrs. Sinclair piled up the crockery and left the room. "I reckon she thinks we'll break her precious china," she said.

"Well, it *is* Royal Albert," Vi said and winked at her friend. Nevertheless, Mrs. Sinclair's behavior had been odd. Why get so possessive over some old plates?

"Don't you think she's a bit...well, odd, I suppose?" she said to Tilly when they got back to their room.

"Dotty. It's the war. It takes people in different ways, especially if they've been through the last lot."

"I suppose so." Vi leaned back on her pillow and picked up her latest book. Dorothy L. Sayers had her sleuth, Lord Peter Wimsey, mixed up in murder and mayhem at a women's college. Tilly was also reading. Some light romance, probably.

It was still early but Vi's eyelids started to close, until she could no longer keep them open. Her book clattered to the floor, startling Tilly.

"I'm going to turn in," Vi said, a huge yawn overwhelming her. "I'll go to the bathroom."

"I'll get changed, but I think I'll read for an hour or so yet." Tilly started to unbutton her blouse as Vi took her toilet bag along the hall to the communal bathroom. The sound of dance music, played by a big band, drifted up the stairs. Mrs. Sinclair was listening to the wireless, no doubt. Probably Joe Loss or Geraldo or similar.

Vi closed the bathroom door, used the toilet, and stood in front of the mirror as she washed her hands and face.

The overhead light cast a dim glow, giving her an almost ghostly halo as she brushed her teeth and stared at her reflection. Mrs. Sinclair's strange behavior kept invading her thoughts. That wildness in her eyes as she snatched that dish back from Tilly....

Her teeth cleaned, Vi rinsed her mouth and dried her face on her towel. She glanced back in the mirror, but instead of reflecting the pale green wall, with black and white tiles running halfway up it, a face swam into view. Close up behind her. Vi held her breath, too scared to move. Like a photographic plate in a developing tray, the image swam before her eyes.

In seconds, the face of a man stared out at her.

That man. Alex.

His lips moved and his voice echoed in her head.

Eligos is waiting....

The image faded and Vi could move. She lurched forward and fumbled with the door, snapped the light off and sped down the landing to their room. She wrenched the door open, dived inside, and shut it, panting as she spun the key in the lock.

"Heavens, Vi, what's happened?" Tilly was beside her in seconds, guiding her to the bed.

Vi couldn't stop trembling. "I saw him. In the mirror. Alex. He's followed us here."

★　　★　　★

Two hours later, Vi still lay curled up, fetus-like, unable to sleep, jumping at every sound. She was sure Tilly thought she had imagined it. But Vi knew. That face she had seen reflected in the bathroom mirror and the man Alex were one and the same.

★　　★　　★

"It's time to get up, Vi. Seven o'clock. Mrs. Sinclair'll have our guts for garters if we're late for breakfast."

Vi struggled up in bed and shook her head, trying to rid it of the sleep that had eventually claimed her. By the time she made it downstairs, Tilly was already finishing a boiled egg and about to start on the golden toast, margarine and marmalade.

Vi's appetite had deserted her and she struggled to get half a slice down, but she did manage two cups of strong black tea.

"I don't know how you can drink it like that," Tilly said.

Vi yawned. "I need something to wake me up."

"I heard you tossing and turning."

"Oh, sorry. I didn't mean to keep you awake."

"You didn't. I kept waking up. I had such strange dreams, really disturbing. I kept seeing that man, you know...Alex. Or my mind's image of him anyway. Clark Gable really. It must have been what you were telling me. Seeing him in the mirror."

"He really was there, Tilly. I'm not making it up and I know I didn't imagine it."

"I never said you did. It's only that...."

"That, what?"

"How could he know you were here? I mean he associates you with Mrs. H., not here."

"Maybe he followed me. Maybe he isn't human, I don't know."

"Are you going to tell Miss Brayshaw?"

"How could I? She'll think I'm barmy. If it hadn't happened to me – to us – I'd think it was barmy. No, we need something more... credible."

Tilly drained her cup. "We'd better get moving. Being late will do us no good at all."

★   ★   ★

"Miss Harrington."

Vi looked up from her typing to see the owner of the clipped voice. A tall, straight-backed woman in her late fifties peered at her from behind round tortoiseshell spectacles that gave her the impression of an earnest owl. Her iron-gray hair was caught into a neat bun at the nape of her neck and she put Vi in mind of a stern schoolmistress.

"May I help you?" Vi asked.

"Mr. Glennister wishes to see you on a matter of some importance, if you would care to come with me."

The whispers behind her, though indistinct, told Vi that Ethel and Nancy would have something to gossip about. She followed the woman out of the office and down the corridor.

"My name is Miss Harvey," the woman said. "And I am Mr. Glennister's private secretary."

"May I ask what Mr. Glennister's role is? They neglected to tell me when he interviewed me."

"No, you may not," Miss Harvey replied.

Vi knew better than to push the point. Last time, Vi had met Mr. Glennister in Miss Brayshaw's upstairs office. This time, Miss Harvey led the way past the officers' mess where, judging by the distinctive aroma, cabbage appeared to be on the menu today. Vi caught a swift glimpse of a sign that read *Fair*. She found it reassuring to know what the weather was doing up there. A lovely spring day, probably. Blossom on the trees. Birds singing as if there wasn't a war on. Yet another beautiful day she was missing. Those carefree days she used to take for granted seemed so far off. Unreal.

Reality hit back as she followed Miss Harvey through a doorway guarded by an armed soldier who checked their ID, and into a corridor Vi hadn't been down before. Here, the only sound was the lightest tap of their shoes on the concrete floor. The air smelled stale and, despite the clanky air conditioning, choked with cigarette smoke – even more so than in her own familiar corridors.

Vi found herself wondering what lay above them. They seemed to have walked for half a mile or more. There was no sound of traffic, but she never heard it where she worked either. A sudden wave of claustrophobia swept over her and she felt nauseous. Just as she thought she would have to tell Miss Harvey that she needed to be sick, the woman stopped in front of a door and knocked.

A male voice she recognized called, "Enter."

Miss Harvey motioned to Vi to follow her as she opened the door and crossed the threshold.

The room was small, in common with the other offices. Big enough to allow for work to be done, too small to be comfortable. In the corner, a simple iron bedstead, with a neatly made-up bed, spoke of a man who worked far longer than normal office hours. Judging from the tiny bit of striped flannel peeking out from under the pillow, the bed was in current use.

The man looked up from a paper he was in the process of correcting or editing. He held his pipe in his left hand, while a gold-and-black expensive-looking fountain pen took up his right.

"Miss Harrington."

"Yes, sir."

"Sit down. That will be all for now, Miss Harvey."

"Very good, Mr. Glennister." The secretary left, closing the door quietly behind her.

"Now, Miss Harrington, I expect you're wondering why I have called you here today."

"I am indeed, sir."

"I am aware of the work you currently do and that you have made a good start. The PM is pleased with your accuracy and efficiency, along with the calm way you approach your tasks."

"That's very kind of him, sir."

"Yes. Indeed." Mr. Glennister cleared his throat. "Now, Miss Harrington. I understand that, until recently, you have been sharing lodgings with a woman by the name of Sandrine Maupas di Santiago and you and your friend, a Miss Layton, who also works here, have expressed serious concerns about the activities of this woman."

"That's correct, sir."

"You believe this Santiago woman is an enemy spy, don't you?"

Vi took a deep breath. "Well...we have no proof, you see, it's just that her comings and goings seem strange. Unusual. Her whole attitude has been quite aggressive, and that man she consorts with—"

Mr. Glennister shot forward in his seat. "Man? What man?"

"I don't know anything about him really. Sandrine – Miss Santiago – calls him Alex." Vi stopped, aware Mr. Glennister was only half listening. He was busy scribbling notes down on a sheet of foolscap.

He stopped and looked up. "Can you describe this man? Height, looks, any distinguishing features?"

"Yes. He's around six feet tall, fairly slim, dark hair, slicked down with Brylcreem or something similar. His face is sort of... craggy, I suppose you'd call it. To be honest, he reminded me a lot of Clark Gable."

"Clark Gable? The American actor?"

"Yes, that's right. He could almost be his double. They say we all have one, don't we?" *Shut up, Vi. You're gabbling.* She clenched her hands in her lap.

"There's no need to be nervous, Miss Harrington. You've done nothing wrong."

Was that an attempt at a smile on Mr. Glennister's face?

"Since you left your previous lodgings at...." He turned over some sheets lying in a neat pile next to him and searched down them. "Ah yes, Boscawen Walk. Since you and Miss Layton left there, have you seen this man again?"

Vi hesitated. He would never believe her. "No, sir."

She wished he wouldn't stare at her so hard. She was sure he could tell she was lying, but what could she do? Risk him disbelieving everything she had said by telling him something totally impossible?

"And, to the best of your knowledge, has Miss Layton ever seen him?"

That was much easier. "No, sir. And I am certain she would have told me if she had."

Mr. Glennister scribbled some more notes, screwed the cap back on his pen and once again laid it down in precisely the same place as before.

After some moments, during which Vi had almost memorized the pattern on the rug at her feet, the civil servant leaned forward again, elbows on the desk.

"Thank you for your co-operation, Miss Harrington. I need not tell you that our conversation has been in the strictest confidence. A need-to-know basis only. This means I would prefer it if you refrained from discussing our meeting with Miss Layton."

"I understand, sir."

"I may ask to see you again but, in the meantime, should you see or hear anything of Miss Santiago or this man – Alex – kindly tell Miss Brayshaw immediately and she will make sure I am informed."

"Yes, sir."

He stood, signaling the end of their interview. He extended his right hand to her and, for an instant, his shirtsleeve rode up his arm a few inches. Just enough for Vi to spot a tattoo she hadn't seen before, on his inner wrist.

There surely couldn't be two of them, could there? Both here? Both with that stylized Odal's rune inked onto their arms?

It took her twice as long to get back to her office, as she managed to take two wrong turns and ended up in the kitchen. An orderly set her right and she gathered she wasn't the first person to get lost.

"These corridors all look the same," she said.

The orderly laughed. "You'll get used to it," he said. "We all do… in the end."

Vi quickened her step, anxious to return to make a dent in her in-tray before lunch. She passed an open door and caught a quick glimpse of the occupant before he shut the door.

It couldn't be…. She leaned against the wall, momentarily winded as if someone had punched her in the stomach. *He couldn't be here. Not HERE.*

She forced herself to take deep, even breaths and then retraced the few steps back to the now firmly closed door. There was no name plate. Just the room number. 338.

That in itself was more than a little odd. Vi wasn't sure how many rooms there were precisely but she had never seen triple figures. Either side of that room were ones marked 81 and 82.

She sped back to her office and arrived, slightly breathless.

Nancy and Ethel looked up.

"You look as if a ghost leapt out at you," Nancy said, laughing.

"Who's in Room 338?" Vi said.

"338?" Ethel looked at Nancy. "There's no such room."

"But there must be. I was there. I went past it. There was a man in there, but he shut the door before I could get a proper look at him."

"Sorry, Vi. You must be mistaken. There is definitely no Room 338 down here."

Miss Brayshaw entered. "What's going on here? Or should I ask, why is nothing going on here?"

"Vi was just asking," Nancy said, "about Room 338. She saw someone in there, or so she says."

Ethel snickered.

Vi sank down in her seat and wished she could disappear under the desk.

"Room 338? Wherever did you get that idea? There isn't one. Never has been. Now come on, everyone, get on with your work. I want those in-trays emptied. And the PM's around, so quietly if you please." Miss Brayshaw left them, pulling the door closed behind her.

At her desk, inserting carbons between sheets of copy paper, Vi inwardly seethed.

Three typewriters made their constant muted *thwumps* and carriages whirred as they were manually returned. Cogs ratcheted as fresh sheets of paper were inserted and wound into them. Printed sheets and carbons rustled as they were deposited in their allotted trays. Occasionally, a well-worn sheet of carbon would be screwed up and tossed into a waste bin at the side of the owner's desk – the noise like scrunched-up tissue paper.

The hours ticked by, measured by the circular wall clock, its second hand moving round and round the Roman numerals.

Vi took her lunch break at one, as Nancy and Ethel returned. She had barely exchanged a word with them since the incident over the apparently non-existent Room 338. Right now, Vi wanted to be on her own. She wanted to retrace her steps.

She reached the end of her corridor and stopped. To the left? Or the right? Why couldn't she remember which way she had come? It had only been a couple of hours earlier.

Vi decided on turning left and looked up at the door numbers. Satisfied she was proceeding in the right direction, she hurried. Her lunch break was only half an hour and she couldn't be late back.

She reached Room 69, guarded as always. Except…. When she passed it earlier, there had been no guard on duty. It hadn't registered at the time because she was still in a flap about the man she had seen. Maybe the guard was only there when the PM was around. But no, Room 69 was the Cabinet Room and was always guarded. Vi hurried past him, to the next room. There was the sign. Number 81. Next door should be….

She stared up in disbelief. Where the number 338 should have been, number 82 was there. Only a short expanse of wall separated the two rooms. There was not enough space for another room – not even enough for the short, narrow passageway she had noticed before. She stood and stared at the two doors, willing the room she knew had been there earlier to somehow miraculously reappear.

"Something I can help you with, miss?"

Vi realized the guard was addressing her. She must look highly suspicious, standing there, with some stupid expression on her face, no doubt. "No, sorry. I got myself a bit…lost."

"Where are you trying to get to? I can direct you. I've been here a few months now. Know my way around pretty well."

Vi forced a smile. "Thank you, but I'm fine now. I know where I need to go."

"Best get off there, then." His polite way of telling her to get lost, but at least he was civil about it.

"Thank you…." She counted the stripes on the sleeve of his khaki uniform. "Thank you, Sergeant. There is one thing…."

"Yes, miss?"

"Were you on duty earlier this morning? Did you see me come past at about nine and then return a few minutes later?"

"I've been on duty since eight o'clock this morning. Yes, I saw you come down here with Miss Harvey. I don't recall seeing you go back this way though. Maybe you took the long way round." He pointed down the corridor past Rooms 81 and 82.

Had she? He was still watching her; a frown had appeared on his face. She would have to let it go, for now at least.

"Thanks again, Sergeant. I'll be getting back now."

"That's the ticket, miss."

There wasn't time for lunch now. Vi settled for a cup of tea, which she took back to the office. Maybe the sergeant was right. Maybe she had gone 'the long way round' as he called it. That would explain how she ended up getting lost.

Ethel and Nancy stopped talking as soon as she opened the door. Let them think what they liked about her. She knew the truth. The only problem was she hadn't a clue how the truth could actually be happening.

CHAPTER TEN

The marine unlatched the locks and yanked the door open.

"You'll sleep down here." Miss Brayshaw led Vi through the bright red iron door she remembered seeing on her first day down here. She had wondered what lay behind it then. Now she was about to find out. Vi followed Miss Brayshaw past another guard, down a flight of stone stairs into a subterranean basement. Maneuvering her suitcase and the box containing her gas mask, which she had slung diagonally across her shoulder, demanded skills of dexterity Vi felt it would need weeks of practice to perfect. But, somehow, she made it to the bottom with her cargo and herself intact.

Vi had packed her suitcase with overnight clothes, toiletries, towel, underwear, nightclothes and change of day wear. She had been told to pack for three days. Shifts would be long, the work would be exacting and, judging by what she was seeing, conditions would hardly be luxurious.

The ceiling was so low, she had to bend her head; warning signs every few yards reminded her to do just that. Vi stood five foot six inches in her stockinged feet and pitied any of the tall soldiers she had seen around here. Some of them were way over six feet.

She followed Miss Brayshaw along the narrow and oppressive corridor. "What's that awful smell?" She wrinkled her nose against the acrid chemical stench, partially masking something that stank like sewage.

"I'm afraid that's from the chemical toilets. There are twenty-two of them down here. Thirteen are for the men and nine for the women. The plumbed-in bathroom is upstairs so I'm afraid you'll be going up and down in your dressing gown if you want a bath. As you can see, you'll have an audience, although they do try to ignore you, but they're only human after all." Miss Brayshaw nodded toward a marine who stood on guard outside a closed door.

"There are offices here as well as sleeping accommodation. If you think *you* have it bad, imagine sleeping *and* working down here for days, perhaps weeks at a time. Some poor blighters have been doing it over the past year or so. You grow accustomed to the smell but…." Miss Brayshaw stopped at a door and opened it. Inside, a small dormitory with three rows of tiered bunks greeted Vi. The beds were simply made up, with a single pillow and a gray army blanket.

"Not what you're used to, I'm sure," Miss Brayshaw said, her voice kind enough to cause Vi's eyes to prickle with tears she had no intention of shedding.

A dull clattering noise echoed through the cramped sleeping quarters.

Miss Brayshaw sighed. "The sound you hear is the air-conditioning."

"Does it go off at night?"

Her supervisor shook her head. "If it did, we would all suffocate. Oh damn!'

Vi jumped. Out of the corner of her eye she saw something black scuttle away under the door. "Was that…?"

"I'm afraid so. Either a cockroach or some other beetle. You'll probably become quite an expert on different species down here, and that's not the worst of it, I'm sorry to say."

"Not rats?"

"Yes. There's no point in shielding you from it. At least you'll know what to expect. Don't leave anything out, and certainly no food of any kind. Not even a crumb. You'll have the hordes descending and everyone will hate you." She smiled. "I know it's grim, Violet, but we're all in it together. I've done my stint down here and I daresay I shall be called on to do it again. One consolation is that your first night will probably be your worst. You've come here well rested from a nice comfortable lodging house so tonight you'll be listening out for every sound, squeak and twitch. You'll imagine the air-conditioning is getting louder, even though it probably isn't, and you'll be concentrating hard on not going to the toilet during the night, which will make it worse until you do have to go. Tomorrow, after a rotten night and a fourteen-hour shift, you'll simply be glad you've got somewhere you can lie down."

Vi glanced around. "How do I know which bed's mine?"

"Pick one that doesn't have a nightie under the pillow and put yours there. You did bring a sensible dressing gown with you, didn't you? Only we had a girl recently who brought an almost transparent piece of French nonsense. Some fancy lingerie set, handmade in Paris. Silly girl had to put her raincoat on to go upstairs to take a bath. Needless to say, the first time she saw a rat she screamed blue murder. At four o'clock in the morning. She made herself extremely unpopular."

"My dressing gown is of the flannel variety, designed to keep out drafts, although it's so hot down here...." Vi fanned herself with her hat.

"As I said, not what you're used to, or many of us, come to that. Some of the girls from Hoxton and Poplar though...." Miss Brayshaw stopped. "Anyway, enough of that. Pop your suitcase on your bed. Yes, that one is as good as any."

Vi pulled the pillow off, holding her breath in case she saw any bugs, relieved when she didn't. She opened her case, pulled out her nightdress, refolded it and put it on the bed, with the pillow over it.

"Come with me and I'll show you where the toilets are and where you can wash your hands."

"I suppose if I forget I can just follow my nose."

"As long as your nose doesn't lead you to the gents'." Miss Brayshaw laughed.

The tall metal chemical toilet with its black seat looked less than inviting.

"This is your nearest convenience. There are others farther along." Miss Brayshaw indicated more cubicles, clearly marked as to whether they were for use by male or female personnel.

"Are the other girls in the dormitory typists as well?"

"Some will be. The rest probably a mix of telephonists and various other personnel, both military and civilian. You *have* brought your flashlight, I hope. It's dark enough now, but at night the lights are mostly switched off in the sleeping areas so you'll need a light to find your way to the toilet and back and, if you're late coming down or early rising, you'll need it then too."

Vi nodded. "I've got it in my handbag in the office."

"Best keep it on you at all times. Right, time to get back to work now. Make sure you note where you are so you'll remember for later."

*   *   *

"How was your first night in the Dock? Grim?" Ethel grinned over at Vi, who nodded. "I can tell by your eyes. You could pack a week's washing in those bags."

"One of the girls I share with snores. Another was so angry with her she woke her up to have a fight with her, thankfully not a physical one though. I swear someone was hammering on that damned air-conditioning and, as if that wasn't enough, a bloody rat ran over my foot as I was getting up this morning."

Ethel laughed.

Nancy came in. "What have I missed?"

"Vi's just spent her first night down in the Dock."

Nancy rolled her eyes. "My turn next week. God I hate it, but you've broken your duck now. Tonight you'll be so tired you'll be happy to sleep on a clothesline."

"After last night, I think I'd rather. And those toilets." Vi pinched her nose with her fingers.

"Even that gets better," Ethel said. "You won't smell it by the end of your time down there. I have a friend who lives in Port Sunlight – near Liverpool. It's where they make Sunlight soap. The whole place stinks of rotten eggs from the chemicals they use. Anyway, I went to stay with her once and I asked her how she could live with that stench. She said, 'What stench?' She couldn't smell it at all, even though she has a perfectly normal sense of smell. You get used to it and eventually your brain seems to decide you've suffered enough and simply switches it off."

*   *   *

Fourteen hours later, Vi wished her brain would switch it off now. She shone her flashlight on her watch. Just after three in the morning. Not that she would have known if it was day or night down here in the Dock. She had finished her day's work an hour earlier. Now it was time to get ready for bed again. Despite the noise, the stench and the heat, Vi was sure she would sleep tonight. Exhaustion made her arms and legs feel heavy. She yawned and made her way upstairs to the bathroom, where she could wash and brush her teeth.

She put her flashlight on the side of the bath and opened her toilet bag to take out her toothbrush and paste as she glanced in the mirror above the sink. The soft light cast a glow that seemed to radiate around her head. Behind her the room was shrouded in shadow. Was she imagining it, or were the shadows growing darker? Vi prayed the bulb wasn't about to give out. She checked the position of her flashlight and reached out her hand for it. Yes, she could grab it in a second.

She spread paste on her brush and raised her hand.

The bulb fizzed. Popped. The room drowned in darkness. Vi threw her toothbrush in the sink and grabbed for her flashlight. She had it; the tips of her fingers brushed its shiny surface. Then she lost it. It must have slipped out of her fingers, but it felt as if someone had grabbed it. It clattered into the bath. Pray God, it wasn't smashed. In pitch darkness, Vi reached into the bath and felt around.

Her hand touched something warm and furry. She gave a little cry and jerked back, quivering from head to foot.

Pull yourself together. You have to do this.

Vi took a deep breath and reached out again, steadying herself with one hand on the edge of the bath. She reached in. *Don't let me touch that rat again.* The enamel felt hard and cold under her fingers, as if she were stroking ice. She patted the surface, trying to move her hand around in logical and ever-increasing semicircles. At the limit of her reach, she took a few tentative steps alongside the bath to explore farther along. Finally, her fingers found what they were searching for. Vi snatched up the flashlight and depressed the switch. It flickered on and off. She shook it. Tried again. This time it worked. There was a small crack in the glass but at least she had illumination now. The bathroom was silent save for an occasional drip from the bath tap.

It's too quiet.

And then it wasn't.

"Good evening, Miss Harrington."

The reflection in the mirror glowed. The man's eyes gleamed as the creature lodged deep within stirred.

Vi's scream brought someone running. Voices – at least one male and one female – called out to her through the door as they banged on it repeatedly. Vi wrestled with the handle, but it wouldn't budge. "It's stuck!" she yelled. "Please. Break the door down. There's someone in here and I can't get out."

Suddenly the door gave way, sending her reeling back against the bath and nearly toppling her. A young woman she had seen working in the switchboard office and two soldiers in uniform dashed in. They grabbed her and pulled her out into the corridor. Vi burst into tears and collapsed against the woman.

The middle-aged telephonist spoke with a north of England accent. "It's all right, love. You're safe now."

One of the soldiers emerged from the bathroom. "There's no one there."

"I'll go and get a fresh bulb," his fellow private said and made off down the corridor.

Vi's cheeks grew hot and she knew she must have turned scarlet with the embarrassment sweeping over her. "I'm so sorry. You must think I'm a total fool making such a fuss, but I heard a voice and I saw...someone. A man. I've seen him before. He called my name and he was standing right next to me. In there." Vi pointed into the dark bathroom.

She knew from the exchange of glances between the soldier and the woman that they didn't believe her. The woman spoke:

"How many nights have you done, love? It's disorientating working and living like this. No daylight. It plays tricks with your mind. I know. I've done my stints in the Dock. How many more days are you on for?"

"Tomorrow – I mean today – is my last."

"That's another thing. You lose track of the days." The woman released Vi and smiled at her. "You'll be fine once you get back home and have a decent night's sleep in your own bed. That's if Jerry will let you, of course. He's been a right bugger this week."

Vi tried to smile. The woman was probably right. She had imagined it. Just like she had imagined Room 338 and seeing that man, Alex. If she carried on like this, she would need to report sick and see a psychiatrist.

"You've been very kind," Vi said to the soldier and the woman. "Thank you so much for helping me."

"Not at all, miss," the soldier said. "Ah, here's Fred now. Soon have that bulb fixed and then you can carry on with…whatever it was you were doing."

"Brushing my teeth. Although I think they can wait a few hours. I need to sleep."

"Will you be all right?" the telephonist asked.

"Yes, I'm fine now. Gave myself such a fright." Vi cast her eyes heavenward.

The telephonist glanced at her watch. "I'd better get back. They'll be sending a search party."

"Thank you again."

Fred came out of the bathroom. "All done," he said and smiled at her.

"Thank you, Fred."

"Anytime." He sloped off, hands in pockets, whistling a nonspecific tune.

Vi gathered up her things and quit the bathroom, making sure her dressing gown was tied tightly around her. Flashlight in hand, she made her way back through the increasing gloom and eventual darkness of the Dock at night.

In her dormitory, Vi couldn't see how many other women were there and took care to point the beam downward so as not to shine it in anyone's face and wake them. She counted the bunks until she came to the one she knew was hers. After pulling back the sheet and blanket, Vi climbed in and switched her flashlight off, placing it on the bedside cabinet next to her.

The heat was oppressive and the room airless. Vi pushed the sheet down so that it only covered her lower half. Thank God this was her last night. By six that evening she would be back at Quaker Terrace. But even there she didn't feel completely safe. She already knew Alex could find her – whether or not she imagined him.

And then there was Eligos.

*   *   *

"Have you ever felt you were going mad?" Vi asked as she and Tilly walked home the following day. It should have been such a relief to get out into the fresh air on such a beautiful warm early evening. The pale pink magnolia trees and bright scarlet camellias lent color and brightness that should have lifted her spirits. Vi had always loved colorful plants and shrubs, but now, they could have been gray for all the restorative effect they were having.

Tilly laughed. "Frequently. I think we all are. It's this bloody war. We'll all be housed in lunatic asylums if it goes on much longer."

"No, I'm serious, Tilly. I seem to be imagining all sorts of things these days. Things I would swear had actually happened. Like seeing Alex at work."

Tilly grabbed her arm. "You did what? You never told me."

"No, because I couldn't have seen him there. He was in a room that doesn't exist. I've been past it almost every day since, simply to check. There *is* no Room 338 on my floor. Oh, you might as well know the rest."

When she had finished her story by recounting the strange incident in the bathroom a couple of days earlier, they had reached their front door. Tilly's face had turned ashen.

Vi inserted her key in the lock. "Are you all right? You don't look well."

Tilly shook her head. "I'll be fine. It's just that.... What you've just told me."

"Yes?"

"It...well, it happened to me too."

Vi fumbled with the key and it fell on the step. She ignored it. "What? All of it? Seeing Alex? Voices in the bathroom? Impossible rooms?"

Tilly nodded. "Only the voices weren't in the bathroom. They were in our room when you were working those nights. I was scared stiff. I would have sworn there was someone in the room with me and then I was sure I actually saw him. Exactly as you described. He didn't speak to me. But the look he gave me." Tilly stopped and the two women faced each other. "I was bloody terrified, Vi. I'm not going to deny that. You know, at first I thought you had imagined him. I mean, someone who looks so much like Clark Gable he could be his stand-in couldn't be real, could he? But now I've seen him for myself...I can't...I *won't* deny the evidence of my own eyes. I believe you. Alex exists every bit as much as Sandrine does – and I believe both of them have a lot to hide and I'm not convinced they're even human. You see, the following day, I saw him again. At the Treasury. I'd gone to get some more paper and he came out of a room. It didn't have a number or a name but it's one I'd never seen before and I thought it was odd because I know that corridor so well. He was too far away to speak to but he's so distinctive-looking, you can't mistake him for anyone else – except Clark Gable of course, and I'm sure as I can be that *he* wasn't visiting the Treasury that day.

"I stood frozen to the spot for a few moments and he strolled down the corridor, away from me. I hurried after him and came up to the spot where he had appeared. Just as I thought though, there was no room there. Only a blank wall. Right along that part of the corridor there *are* no doors. Only that one time. I wasn't going to tell you any of this because I know how upset you've been, but.... You deserve to know. Either we're both mad, or neither of us is."

Vi stared at her friend. "So, does this mean we're having some kind of joint hallucination?"

Tilly shook her head. "I've never heard of such a thing. Isn't the simplest solution usually the best?"

"What?"

"That it actually happened. I don't know how, but I can't think of any other explanation."

CHAPTER ELEVEN

Vi and Tilly stood in the empty kitchen. Vi touched the kettle. It was stone-cold. "This hasn't been boiled all day. I don't understand where she could have gone. Mrs. Sinclair's the most punctual person – a stickler for timekeeping – but it's nearly seven and there's no sign of her."

"You'd think she would have left a note," Tilly said, "but there's nothing. You don't think she's had an accident, do you?"

"I'm going outside," Vi said. "The outdoor toilet and the wash house – maybe we can find some trace of Mrs. Sinclair there. If not, I suggest we try the neighbors. See if they've seen her at all today."

"I'll grab my shoes and join you."

Vi opened the door and stepped out into the still-warm evening air. It was light enough to see without a flashlight, but she took one from the windowsill above the sink. The interiors of the outbuildings would be gloomy, and she didn't want any dark shadowy corners this evening.

The catch on the wash house stuck as usual but a little persuasion and it unhooked. Vi stepped in. The lingering clean smell of laundry soap greeted her. She stepped onto the stone floor and shone her flashlight around.

Vi caught her breath at a sudden scurrying movement in the far corner. Too big for a mouse or even a rat.

"Who's there?" she called.

From the kitchen doorway, Tilly called. "What is it? What's going on?"

Vi turned back to the entrance and poked her head around the doorway. "I thought I saw something."

Something warm and animallike – maybe even human – brushed up behind her. Vi shot out of the entrance and stood, panting, on the path.

Tilly rushed over to her. "What is it?"

"Something...someone...touched me."

Tilly grabbed the flashlight and strode into the wash house. She shone the light around wildly, the beam dancing off the walls. "Come out, whoever you are. We're not playing games here. This is private property and you have no business being here."

"Oh, I think you're wrong there."

*   *   *

Alex's voice was the last thing Vi heard until she woke up in bed the following morning to find Tilly stretching herself and yawning.

"Hello," she said. "Sleep well?"

Vi shook her head, trying to clear the fog that seemed to have settled on her brain. "I don't know. I.... Any sign of Mrs. Sinclair?"

"What?"

"Mrs. Sinclair. Has she come back?"

"Back from where?"

"What do you mean? She's *missing*. The last thing I remember was going out into the backyard to see if I could find any trace of her. Then I heard Alex's voice and I must have blacked out or something."

"Vi, you're not making much sense."

What now? Was Tilly playing games with her?

"Don't you remember telling me that you had seen Alex here when I was working nights last week? The same man who turned up at Mrs. Harris's and who I also saw at the Treasury?"

Tilly scratched her head. "I don't know what you're talking about. Who's Alex?"

"Alex. Sandrine's friend, or partner in crime, or whatever he is. Come on, you remember. I know you do."

"Who's Sandrine?"

Vi threw the covers off. "I don't find this at all funny."

Tilly raised her hands defensively. "Hey, whoa, girl steady on. Go back to the beginning. Tell me about this Sandrine and her Alex chap, and while you're at it, tell me who Mrs. what's her name…Harris? Who's she?"

"This is insane. I'm getting ready for work."

"It's Sunday. You're not back at work until tomorrow."

"In that case I'm going out for a walk. I need to clear my head."

"Make sure you come back in a better mood then. And don't forget, we're supposed to be going to the cinema tonight. *Rebecca*'s playing at the pictures."

"I had no idea we had any such arrangement." Vi knew she sounded as if she was talking to a stranger but right now, Tilly was acting like one.

Downstairs, Mrs. Sinclair was carrying toast and tea into the dining room, acting as if nothing had happened. As if she had been there the day before. Well, so be it.

"Good morning, Mrs. Sinclair. Did you enjoy your day out yesterday?"

"Good morning, Violet. My day out, you say? I didn't have a day out. I was here as usual." She set the breakfast things down and moved over to the window. Vi watched her in stunned silence.

Mrs. Sinclair tweaked the net curtains and peered out. "Another lovely sunny day. One to make the most of if you don't have to work."

Vi forced a smile and sat at the table. "It's my day off and I thought I'd take a walk around the park."

Mrs. Sinclair smiled and poured out tea.

Vi picked up the milk jug and then set it down again. Better to have her tea as strong as possible this morning.

Tilly joined her, sitting down opposite and eyeing her with a look that mixed suspicion with pity.

"Before you say anything," Vi said, "I know what happened last night. My last memory is of you and me outside the wash house. Alex spoke to us."

Tilly slammed her knife down, making the cups rattle. "For the last time, Vi, I don't know any Alex and I certainly don't have any recollection of any clandestine trips to the wash house."

Vi said nothing, sipped her tea, ate her toast and left the room. Tilly could go to the pictures alone. She certainly wouldn't be accompanying her.

Vi took the Tube to Hyde Park, where birds greeted her with their tuneful spring chorus. Trees were sprouting cherry and apple blossom; leaves were budding. Everywhere she looked were sights and smells of the earth renewing itself. It didn't matter that at any moment, the sirens could sound and the whole park could be blitzed into oblivion. Nature didn't wait and see; she simply got on with things.

After half an hour or so, Vi sat down on a bench and watched a pair of blackbirds foraging in the undergrowth nearby. Events of the past few days and weeks spun around in her head. Whatever was happening to her, was happening to her alone. Alex – or whatever his real name was – had done something to Tilly and probably Mrs. Sinclair too. He had wiped Tilly's memories clean of anything that could relate to Sandrine, Mrs. Harris and maybe even Boscawen Walk itself. If Tilly didn't remember Mrs. Harris, then she presumably didn't remember living there either.

For now, at least, it seemed that only Vi was permitted to know that certain people existed, but one thing she could prove....

Vi stood and made her way to the nearest Tube station. Soon, she was walking down the familiar streets that had led to her former lodging house. She turned into the next street as she always had. Boscawen Walk.

She looked down at the sign and did a double take. She had turned into Bottomley Way.

Vi stared at the sign in disbelief and confusion. She had never heard of Bottomley Way. Where the hell was she? She turned back on herself and gazed around wildly. The houses didn't look familiar. The people didn't look familiar. Where the corner shop should have been, there was another house – boarded up, following a bomb blast.

Vi retraced her steps, back toward the station. She didn't deviate from the direction that she would always have taken if she was going to the Tube. Sure enough, she arrived back there within a few short minutes.

No, she must have gone wrong somehow.

Vi painstakingly made her way back toward Boscawen Walk – or at least where it should have been. She checked each sign.

Finton Street…Getting Street…Walkden Way. Not one of them was familiar.

But this is all wrong. I'm going the right way but the streets are all wrong.

Sure enough, she arrived back at Bottomley Way.

A young woman in ATS uniform approached her. "Excuse me, but are you all right? You look a bit faint."

Vi struggled to pull herself together. She pasted a smile on her face. "Yes, I'm fine. Really. Just had a bit of a shock, that's all."

"Oh dear, do you want me to walk you to the nearest café? Doris's is just around the corner. A good strong cup of sweet tea should put you right and she makes tea you could stand your spoon up in."

"That's very kind of you."

Vi walked with the stranger, grateful for her company. At least she seemed normal, even if the rest of the world was going crazy.

They carried on along Bottomley Way, round the corner and into the small establishment the woman had recommended. The middle-aged woman behind the counter – Doris presumably – greeted her. "Hello, Agnes, brought a friend with you?"

"Hello, Doris. This is…." She turned to Vi. "I'm sorry, I don't even know your name."

"Vi. Vi Harrington."

"And I'm Agnes Boothroyd. Pleased to meet you, Vi."

"Pleased to meet you too." Agnes turned her attention back to Doris. "I met Vi round the corner in Bottomley Way. She's had a bit of a shock."

"You sit yourselves down. I've got just the thing for that. A nice pot of tea and a slice of my Dundee cake."

"Dundee cake?" Agnes exclaimed. "I haven't had any of that since before the war. How did...? Ah, best not ask." She laughed as Doris tapped the side of her nose with her forefinger and winked.

Vi managed a smile and sank down on a wooden chair at one of five tables, each laid out with red-and-white-checked tablecloths. Everything in the place was pristine and the tea and cake, when they arrived, soothed her.

Agnes took a bite of cake and Vi sipped the hot tea. It had the instant effect of reviving her. Hot, strong and quite sweet, it soothed her frayed nerves.

"So," Agnes said. "What was the shock?"

"Sorry?"

"You said you had just had a bit of a shock and that's why you were so pale and looked so lost."

Vi set down her cup on its saucer. "It's a bit difficult to explain. You see I was looking for the place where I used to live until a few weeks ago. Boscawen Walk. I came out of the Tube station and walked exactly the same way I always did...but I ended up in Bottomley Way."

Agnes frowned. "Boscawen Walk? Can't say I've ever heard of it. Do you know it, Doris?"

The older woman paused in the act of pouring out a mug of tea for a burly workman who was also taking an interest in the conversation. "Boscawen Walk? No. I don't know it and I've lived here for thirty years. How about you, Bert?"

The workman was rolling a thin cigarette. "No, there's no Boscawen Walk around here."

How could they say that? Vi stared from one to the other. They all seemed perfectly ordinary, nice people. Why would they lie? "But there must be," she said. "I was living there."

Bert raised his eyebrows and Doris wiped the counter surface unnecessarily as it was spotless.

"You really don't look well," Agnes said. "It's the war. It's getting to all of us. Making us say and do all sorts of things we wouldn't normally dream of doing."

Vi pushed her chair back and stood. Tea slopped in her saucer. She didn't care. She had to get away from here. This was madness, surely?

"I'm telling you. I lived there. It should be there. It used to be there. But now it isn't."

Agnes stood and came round the table to put her arm around Vi's shoulder. Vi shrugged her off.

"Vi—"

Vi gave them all one last look and raced out of the café. She ran most of the way back to the Tube station, where a train was pulling in. She scrambled in, squeezed into a seat and cast her eyes downward at her hands, clasped in her lap. As usual, the train was packed. It reeked of tobacco and unwashed bodies. Her stomach churned and she swallowed hard and repeatedly, the sour taste of bile tainting her tongue.

Within a couple of minutes the train reached her stop and Vi pushed her way through the throng and down onto the platform. She glanced at her watch. Ten past four. No doubt Tilly would be getting ready to go to the cinema with her. Vi had resolved not to go with this person who had overnight become a stranger. Now, she thought she might. Maybe, somewhere along the line, Tilly would let down her guard and reveal that she did indeed remember living at Boscawen Walk in Mrs. Harris's house. They would talk about Sandrine and all the strange events that had occurred. Life would return to normal. Or as normal as it could be in these bizarre circumstances.

★   ★   ★

Vi immersed herself in the drama of Daphne du Maurier's Gothic tale and Hitchcock's impeccable direction. He managed to wring every ounce of dramatic tension and sinister scariness out of the story. The chilling Mrs. Danvers, obsessed with her late mistress. The frightened and lonely second Mrs. de Winter and the husband who appeared to be aloof and uncaring but who harbored a terrible secret.

Even before the lights went down and the film started, Tilly and Vi barely spoke to each other. All their usual lively chatter seemed a thing of the past. They behaved like two people – almost strangers – who had paired up to go out for the evening rather than go alone.

It was still light when they walked home. Finally, Vi broke the awkward silence. "I went to Boscawen Walk today."

"Where's that?"

"Where we used to live."

"I don't know what you mean, Vi. I've never lived anywhere called Boscawen Walk."

Vi bit her tongue. There was no use protesting. She let it drop and carried on. "I ended up in Bottomley Way instead."

"Now, *that's* a road I *have* heard of. Not far from here. Couple of stops on the Tube."

"How do you know it?" Maybe Tilly would reveal something that would shed light on why she was lying.

Tilly was quiet for a moment. "I'm not sure. Maybe one of the girls in the office lives there. I've certainly heard of it."

"So where did you live *before* we came to Quaker Terrace?"

"Great Yarmouth. You know that. Then when the war broke out, I came to London. You and I met in a Lyons Corner house and, as we were both in pretty awful digs, decided we could get along together so we looked in the paper and there was an advertisement for Mrs. Sinclair's place. We've lived there ever since. That was two years ago."

It was as if a whole chunk of Tilly's life had been rewritten – or maybe hers had. At that moment, Vi doubted herself. Tilly seemed so definite, so certain. Could she be right? Could Vi have imagined Mrs. Harris and Boscawen Walk? And if so, what else had she dreamed up?

Neither of them spoke until they arrived back at Quaker Terrace.

"Home, sweet home," Tilly said, retrieving her key from her coat pocket and letting them both in.

★   ★   ★

The next morning, Vi deliberately left earlier than Tilly. She had no desire to walk with someone who had so recently been a friend and was now behaving like a complete stranger. If she could afford it, she would look for somewhere else to live but, with London rents as they were, she would be hard-pressed to find anywhere she could afford on her own. Mrs. Harris's had been unusually cheap.

In the office, Nancy and Ethel arrived a few minutes later and treated her as they always did. Normal cheery 'Good mornings', usual topics of conversation about the weekend they had enjoyed. Vi joined in, talking mainly about *Rebecca*. The relief at finding that not everything had gone topsy-turvy meant she had to fight off the urge to hug both girls.

When Miss Brayshaw dropped by to say Vi was requested to go to Mr. Glennister's office, she was feeling much calmer. Almost back to normal in fact.

Miss Harvey opened the door of Mr. Glennister's office, announced Vi, and stepped back to let her through.

The cheerful smile on Vi's face vanished in an instant as she saw who was standing by the fireplace, tapping tobacco ashes out of his pipe.

"*You.*"

The man she knew as 'Alex' grinned at her. "Have we met somewhere before? I'm sure I would have remembered."

She was aware of Mr. Glennister staring at her and she struggled to pull herself together. Before she accused him of anything, she had to know where she stood.

Mr. Glennister spoke. "Miss Harrington, this is Mr. Leopold Rance from the Foreign Office. He would like to talk to you on a matter of the utmost importance."

"But he's...."

"Yes. Miss Harrington?"

She couldn't hold back any longer. Mr. Glennister was standing, papers in his hand. It was clear he intended to leave the two of them alone together and that was the last thing she wanted. "He's the man I told you about. The one Sandrine called Alex...." Her voice tailed away as she saw both men exchange bemused glances.

"Leo? Have you any idea what Miss Harrington is talking about?"

"Not a clue." Oh, he was smart, that one. He played his part well. Vi felt a wave of anger curl upward. Pretty soon she wouldn't be able to stop herself.

She fought for control of her voice and temper. "Mr. Glennister, this man is not who you think he is. He and Sandrine Maupas di Santiago are allies and, I believe, Nazi spies—"

Vi was interrupted by a roar of laughter from the man by the fireplace.

Mr. Glennister didn't laugh. He sat down again and motioned Vi to a chair on the other side of his desk. "Miss Harrington, Leopold Rance is a distinguished politician and member of His Majesty's government. He comes from a family who can trace their lineage back to William the Conqueror. His credentials are impeccable and to suggest he is an enemy spy is preposterous."

"I'm sorry, Mr. Glennister, but frankly I couldn't give a fig for his family tree. All I know is that he and a woman I shared a house with – and who is a person of interest to the Prime Minister himself, as a result of her suspicious activity – are involved together in some sort of occult plot. I've heard them and I've seen them."

"These are most serious accusations, Miss Harrington, and I must insist you take back what you have said and apologize to Mr. Rance immediately."

"Oh Derek, old boy," Leopold said. "There's no need. The girl has just got confused, that's all. I probably look like this chap...Alex, is that his name? Easy mistake to make. I've been told I look a lot like Clark Gable. Can't see the resemblance myself but enough people have mentioned it so I suppose it must be true."

Mr. Glennister placed his hands palms down on the desk and stood. "Consider yourself fortunate that Mr. Rance has chosen not to take matters further, Miss Harrington. However, in light of your unfounded accusations, I no longer feel we have anything further to say to one another. What say you, Leo?"

"Probably wise."

Vi didn't like the way the man's eyes seemed to bore into her. He had left his position propping up the mantelpiece and was now standing alongside Mr. Glennister – and he was no longer smiling.

Mr. Glennister pressed his buzzer and Miss Harvey responded immediately. "Miss Harrington is leaving. Kindly escort her back to her office."

Vi knew the way perfectly well. The fact he required Miss Harvey to escort her was symbolic. There would be no return visits.

She mustered up every ounce of dignity she could find, held her head high, and forced herself to walk steadily out of the office, feeling two pairs of eyes watching her every move. She had really done it this time and would be lucky to keep her job. An image of a production line in a noisy munitions factory played like a newsreel in her head. Rows of women, their heads wrapped in knotted scarves, identical overalls, handling dangerous explosives.... She would be joining them soon unless she got lucky.

Miss Harvey said nothing on the walk back. She inclined her head when Vi thanked her for walking with her, and immediately started making her way back to her own part of the building.

Nancy stood up from her desk.

"Are you all right, ducky?"

Why did she have to be so nice? Vi burst into tears.

Ethel walked in, took in the situation and did what she always did. "I'll make us all a cup of tea."

Nancy steered Vi to her desk and she sat down on her chair.

"I'm sorry to be such a baby."

"Don't worry about that. A good blub is sometimes all we need to get us back on track. What happened? Did they have bad news for you?"

Vi blew her nose on her handkerchief. What could she tell her that she would believe? "In a way. Yes, some bad news. Oh, no one has died or is lost or anything. As far as I know my brother's fine. I can't really tell you anything else."

"Ah, right, I see. Keep mum and all that."

Vi nodded. This was one time when the wartime maxim had come to her rescue. No one probed any further when you indicated you were privy to a secret.

Tea and Ethel arrived and, a few minutes later, all three were busy, tapping away at their typewriters.

The expected summons came just after three that afternoon. A serious-looking Miss Brayshaw called Vi to her office.

Vi's heart thumped harder than ever as she took her seat and smoothed her skirt rather more times than usual.

Miss Brayshaw leaned forward and steepled her fingers. "I have had the most uncomfortable and unpleasant interview with Mr. Glennister. What were you thinking, Violet? Leopold Rance is one of the most respected politicians of his day and you accused him of being a Nazi spy?"

"It seems I was wrong. Mistaken identity."

"That's as may be and you're lucky that Mr. Rance is of that opinion as well. Have you any idea how serious such an accusation is? If anyone had believed you for one instant...." She shuddered. "As it is, I have had to fight tooth and nail to keep your job here. Mr. Glennister wanted you thrown out of the Civil Service altogether. As things stand, you can keep your position, but an account of the incident will be kept on your record for the duration. It may yet come back to haunt you when – and if – promotion is being considered. That's the best I can do. Frankly, if Mr. Rance himself hadn't come to your defense, I doubt even my efforts would have won the day."

"You mean...you mean Al—I mean Mr. Rance defended me?"

Miss Brayshaw nodded. "Fervently. He said anyone could make a mistake and you should be given a second chance. Especially as your record so far had been unblemished and your work had earned the praise of the PM. You have a lot to thank him for. Mr. Rance, I mean. Now go back to work and never, ever do anything like that again."

"No, Miss Brayshaw. Thank you. Miss Brayshaw, I must see the PM about something."

"Out of the question."

"It's to do with national security."

"Then you can tell me and I shall decide whether or not the PM needs to be troubled."

Could she trust her? She wanted to. Miss Brayshaw had been kind, and she had defended her against Mr. Glennister's wishes. Then there was the other question; would the PM even believe her?

"I'm sorry, Miss Brayshaw, what I have to say I can only say to the PM himself."

"Then it will have to remain unsaid. Go and get on with your work."

On the other side of Miss Brayshaw's office, Vi leaned against the cool wall, filled with mixed emotions. Relief that she had kept her job, but fear of what Sandrine's accomplice was up to. Why would he defend her? She had to see the PM.

Two days went by. It seemed Miss Brayshaw was determined Vi should never be alone in the office. It was all very subtle and Vi didn't know how much she had told Ethel and Nancy. But the two friends never went on lunch breaks together anymore and always waited behind until she had left before they went home.

Finally, on the third day. Vi decided to play them at their own game. She had overheard Churchill's male private secretary grumbling to a senior colleague about having to work late that evening.

"The PM's put in a call to the White House for seven this evening. Damn nuisance. I was hoping to get a round of golf in. Old Biff Fontenoy and I have a bet on. Oh well, can't be helped, I suppose. I hate being around this place after everyone's gone home. Pretty bloody spooky."

"You don't know the half of it," Vi whispered to herself.

"Night," she said, after covering up her typewriter and grabbing her coat, hat and bag.

"Good night," Ethel and Nancy chorused.

Vi hurried down to the ladies' and made for a stall. She locked the door and waited, checking her watch every few minutes. Women came and went. Some lingered to touch up lipstick or have a final gossip before leaving for home. When all had gone quiet, Vi dared to emerge.

She checked her watch again. Ten minutes to seven. The PM would be coming out of his office any second now to make the short journey to the door that looked like it belonged on a public lavatory, complete with a *Vacant/Engaged* sign. Above it, the sign reading, *Private* had led many to speculate that it was Churchill's own private WC. Or 'W.C.'s WC' as rather too many had quipped.

Vi knew it existed for a much different purpose. Here was the intricate telephone system that ensured every call was scrambled and no one could overhear conversations between the PM and President Roosevelt, or anyone else for that matter.

She would have a few seconds at most to collar the PM on his way to that room.

"Oy, miss, what are you doing here at this time of night?" The soldier barred her way.

"I have to get an urgent message to the PM. I work here," Vi said.

"I know you do, but you're not supposed to be working late tonight, are you? ID please."

Vi showed him her pass. "I got caught up. I'm running late. It's really important I give him this message before he makes his call."

"Oh, you know about that?" The soldier seemed surprised.

"Yes," said Vi.

The soldier considered for a few seconds, then stood back. "Very well, off you go."

"Thanks, Sergeant."

Vi scurried up the corridor. A few yards away, Churchill was already making his way to the telephone room. It was now or never. He was on his own. There would never be a better opportunity.

"Sir!"

The PM stopped and turned. He didn't look pleased. "What is it? Is the House of Commons on fire?"

Vi caught up. A little breathless and with adrenaline coursing through her body, she said, "You told me I should tell you if I saw anything suspicious relating to a certain person and her accomplice."

Churchill nodded and ushered Vi back into his office. He shut the door firmly. "You have precisely twenty seconds before I must leave."

"Sir, the man – Alex – I saw him here in Mr. Glennister's office. He's Leopold Rance, the MP. At least, that's who he is when he's here."

Churchill stared at Vi so hard she felt herself squirm. "Young lady. Unless I am becoming totally gaga, I distinctly recall you described the man you called Alex as bearing a remarkable resemblance to Clark Gable."

"That's right, sir. The very image of him."

"Have you ever seen a photograph of Leopold Rance? The man is sixty if he's a day and looks more like a rumpled old stuffed rabbit his nanny couldn't bear to part with. If you seriously believe *that* description befits a Hollywood heartthrob, I suggest you visit an optician post haste. As for Derek Glennister, he is a high-ranking civil servant who, I am certain, would hardly associate himself with people of dubious character. Now, if you'll excuse me, I have an important call to make."

Vi followed the PM out. She had made such a mess of it. Could she feel any worse?

The Prime Minister disappeared behind his private office door, ready to make his telephone call.

The sergeant was back at his post. "Job done, miss?"

"What? Oh...thank you. Sergeant, how would you describe Leopold Rance?"

"The MP? Not a bad sort, for a politician. Face like a smacked arse, but at least he's always civil. A lot of them aren't."

"So, he doesn't look anything like Clark Gable?"

"You're joking, right?" The sergeant let out a roar of laughter. "That's a good 'un. I'll tell my girlfriend that. She'll have a good laugh too."

Vi could still hear him chuckling to himself halfway down the otherwise silent corridor.

The next day, she visited the nearest library and looked up Leopold Rance. Even his professionally posed studio portrait couldn't hide the wrinkles and bulbous nose. Far from resembling Clark Gable, he looked more like W.C. Fields. But, in Mr. Glennister's office, Rance, or Alex, or whatever his name was, had said he was often mistaken for Clark Gable – and Mr. Glennister hadn't shown one flicker of surprise.

★   ★   ★

Second time around, the Dock didn't seem quite so daunting. Vi felt almost like an old hand at it, especially when a shy, mousy girl with wide, frightened eyes sidled into her dormitory.

"First time?" Vi asked, and the girl nodded. She looked as if she might burst into tears at any second and Vi took pity on her. "You can have the bed next to mine if you like. No one's grabbed it yet."

"Thanks."

"I'm Vi, by the way."

"Philippa. Everyone calls me Pippa."

"Nice to meet you, Pippa. Where do you work?"

"I'm a telephonist. I mean I will be when I know what I'm doing. At the moment, it's all wires and plugs and I haven't a clue. Everyone tells me I'll soon get the hang of it, but I really don't see how. It's a nightmare. Where do you work?"

"I'm a secretary. Well...a typist, really."

"Oh." Pippa laid her suitcase on the bed and looked around her. "It's awfully cramped and stuffy, isn't it?"

"Yes, I'm afraid so. Have they warned you about the...wildlife around here?"

Pippa nodded. "That doesn't bother me. I grew up on a farm, so I'm used to rats. I wasn't expecting it to be a mixed dorm though."

"It isn't. These are the women's quarters. The men's are down another corridor."

"But I thought I saw…." Pippa shook her head and opened her case.

Vi's curiosity was aroused. "Thought you saw what?"

"Nothing. It doesn't matter. I obviously misunderstood."

"Did you see a man down this corridor?"

"No, I couldn't have, could I?"

Pippa opened the drawer of her bedside cabinet and stuffed underwear into it.

Vi couldn't let it go. "Did you see a man?"

Pippa looked and blinked. "No, I told you. I got it wrong."

★　　★　　★

That night, Vi lay in the stifling dark. The pipes groaned and creaked. In the bed next to her, Pippa shifted from side to side. Elsewhere, other girls slept, snored lightly or, probably, also lay wakeful far into the night. Vi thought she had more or less got used to the stench but, having been away from it for a couple of weeks, found it worse than ever tonight.

A series of squeaks came from the corridor. Ratty was up and about, maybe taking his girlfriend out for a late-night trot. Vi tucked her legs up.

"Hello, Violet." The man's familiar voice came from nowhere and everywhere at the same time.

Vi shot up in bed and reached for her flashlight.

Pippa stirred. "What is it?" she whispered.

"I thought I heard…a man's voice."

"So did I," she said. "He's standing next to your bed."

"*What?*"

Vi shone her flashlight as her cry and the sudden beam of light woke the other girls.

"Switch that bloody flashlight off," one of them cried.

"What the fuck?" another one protested.

"I'm sorry," Vi said. "But there's a man in this room."

"Don't be bloody ridiculous." This from the girl who had sworn previously.

All round the room flashlights were on and being swept around.

"There's no one here," one girl said. "Now shut up and let's get some sleep."

Choruses of agreement joined her. Flashlights were switched off, until only Vi's remained on. She lowered it and clambered out of bed. Pippa was still sitting up. Vi joined her and whispered, "Did you get a good look at him?"

"Not really. He was in shadow. He was tall, with black hair, slicked back. I think he had a moustache. He looked a bit like Clark Gable, but that's probably my imagination. I only saw him for a few seconds. He was bending over you. I don't know how you didn't see him. I mean, I know it's dark in here, but there was a little light seeping in from the corridor."

A movement made them both jump. The girl who had sworn at them earlier was puffing and clearly not amused. "Will you shut the fuck up? Some of us have to be up early in the morning."

"Sorry," Vi said.

"And switch that bloody flashlight off. Batteries don't grow on trees."

"Sorry," Vi repeated and switched off the flashlight, before feeling her way back to her own bed.

For the rest of the night, she lay awake, listening to the clamor of the pipes, alert to any other sound. So Pippa had seen him but, this time, Vi hadn't. What did that say about Pippa?

*   *   *

"I've always been able to see things other people couldn't," Pippa said as she sipped coffee with Vi in the mess. "Mum was the same and her mother before her. Not one of my brothers can, though. It's only the women."

"What I don't understand is that I've seen him, large as life. I've been in an office with him and a senior civil servant. Everybody could see him then, although he was called by a different name and it may have been only me who saw him as you did. I've seen him in my home too. My friend Tilly—" Vi stopped herself. Tilly would deny any knowledge of him now though, wouldn't she? "The thing is, you say he was standing right next to me, bending over me, but I couldn't see him at all. I had no idea anyone was there. All I heard was his voice."

"That's certainly odd. But that's probably what he wanted. He manifested himself in that way."

"Manifested? So, you think he's not...."

"Not human? Quite probably. He wouldn't be the first ghost I've seen. Or he might be able to project himself. That would mean he leads a perfectly normal human existence where everyone can see him, but he has a second life. A spirit life, if you like. There are people who can project an essence of themselves. They are usually deeply into the dark arts. Black magic, if you prefer."

Vi blinked. Pippa had said that as if it was the most natural thing in the world. Gone was all trace of the frightened girl from yesterday. Talking about spirits and ghosts brought out her confidence, while it scared the hell out of Vi. But, if what she said was true, it could explain a lot.

"Could he have the power to make people forget they ever met him?" she asked.

"The spirit part of him could, almost certainly. Why? Has that happened?"

Vi told her about Tilly's denials and, as Pippa continued to listen attentively, went on to tell her about Sandrine. When she had finished, she took a sip of her, now-cold, coffee.

Pippa glanced up at the clock. "Look, I'm going to have to go now, but meet me after your shift. There's some stuff you need to know. I'll see you back here."

"I'll be here." Vi watched her go.

* * *

At five, Vi left her office and returned to the mess. At half past she was still there, nursing a lukewarm cup of tea. No sign of Pippa. Maybe she had had to work late? It happened a lot.

Vi finished her tea, picked up her bag and gas mask and made her way down the corridor to the switchboard room.

A cacophony of voices met her yards away. In the room itself, no one took any notice of her as they busied themselves connecting calls. There was no sign of Pippa.

A tall, officious-looking woman approached her. "Are you looking for someone?"

"Yes. Pippa. I was supposed to meet her at five."

"Pippa Yates was admitted to hospital suffering from severe appendicitis three days ago."

Vi stared at her. "But that's impossible. She shared a dormitory with me last night in the Dock. I had lunch with her today."

"You must be mistaken. Pippa is in hospital. She's really quite ill at the moment. They took her appendix out, but it had already burst. We're all hoping for the best, but…." The woman spread her hands expansively.

Vi mumbled a perfunctory, "Thanks." As she left the room, a young woman with eyes reddened from crying brushed past her and dashed inside. Vi stopped and listened. She heard the woman speak, her voice trembling with emotion.

"It's Pippa."

Vi slipped back into the room. Several of the women had stood up from their switchboards. Lights flashed angrily as calls went unanswered.

The young woman's colleagues had gathered around her.

"Pippa died during the night. She never regained consciousness after the operation." The woman broke down, sobbing.

Vi left them to their grief. She hurried down to the Dock. She would have to be back on shift again in less than an hour but right now, she needed to see someone. She hoped and prayed she would be there.

She was.

Hearing her footsteps, the older woman turned round from where she was folding clothes on her bed. "Oh, it's you. I trust we're not going to have another bloody repeat of last night. Man in the room indeed. Chance'd be a fucking good thing."

"Look, I'm really sorry about that. I need to ask you something. Do you remember the girl in the bed next to mine?"

"Girl? What girl?"

"She was quite short, brown curly hair. She had this bed." Vi pointed at the bed in question.

"I don't know what you're talking about. There was no one in that bed last night."

"But you came over to us. I had my flashlight on and you told me to switch it off. I was talking to her."

"You were muttering all right. Talking to yourself about some man or other."

"But you must have seen her. She was right *there*."

The woman's face colored. Her voice rose. "Now look here. I don't know what's the matter with you, but I don't have time for this nonsense. Get yourself off to the doctor if you're having delusions." She pushed roughly past Vi, nearly knocking her off balance.

Vi sank down onto her bed. She thought over what Pippa – or maybe it had been Pippa's spirit – had told her. Because that would be the proof of it, wouldn't it? The sick girl lying close to death in a hospital bed, but with her psychic gifts intact, reaching out to a stranger in need of her help. Well, now maybe Pippa had led her to one possibility. Leopold Rance and Alex. Could they be two halves of the same person?

*   *   *

That evening, she shared the office with two girls she had never met before. They were also sleeping in the Dock, farther down the corridor from her. They seemed pleasant enough but Vi was grateful that they were all too busy to indulge in much idle chatter. She simply wasn't in the mood.

Finally, at around eleven, she packed up for the day and made her way down to the Dock.

Vi climbed into bed and felt so exhausted, the lumpy mattress seemed cozy and welcoming for a change. She peered through the gloom at the empty bed next to her before her eyes grew heavy. She thought she detected a slight movement, a rustling of the sheet, and a body shifting to a more comfortable position. Just as sleep claimed her.

The voice drifted into her dreams. That familiar male voice she felt she had known all her life:

Eligos is waiting. They'll never believe you. You're on your own. Come to us and be safe. Come to us. Fulfil your destiny....

It seemed to echo all around her. Vi opened her eyes and found herself in a strange room, draped with floor-to-ceiling deep violet curtains. They fluttered in a slight breeze. One stroked her arm, its touch like velvet.

Vi took a tentative step forward and felt smooth wood beneath her bare feet. Gone was the incessant rattle of the air-conditioning, gone was the dormitory with its unrelenting concrete floor. Now, in a soft half-light, curtained walls, stretching out as far as she could see, lining her route. The urge to move ever forward overpowered her and she took short, jerky steps. The only sound now was the soft whistle of the breeze and the swish of the curtains. She should have felt scared, but she didn't. Instead, an inner calm filled her and she pressed on, along the seemingly endless walk.

Vi must have been walking a full ten minutes before a flickering light ahead indicated that she was coming to the end. It grew stronger and brighter the closer she drew to it. She could barely make out two adult figures. One male, one female. The light shone from behind them, silhouetting them but making it impossible for her to make out their features. It didn't matter. She didn't need to see more. Instinct told her who was waiting for her.

As she approached, they stood aside and her suspicions were realized.

"Good evening, Violet." Sandrine smiled at her. The first time Vi had ever seen that woman properly smile. "Please sit. We have been waiting for you to arrive and there is much to discuss."

Vi sat where indicated. Apart from feeling slightly incongruous, dressed, as she was, in her pajamas and with bare feet, she felt no emotion. Neither fear nor trepidation.

The man stepped forward and smiled, his white teeth flashing. Alex. Leopold.

"What *is* your name?" Vi asked. "I mean, really?"

The man merely smiled again and said nothing. He stepped to one side, allowing Vi to see that there was a third person in the room with them.

"Good evening, Miss Harrington."

Vi stared in disbelief – the first active sensation she had experienced since waking up in this strange place.

"Mr. Glennister!"

"The very same."

"But...."

"It will all become clear. Sandrine, my dear, bring Miss Harrington a glass of water. She looks a little pale."

Sandrine nodded and left the room by parting one of the curtains. There was no sign of an actual door. She returned almost immediately and handed a full tumbler of water to Vi, who gulped it down gratefully. She hadn't realized she was so thirsty.

"Feeling better now?" Mr. Glennister asked.

Vi nodded, putting the empty glass on the floor beside her. Sandrine retrieved it and went to sit beside Alex, at right angles to Vi. Mr. Glennister remained standing.

"You have some questions, I am quite sure," he said.

'Some questions' was an understatement to describe the jumble of thoughts crashing around Vi's brain.

"Miss Harrington, you have no idea what's going on here, have you?"

Vi shook her head.

Mr. Glennister leaned closer toward her. A little too close. Tiny hairs on the back of Vi's neck prickled. "There are forces at work here," he said. "Dark forces that have been at work since the dawn of time itself. In the depths of the earth exists a realm far removed from this one, yet able to commune with it if the circumstances are right. Some of us are gifted in special ways and have to use our gifts wisely and well. In your case, you have untapped knowledge and we have need of that knowledge."

For the first time since she had arrived here, a twist of fear began to form in Vi's stomach, like a serpent uncoiling after a long sleep. "What do you mean?"

Mr. Glennister raised his arm and unbuttoned his shirtsleeve, revealing the tattoo of Odal's rune. "What does this mean to you? Don't deny you recognize it. I saw the expression on your face when you first caught sight of it."

"Oh, I recognize it – an ancient Viking symbol – but I don't know a lot more than that. My brother was fascinated by runes and he taught me the runic alphabet."

"Yes. Your brother…."

Vi didn't like the way he said that, as he re-buttoned his shirtsleeve and adjusted his jacket.

"You are close to your brother, I believe?"

"Of course. He's…family."

"Exactly. And family is most important, isn't it, Miss Harrington? The *most* important thing."

Vi wished he would get to the point. She didn't like the direction this conversation seemed to be taking. "What do you want from me?"

"Of course. Direct and precise. I like that. Those are valuable qualities to possess."

"Then, please, would you tell me why you brought me here and what you want from me."

"Brought you here? Brought you where, Miss Harrington?"

"Here. To this room."

"Miss Harrington, you have never left your room."

He clicked his fingers and Vi shot up in bed.

CHAPTER TWELVE

The days slipped by and, while the air raids still frequently disturbed their nights, the Nazis seemed to have turned their attention to other parts of the country. No doubt they felt there was little left standing of any importance in London. Only St. Paul's Cathedral remained as a beacon of hope. If they had realized how important that one building was to the morale of Londoners, they might have tried a bit harder to demolish it. At least, that was what Vi thought.

In Mrs. Sinclair's tiny front border, a couple of yellow roses, tinged with pink, blossomed.

Peace, Vi thought as she admired them. *Mother's favorite rose. One day, maybe they'll bloom when there's no more shelling. No more bombs. Maybe this year. Maybe this year everything will make sense again.*

★   ★   ★

At work, Vi got on with Nancy and Ethel, did her work sufficiently well to earn Miss Brayshaw's praise, but never seemed to be called on to do anything for the PM anymore. This had gradually dawned on her as the days became weeks and the summons 'Miss' never seemed to apply to her.

The strange dream she had experienced, when she was last in the Dock, stayed with her long into the wakeful nights. Apart from that, she hadn't seen Mr. Glennister since that last awful meeting. She had no reason to venture down his corridor and there would be no need for him to come to this side unless he had a meeting with the PM, but that didn't seem to be part of his duties.

One lunchtime, she found herself alone in the office for the first time in a couple of weeks. The familiar gruff voice echoed down the corridor.

"Miss!"

Vi grabbed her notebook and pencil and hurried to the Prime Minister's office. He looked up from some papers he was signing.

"Miss Harrington. Take a seat. Where have they been hiding you?"

"Oh, nowhere, sir, I've been in the office, working away."

"Glad to hear it. I shouldn't want to think of you sitting there twiddling your thumbs or getting into some form of mischief."

There was a twinkle in his eye as he spoke those words but Vi wondered if he knew more than he was letting on. Probably. She doubted much of anything got past Winston.

"I trust you have kept your speed up. I should hate to have to repeat myself."

"No, indeed, sir. I'm sure I shall be able to keep up."

"Good. Good. To business...."

Churchill proceeded to dictate three letters – one each to the heads of the Army, Air Force and Navy. The letters were sharp, direct and merciless. The PM was clearly not happy with the chiefs of staff of any of the armed forces.

When he had finished, Vi stood up.

"Before you go," Winston said, "any news of that Santiago woman? Our trail appears to have gone somewhat chilly. Is she still in circulation?"

"I don't know, sir. I think she may be." After their last meeting, Vi refrained from any mention of Alex – or Leopold Rance.

Winston nodded and puffed more on his cigar. "Very well. You may go now. Let me have those when you've typed them up."

"Yes, sir. Thank you."

Outside his office, Vi leaned against the wall, relishing the coolness of the concrete. She hadn't dared to question the PM further, but one thing was for sure. She hadn't imagined Sandrine, which probably meant she hadn't imagined most of what had happened. Tilly *had* to remember, but if Alex and Sandrine, along with whoever else they were working with, *had* exerted some kind of mind control over her, how on earth could Vi break it?

★ ★ ★

On her way home, Vi checked her purse for change. She had enough pennies for a short phone call to her mother and longed to hear her voice. Letters were all very well, but so one-sided. Besides, there was something she needed to ask her.

The phone was answered on the third ring and her mother recited Lilian's Cheltenham number in her usual singsong rendition. "Five, seven, six."

"Hello Mother, it's Vi. It's so good to hear your voice. How are you?" Having established that Mother and Dad were well, as were Lilian, the children and Scottie the dog, Vi was able to get on to the main point of her call. "Do you remember where I lived before? You used to send letters there."

"Yes. Boscawen Walk, wasn't it?"

Vi wished she was closer so she could give her mother a big hug and kiss. Why hadn't she thought of doing this earlier? "That's right. Only I went there recently and it wasn't there anymore. Oh, I know a lot of the houses were destroyed, but this is the street itself. Its name. Everything. Gone as if it had never been there and no one seems to have heard of Boscawen Walk."

"Really?"

"There's a road called Bottomley Way there instead. People say it's been there for generations. Mother, how can that be possible?"

There was a crackling silence on the other end of the phone. Then her mother spoke. Her voice was hesitant.

"I...don't know, dear. Have you been sleeping properly? And eating well?"

"It's not that, Mother. I just don't understand.... Have you heard from George?"

"Yes. Last week. He sends his love."

The pips sounded. Vi didn't have any more change. "I'll have to go now. Lots of love to you, Dad, Lilian and everyone."

The phone went dead.

Vi stared at it for a few moments before replacing the receiver and pushing the door of the phone box open.

She hadn't meant to worry her mother, although she clearly had, but at least she knew she hadn't imagined Boscawen Walk. Armed with her mother's recollections of sending mail to her there, she was ready to confront Tilly.

★   ★   ★

Tilly looked up from her knitting – not an occupation Vi had ever seen her pursue before.

"Hello, Vi. Had a good day at work?"

"Not bad."

"Mine was all right too. Busy as always. Oh, this damn knitting. I've got about ten more stitches than I started off with. The bloody wool keeps splitting. Are you any good at it?"

Vi shook her head. "Hopeless. I'm better at sewing and I'm not very good at that. Mrs. Sew and Sew gave up on me. She'll have to 'Make Do and Mend' without me."

Tilly smiled and threw her knitting aside. "I daresay I can do without a new jumper. The weather's too warm for woollies now anyway. I just thought I'd get a head start before autumn."

"Tilly, can I ask you something?"

"Fire away."

"Why do you keep denying any knowledge of Boscawen Walk or Mrs. Harris? I have proof positive today that both exist – or at least existed."

Tilly stared at her. "Vi, I honestly don't know what you're talking about. I thought you were done with this."

"And you still deny knowledge of Sandrine Maupas di Santiago and her accomplice?"

"I'm not having this conversation again, Vi. I'm sorry but I do think you're ill and need to see a doctor. Please do something about it, or I may have to, for your own good."

"Is that a threat?"

"No. More of a promise."

Tilly got off the bed and strode out of their room.

The world around Vi felt as if it had suddenly turned a deep shade of red. A bloody mess of deceit, lies, false identities, memories which might or might not have been true. She glanced over at Tilly's bed, unmade, messy, the discarded knitting thrown aside, an untidy ball, half unraveled on the floor.

Vi caught sight of something on Tilly's bedside table. She recognized it instantly and, without hesitating, leapt off her bed and grabbed it.

Tilly's Mass Observation pad – and she had been writing in it today. The date was underlined at the top of the sheet:

Thursday, May 22nd, 1941

Vi read on:

V. continues to behave oddly. She isn't the girl I first met. All the life seems to have drained out of her. Of course, it could simply be the war, her work, or being away from her family, but she has definitely changed this past couple of weeks or so. She hasn't mentioned that woman, Sandrine, for a little while, which is a blessing, but I miss our friendship. She said hardly a word to me when we went to the pictures to see Rebecca. I couldn't even say whether she enjoyed it or not. Maybe she'll buck up when she gets some leave and can go home to visit her family....

Vi set the pad down where she had found it. At least Tilly was consistent. It looked very much as if she believed what she wrote. Somehow, she had no recollection of events and people that were all too vivid and real to Vi. Tilly always sent the original reports off to Mass Observation and didn't keep any copies, so there was no way of tracing back to see if or when her recollections changed.

Vi remembered the last time she and Tilly had been together before her friend's memory changed. The wash house. Alex. If he was capable of projecting his spirit, then surely a small matter of manipulating a person's mind so that their version of the truth became radically altered would be a small feat. Pippa had certainly believed it possible. Or, at least her spirit did. Maybe he was even capable of eliminating all trace of Boscawen Walk, making it as if it had never existed. Except... Vi remembered it. Her mother remembered it.

So the overarching question remained.

Why?

★   ★   ★

"Telegram for you." Tilly handed the manila envelope to Vi across the breakfast table.

Vi took it, her hands trembling. In wartime, these envelopes more often than not contained bad news. She struggled to tear it open while Tilly watched her. At least the girl looked concerned.

George home on leave tomorrow. One week. Can you come? Mother.

"Thank the Lord." Vi reread the telegram again to be sure she hadn't misunderstood.

"Good news?" Tilly asked, smiling.

"The best. My brother's coming home on leave for a week. Mother wants me to go home. I need to ask Miss Brayshaw for leave. Trouble is, it's not the best timing."

"Surely she'll let you have a couple of days at least. When did you last see him?"

Vi had to think. "It's so long. A year maybe. He's been abroad... somewhere. Oh, Tilly, I don't know what I'll do if Miss Brayshaw says I can't go."

"Never meet trouble halfway, that's what my old nan used to say. And she was right. Go and see your Miss Brayshaw as soon as you get in – and lay it on thickly."

The girl's voice was warm. Right now, it was almost like it used to be between them.

"I will," Vi said. She gulped down her tea, grabbed her things and dashed off to work.

★　　★　　★

"I'm sorry I can't spare you for the entire week, Violet, but you may have seventy-two hours' leave commencing from the end of your shift this afternoon."

"Thank you, Miss Brayshaw. I know this isn't the best of times to be on leave."

Miss Brayshaw smiled. "I'm sure we'll cope. Try and clear your in-tray before you go and hand anything that still remains to be done to Ethel."

Vi nodded. For the rest of the day, she fought hard to contain her excitement. Finally, some good news.

The PM was in good humor when she handed some documents to him for signature. He duly read them, signed and returned them to her. "I understand we are to be deprived of your company for a few days," he said as she accepted the last sheaf of papers from him.

"Yes, sir. My brother is home on leave from the RAF and Miss Brayshaw has kindly allowed me some leave to go and visit him at home."

"Excellent. Excellent. You must be very proud of him."

"I am indeed, sir. We all are."

"Flight lieutenant, I believe. Next step, squadron leader."

"Yes, sir."

"Good. Good. Well, enjoy your leave, Miss Harrington. We shall look forward to seeing you on your return."

"Thank you, sir."

Vi returned to her office, sat at her desk and picked up the next document ready for typing. As she loaded the paper and carbons into her machine, she pondered her latest encounter with the PM. It was quite extraordinary how such a busy man, with the weight of responsibility Churchill carried, was still able to concern himself with the lives of his staff, even junior ones such as her. She had never told him anything about her brother, yet he knew his rank.

*   *   *

"Enjoy yourself," Ethel said, and Nancy nodded in agreement. "Don't think about us for one second, beavering away down here in the bowels of the earth while you have fun in the bright lights of Cheltenham."

"Don't worry. I won't," Vi said as she put on her hat and light raincoat. The sign in the corridor warned of *Light showers*. She dashed home, arriving just as the heavens opened.

She threw clothes into her suitcase and found Mrs. Sinclair in the kitchen, laboring over an aromatic stew. The landlady grumbled a bit over the short notice but eventually wished her a safe trip, and Vi left with a spring in her step.

*   *   *

The Cheltenham train was overcrowded, smoky and dirty. Vi managed to squeeze herself and her small case into a corner of a carriage as the massive locomotive puffed and lurched its way out of the station. It stopped everywhere – including places Vi had never even heard of and which seemed to lie in the middle of nowhere with barely a house in sight. By the time she reached her destination, she was hot and in dire need of a bath.

Her sister, Lilian, lived about half a mile away from the station, and the sight of her neat white gate and shiny green door was so welcome, Vi felt she could have knelt down and kissed the scrubbed front step.

She knocked on the door and her sister's beaming smile told her all she needed to know. "Is he here?"

Lilian nodded, hugging her sister. "Come in. You look exhausted. I'll make you a cup of tea. We're all in the living room."

Despite her weariness, Vi almost skipped down the hall. In the living room, all eyes turned toward her. Her father and mother grinned broadly, although from the red-rimmed eyes and handkerchief dabbing at her nose, Mother had obviously been having a little weep.

"Hello, sis." George, dressed immaculately in his uniform,

unwound his long legs and stood up before advancing toward her and enfolding her in one of his massive bear hugs.

"George, watch it, you're crushing the breath out of me." Vi struggled to breathe and George relaxed his hold. She immediately hugged him to her. He smelled familiar, a combination of whatever he used on his hair and pipe tobacco. Tears welled up in her eyes as the years fell away, the war seemed a distant nightmare and she was thirteen again, with her big brother defending her from the school bully.

"You're a sight for sore eyes and no mistake," George said as he released her and held her at arm's length. "Look at you. All grown-up, working, and so pretty, I bet you're fighting them off."

Vi laughed. "I wouldn't go that far."

George's smile faded. "You've got dark circles under your eyes, though. Are they working you too hard?"

"No more than anyone else. We do some long shifts and I sleep there sometimes. It's hard to get a decent night with the noise and...." Vi became aware that everyone was listening intently. Her mother looked worried. This was her brother's time and she was monopolizing it. "Anyway, there *is* a war on, you know." Her attempt at levity worked, and laughter rang out around the room. Lilian dispensed liberal quantities of tea, and Vi sat on the arm of George's chair.

"I've only got seventy-two hours, I'm afraid," Vi said. "And I know we're going to be a bit cramped here."

"Oh, don't worry," Lilian said, brandishing the teapot. "The children are staying with a friend of theirs a couple of streets away. If you don't mind sleeping on the settee, Vi, I've given George their bedroom."

"Oh no," George said, "I won't hear of it. Vi shall have that room. I'm quite all right on the settee." He squeezed her arm. "I have a week to catch up on my sleep, but you've only got a couple of nights. Go on, take it. I shan't get a wink's sleep if I'm up there and you're down here."

Vi couldn't deny that some decent sleep away from either the

Dock, or the roommate who had become such a stranger, would be welcome. "Thanks, George. That's really good of you."

"Very well then," Lilian said. "That's settled."

★   ★   ★

For the first time in days during this dull and colder than average spring, the sun shone the following morning as Vi joined George outside in the backyard, where he was enjoying the morning air and smoking a cigarette.

"Has it been really bloody for you?" Vi asked.

George gave a short, mirthless laugh. "Not the best of times. I've been lucky but I've lost friends. Good friends. And I've looked into the terrified eyes of a German boy younger than you, right before our gunner shot him out of the skies. That's not a sight I want to see again, although I have a horrible feeling that, if I'm spared, I will do. It's a bloody evil affair, this war."

"I'm lucky I don't have to face that, and I don't know how you cope with it."

George shrugged and stubbed his cigarette out under his toe. "You get on with it, Vi. It's your job and, if you don't, then it's your turn next and some Nazi officer is staring at you right before he makes an end of you."

"Yes, I understand that…." Vi hesitated.

George touched her arm. "What's wrong, Vi? You know you can never hide anything from me. Remember when you broke that vase?"

"The one with the strange weeds growing on it?"

George laughed. "You used to call it the weedy vase. I think it was supposed to be honeysuckle and it was painted on."

"It looked very realistic."

"You were only four years old at the time. I remember Mother accusing me of smashing it and then she had a go at Lilian. She never thought of you. You were her little blue-eyed baby, but I asked you outright and you went beetroot and admitted it."

"You still took a smacking for me though."

"You're my kid sister, what else is a chap supposed to do?"

"I did tell Mother it was me. In the end."

"Oh? She never said. When was that then?"

"About six months ago."

George punched her arm and the two laughed.

George lit another cigarette. "Seriously though, there *is* something wrong. Tell me, Vi. Maybe I can help."

"I don't see how, I'm afraid. It's all so…incredible."

George listened and said nothing until she had finished. Mother popped her head out of the kitchen door, saw the two in deep conversation and went back inside.

When Vi had finished speaking, her brother lit yet another cigarette. For once, she found it hard to read his expression. "You see?" she said, "It's crazy, isn't it? I must be going mad or something. I accused Tilly of deliberately lying and now, from her MO entry, I can see that, as far as she's concerned, *I'm* the one with the problem."

George looked her straight in the eyes. "But you're not."

"You can't be so sure of that. Not after what I just told you."

"The PM believes you. He asked you about Sandrine Maupas di Santiago and Alex only the other day, didn't he?"

"I said he asked about…." She *had* mentioned Sandrine by name, but she *hadn't* used the name 'Alex'. Instead, she had spoken of Leopold Rance.

"How did you know his name? Alex, I mean?"

George inhaled deeply. "Because I've met them. Both of them. And I hope never to see either of them ever again for as long as I live."

"Are you two planning on staying out there for the rest of the day?" Lilian's smile was friendly enough but her voice betrayed frustration. "It's not raining for once and it would be good to go out for a walk. We can take a picnic down to the park and watch the ducklings."

George squeezed Vi's arm. "Tell you later." To Lilian, he said, "Coming, Lil."

Vi stared after him, stunned. How on earth had he met those

two? He had been stationed God knows where while they had been in London.

She shook herself and made her way back indoors. George said he would tell her later. She would make sure that was sooner.

*   *   *

Sitting on the grass, eating cress sandwiches and drinking tea out of a Thermos, seemed a world away from the Cabinet War Rooms and ever-present secrets, dark corners and unexplained events. Lilian chatted to them all about trivial day-to-day things. Who had said what to whom, of Jack and Nellie, who owned the local shop and who seemed to be constantly under siege from disgruntled customers demanding food that was either not available or on ration and of which they had already had their maximum.

Vi was only half listening but hoped her sister wasn't aware of that. From what she heard, Lilian's problem was mainly boredom, the sheer repetitiveness of her daily life, housework, shopping, washing, cleaning, looking after the kids…. She had recently joined the Women's Voluntary Service and distributed basic food to the elderly, infirm and generally housebound, but even that didn't absorb her mind, even if it occupied hours of her time.

"Trouble is, there's so much I can't volunteer for because I can't leave the children in the evenings, and things like fire watching…well, it's the nighttime they need you the most."

"Oh, I shouldn't like to think of you doing that, Lilian," their mother said, shifting her position on the blanket she had appropriated from the car. "You remember Annie next door to us back home? I had a letter from her the other day. Her daughter, Sheila, does the fire watching and she was nearly burned herself last week. A bomb landed nearby and exploded, killing one of the chaps on her shift. She was lucky it wasn't her. And some of the places they have to do their watching…well, they're not the most salubrious. Sheila and a couple of girls had to barricade themselves in from some drunken soldiers who shouted through the keyhole and made lewd suggestions. It's not funny, Vi."

Vi struggled to control the giggles – evidence of which had leaked onto her face.

"Did they say what sort of lewd suggestions?" George asked, his face a picture of innocence.

This was too much for Vi. She jumped up. "Just going for a stroll," she managed.

"I'll come too," George said.

The two ran off to the water's edge, where a flotilla of tiny fluffy ducklings was trying to keep up with their mother as she sailed regally across the lake.

"I'll give you ten to one they said, 'Show us your knickers,'" George said.

Vi burst into fits of laughter until the tears streamed down her face. "Oh, that feels good. To laugh I mean," she said when she had recovered herself sufficiently.

George wiped a tear from his cheek. "It does indeed."

Vi blew her nose and tucked her handkerchief into her skirt pocket. "So, you were telling me about how you met Alex and Sandrine."

The smile vanished from George's face. "Yes. I was, wasn't I?" He drew a deep breath. "I imagine we're far enough away from anyone for me to tell you that I've been stationed almost as far north as you can get before you hit Norway. Orkney. Beautiful place – if it wasn't for all the mud – and pretty remote. Not the sort of place you would expect to find someone like Sandrine. Well, *you* know, you've met her. Like some exotic tropical creature."

"You're right. I can't imagine her in a place like that. Not that I remember ever even seeing a photograph of Orkney."

"Apart from a couple of small towns, it's sparsely populated – except for all the military of course – quite desolate in parts and there's precious little to do when you're off duty. There's a cinema of sorts and a few pubs, but that's about it. The locals do their best, but even the accent is difficult to decipher. It's not like Glaswegian even. You remember old Jocky?"

Vi smiled. Jocky McGregor had been a teacher in their primary school. He hailed from the insalubrious Gorbals in Glasgow, with an accent you could slice with a meat cleaver. All the kids used to imitate him, but he took it in good heart.

"Well, I reckon old Jocky himself would have had problems understanding some of the older Orcadians. That's what they call someone from Orkney. Anyway, you see the same faces day in, day out, so when this beautiful, dark-haired, black-eyed beauty turned up one day, you can imagine the reaction. She was a civilian attached to the RAF. Some kind of desk job, but I never really found out what. Wasn't all that interested, if I'm honest. I was more interested in *her*. The thing was, it was like that old movie cliché of two pairs of eyes meeting across a crowded room. Our eyes met across the smoky village hall and that was it. I was smitten. Never thought I had a chance, of course. I mean, I'm only an average-looking flight lieutenant. She could have had her pick of squadron leaders and even the odd wing commander or group captain if she hadn't minded them married. As it happens, I don't think that would have put her off, but I'm getting ahead of myself. To cut a long story short, we began seeing each other and things progressed very rapidly. Far more rapidly that I have ever experienced. I fell in love with her and I thought she felt the same way.

"Two weeks into our relationship, I asked her to marry me. When I look back now, I realize how stupid I was. So swept away by her charisma." George stopped and stared over the lake; his eyes misted up.

"What did she say? When you asked her to marry you?"

He paused and Vi began to think he had either not heard her or didn't want to reply. She was about to prompt him when he spoke.

"She laughed in my face, Vi. Told me to stop being ridiculous. She said she only wanted to have a good time. That's all. Then she dropped the real bomb. She told me there was someone else. There always had been someone else, and he would be arriving the following day. She'd intended to tell me that evening. Then she left me there. In the pub, clutching a pint of weak beer and feeling like the biggest idiot."

"That's awful, George. She's a horrible person. Really horrible. But when did this all happen?"

"About two months ago. But that's not all. The next day, that man did turn up and she brought him to meet me. It turned out he knew all about our affair and was perfectly fine with it. Of course, I could see what she saw in him. The man is the spitting image of Clark Gable. Much more the sort of suave bloke a woman like her should have on her arm. Obviously wealthy and well-connected too. He offered me a cigarette from a gold case. 'Handmade. My own blend,' he said. Actually, they tasted foul. Like those French things. Gauloise. They stank."

"Did he say anything about who he was or what he was doing there?"

George shook his head. "Not at first. I was too flabbergasted to ask any questions. The whole thing seemed unreal somehow. As if I was dreaming it. In fact, I became convinced I was, until I kept on seeing him around the base and, every time I caught a glimpse of him, he was staring at me. Then one evening, I was strolling back from the pub – on my own, which was unusual. I had drunk a little too much. The landlord had managed to get hold of a barrel of Scotch. No one asked where from. They do get shipwrecks from time to time and the night before had been rough, with storms and an exceptionally high tide. I was a bit unsteady, walking along in the dark with my flashlight barely flickering, and suddenly, there he was in front of me.

"What happened next is something I'll never forget, but which I still don't know existed or was created by my alcohol-fed brain."

"Tell me."

George lit a cigarette. "At first he was all smarmy solicitation as he had been since the first time we had met. 'Don't worry, old boy, I'll get you back safely. Here, take my arm.' You know the sort of thing. So, I went along with him until I realized we weren't going the right way. He steered me off course to some deserted and derelict barn. Inside, a couple of oil lamps illuminated it quite well. I remember a sharp smell of fresh tar and I saw the floor timbers had been covered over with something – probably tarpaulin or similar, which I guess they had coated in bitumen.

"Someone moved in the far corner and I recognized Sandrine. Behind her was some kind of altar. There was a massive curtain that went from floor to ceiling and was decorated with – remember Odal's rune?"

Vi nodded.

"By now, the alcohol had weakened my balance to the point where I could barely stand upright. It was simple enough for Alex to rip off my jacket, half carry me to a chair, sit me down in it and tie my legs and hands with rope.

"I tried to speak, to protest and tell them to let me go, but my words were slurred and indistinct, and Sandrine stood there, mocking me. Laughing at me. Until she produced a sharp knife. It resembled a dagger, but really thin. Like an Italian stiletto. Before I knew what was happening, she mumbled some gibberish, raised the knife high in the air and brought it down on my left forearm. The pain was excruciating. I cried out and felt warm blood dripping down my wrist. I must have passed out at that point. When I came to, it was early morning and I was lying propped up against the barrack room. How I'd got back there I haven't a clue. I managed to stagger inside, to my room. I was wearing my jacket, but as I looked down, I could see the left arm was stained with blood and it was throbbing too. I eased off the jacket and nearly fainted when I saw the mess. Dried blood streaked all down my arm. I washed it off as best I could, fighting the urge to give way and pass out. That's when I discovered what they'd done to me." George removed his jacket and handed it to Vi. He undid the wrist button of his shirtsleeve and rolled it upward. When he turned his inner arm out to face her, Vi caught her breath.

There, tattooed neatly and evenly, was Odal's rune, but with the ends turned up so that it was identical to Mr. Glennister's.

"That was no dream," Vi said.

"It's possible I could have done it to myself but, no, it wasn't a dream, was it? Those two really did that to me. But the question is, Vi, *why* would they do it? They disappeared after that and even odder, whenever I mentioned either of their names to anyone – my fellow officers, civilians, it didn't matter who – no one knew who the hell I was talking about. I began to believe I was imagining it all, until I came home on leave and you told me what had been happening to you." George sighed. "Well, that's my story. Sound familiar?"

"All too familiar. The thing is, what happened to you took place in March, didn't it?"

George nodded.

"But in March those two were in London. Sandrine living at Boscawen Walk. Alex turning up from time to time."

"So, they were in two places at the same time?"

"Sandrine did used to disappear, usually around the time of an air raid. She was also away when I first moved there, so it isn't impossible. Besides, someone told me that there are people who are more than capable of transporting a part of themselves – their spirit, for want of a better term – and I'm as sure as I can be that Alex is particularly adept at this. Probably Sandrine is too. And it is entirely possible that they aren't even human."

"It all sounds so absurd. Like something out of a really bad movie."

"I agree, but I happen to know it's possible because the person who told me was as real to me as you are now, but when she told me what she knew, she was actually lying in a hospital bed a few miles away, dying from a burst appendix."

George blinked a few times. "Seriously?"

"Seriously. These people are far from normal human beings, and for some reason, they've attached themselves to the two of us."

"This is messed up. Really messed up."

"And I probably shouldn't have told you half of what I've told you this past twenty-four hours," Vi said. "In fact, there's no probably about it. I'm not supposed to talk about any aspect of my work, or who I work for."

"Your secrets are safe with me, sis, you know that. I think the fact that Churchill knows about them when everyone else is denying their existence proves what you're saying is true. They haven't manipulated him – yet. But whoever they really are, they're dangerous and they've got to be stopped. If they're working for the enemy...." George shook his head and dragged deeply on his cigarette, exhaling a cloud of smoke that billowed around him in the light afternoon breeze. He flicked his cigarette end into the lake. "We'd better get back to the family. They'll be wondering where we've got to."

Vi linked arms with her brother and they wandered back, each lost in their own thoughts.

⋆   ⋆   ⋆

"I'll walk you to the station," George said. "You don't want Mother drowning you in tears."

"Thanks, George."

Her mother, father and sister were waiting for her in the living room. Sure enough, her mother had her handkerchief in her hand and the first tears were brimming over her eyelids.

She grabbed Vi and held her tightly in a suffocating bear hug.

"Come on, Mother, I'm only going back to London. It's not like...." Vi caught George's eye and let her words hang in the air, unfinished. Mother didn't seem to have noticed anyway. She was far too preoccupied with losing her baby girl. With a sudden pang, Vi realized how poignant this was. Her parents should have been in London in their neat little home where she had grown up and lived until the war had intervened, turning their lives upside down. That house was a pile of rubble. Her parents were, essentially, homeless. What they would do when peace eventually came, she could only imagine. All being well, Lilian's husband would return from the navy and there really wouldn't be enough room for them all here. So, let her mother have her little weep. She'd earned it. She had never complained once in Vi's hearing about the bombing that had robbed her of so much.

Vi's dad gave her a perfunctory hug and turned away. She knew he too was tearing up and that wouldn't do at all. It simply wasn't done for a man to cry.

The train steamed into the station. George opened a door to third class and Vi clambered up the steps. Unusually, it wasn't packed, and she had her choice of three seats in the six-seater compartment. She placed her handbag and gas mask on one and returned to the window to lean out and exchange her last few words with George. Who knew when they would get the chance to talk again?

"You take care of yourself, sis. Don't forget to write. Let me know if anything else happens, but be careful."

"You too." They touched fingers and fear struck her with the force of a mallet. A vivid image flashed through her brain. An RAF plane, spiraling downward, both engines ablaze, thick black smoke creating a labyrinthine trail. She snatched her hand back and the vision left her.

"What's the matter, Vi? You've gone pale."

"Nothing, George. Nothing at all." She forced a smile. "Cheerio and be good."

He delivered a mock salute and smiled. "Cheerio, sis."

The guard blew his whistle, the noise shrill and unwelcome. The train huffed and puffed as it built up its head of steam. It lurched and Vi nearly ended up in the lap of a surprised elderly clergyman. By the time she recovered her balance, they were off, and she could no longer see George. The strongest feeling that she would never see him again overwhelmed all sense of reason as she took her seat by the window and stared out at the passing countryside.

★   ★   ★

Vi must have dozed because a sudden violent jolt of the train woke her. They had stopped at a station, but she couldn't see the name. She leaned over to the clergyman, who was reading a newspaper. He was dressed in an ankle-length black cassock with a black shirt and broad dog collar, his wire-rimmed circular spectacles perched precariously on the end of his broad nose. "Excuse me, sir, I dropped off to sleep. Which station is this?"

"Swindon." He seemed annoyed to have been interrupted.

"Thank you, sir, sorry to have troubled you."

He rustled his newspaper and didn't reply. The compartment door opened and Vi looked to see who had entered.

Sandrine Maupas di Santiago, elegant as always, smiled at her as she took her seat diagonally opposite, next to the vicar. She removed her gloves. "Hello Violet, how nice to see you again."

"No, you can't be here. You can't."

The clergyman folded his newspaper. "Young lady, who are you talking to?"

"The woman who has just come in. The woman sitting next to you."

The clergyman removed his spectacles. "There is no one sitting next to me."

"What? You must be able to see her. She's right there." Vi appealed to the other two people in the compartment – an army private and an elderly woman engaged in crocheting. They both looked bewildered.

The private spoke. "Look, miss, there's only the reverend here, me, this lady next to me and you."

Vi looked at the elderly woman, who nodded, a smile of pity playing at the corners of her lips.

Sandrine spoke. "You're the only one who can see me at this moment," she said. "And I wouldn't speak if I were you."

Vi shut her mouth.

"That's better. We don't want everyone thinking you're insane, do we?"

Vi continued to stare but said nothing. Inwardly she longed to wring the woman's neck. The elderly woman went back to her crocheting, but her face was set in a frown, and Vi was aware of her shooting furtive glances in her direction, probably wondering what she was going to do next. The clergyman went back to his newspaper. For a vicar he showed remarkably little concern for a fellow human being so clearly in distress. The soldier reached in his pocket and drew out a small pack of Woodbines. He leaned across and offered her one. She declined.

"Are you sure? It looks like your nerves could do with some calming and these usually do the trick for me."

"Thanks, but I've never smoked."

"Do you think your invisible friend would like one?" He mockingly offered Sandrine a cigarette.

She laughed and shook her head. "Don't worry," she said. "He can't see me. He's having a joke at your expense."

"I know." The words were out before she could stop them.

"Know what?" the private asked, lighting up.

"Nothing," Vi said.

"I'd see a doctor if I were you. There's something not right." He tapped his forehead.

Vi ignored him. What was Sandrine doing here? What did she want from her? Why wouldn't she go away and leave her alone?

"I know you have many questions," Sandrine said. "And they will be answered in the fullness of time. You may not like the answers, but they will come anyway." She stood, made her way to the compartment door and opened it.

"There," Vi said, pointing at the half-open door. "Surely you can all see that. The door didn't just open by itself."

Sandrine's laughter rang out as, once again all eyes in the compartment turned to Vi. This time it was the vicar who took up the gauntlet. "The door didn't open at all. It has remained shut as it is now."

She looked from one to the other. Their stares said it all.

★   ★   ★

Vi was alone in her room that night. Tilly had obtained leave to visit her grandmother, who had been injured in a bomb blast in Great Yarmouth.

She lay awake long into the night, her mind churning over and over; fears that wouldn't go away assaulting her from every angle. All she had was questions. Not one single answer.

When she finally fell asleep, images of Sandrine and Alex mocking her, laughing at her, mingled with the passengers she had shared the compartment with. They were all pointing, jeering. In her nightmare they could see Sandrine as clearly as she could.

And it all seemed so horribly real.

★   ★   ★

The next morning, she met the postman on the doorstep. He handed her the brown envelope everyone feared.

She ripped it open. The telegram was short. *George killed. Come home. Mother.*

The world seemed to stop. Traffic noises, blaring horns, horse-drawn carts, all faded into the background. She was vaguely aware of Mrs. Sinclair at her elbow.

"Bad news?"

Vi thrust the telegram at her.

Mrs. Sinclair read it. In one second, she seemed to have a total personality switch. From inside the tight, buttoned-up, cold exterior, a warm wave of concern poured out. "Oh, my dear, I'm so sorry. Come back in and I'll make you a nice cup of strong tea."

"You're very kind, but I have to go to the phone box and ring Mother. And I'll have to let them know at work."

"Of course, but when you've done that, I'll have that tea ready for you and then you can pack and catch the next train."

Vi acknowledged her and dashed down the street to the red telephone box. She fumbled in her bag for her purse, found it and prayed she had sufficient coins. Then she dialed the operator.

She spoke to Miss Brayshaw, who was almost too kind. Vi didn't want to break down now, so she quickly thanked her and ended the call. She swallowed hard, trying to get rid of the enormous lump that had formed there. Then she made the call she had always dreaded.

Lilian answered the phone, her voice wavering. She could barely recite the number. Vi interrupted her. "Whatever happened?" The image of that plane crashing in a ball of flame flashed into her mind.

She could tell Lilian was struggling to get her words out. "Tommy Grayson's bloody motorbike. That's what happened. George's old school friend.... He came round.... George asked to go for a spin... that's the last...."

"He was killed riding a *motorbike*?" Even speaking the words out loud didn't make them any more real. It was so senseless.

The only sound from the other end was Lilian sobbing. Vi waited. The pips went and she shoved more pennies in the phone. Finally, her sister recovered herself sufficiently to speak. "The sun was shining. It was early yesterday evening.... We waited an hour, when he said he'd only be gone ten minutes. Tommy was getting anxious and he set off walking. He knew where George would have gone. About a mile up the road, he saw an ambulance and someone crouching over something on the road. He ran up to them and saw his bike, mangled at the side of the road...." Lilian broke down again.

Vi couldn't listen to any more. She had to get there. "We'll talk about it later. I'll pack a few things and catch the next train."

"I'm so glad you're coming. Mother's hysterical. The doctor's given her something to calm her down but it hasn't taken effect yet. Dad's sitting at the table, staring off into space. He doesn't speak or respond to anything. The doctor's given him something too, but it seems to have made him worse. He won't go to bed. I really need your help, Vi."

"I'll be there as soon as I can." She replaced the receiver.

Killed on a motorbike. Of all the stupid, idiotic ways to go.

Into her mind came a picture of Sandrine.

She was laughing.

CHAPTER THIRTEEN

The next few days passed in a blur. The funeral. The vicar speaking of a young life cut tragically short. Mother's eyes perpetually red. Dad looking as if he had aged twenty years. Haggard, gaunt, barely speaking above a whisper.

And in the middle of it, Lil had cornered Vi. A little too much sherry had loosened her tongue. "That was no accident that killed our George...."

After her sister had finished her frenzied account, she raced out of the room, her hand cupping her mouth. She really should have eaten something with all that alcohol.

But she left Vi with much to consider.

Then back to London. Getting back to normal. It had to be done, however little she felt like it, however surreal life was at that moment. Returning to work helped. Ethel and Nancy were kind, expressed their condolences, even made sure her in-tray was manageable for her first day back in harness.

Miss Brayshaw told her how sorry she was, what a fine young man her brother had been and how Vi could always be proud of his service to her country. Even the PM smiled at her when their paths crossed in the corridor that first morning, but to Vi it seemed she was surrounded by a nebulous cloud, creating a seemingly constant echo chamber through which people's voices came and went. She moved through the day, but that's all it was. She went through the motions of living and feeling as if she were observing from a distance.

Vi loaded up her paper and carbons in her typewriter, read the scrawled handwriting on sheets of lined foolscap, transcribed them, unwound them from her typewriter, collated them, put them in her out-tray and moved on to the next task. At one p.m. precisely, she downed tools and made her way, alone, to the canteen. There were faces she recognized, people she could have shared a table with, but they all seemed too far away, in a different world to hers. She responded to greetings and conversation like an automaton, until a voice pierced through the engulfing cloud.

"Violet. Come with me."

Vi looked up from her cup of tea. Sandrine stood next to her. Suspended in a dreamlike state, Vi stood and followed her out of the canteen and down the corridor, past familiar rooms, until they stopped outside a door. Vi stared at the number. The impossible room. Number 338.

"In here." It wasn't a request. Sandrine opened the door and Vi walked in. She almost knew what to expect and wasn't surprised to see Alex and Mr. Glennister sitting behind a solid mahogany desk. Sandrine followed her in and closed the door before taking her place next to the two men.

No one smiled. Still feeling as if she was in some form of suspended animation, Vi sat where Mr. Glennister indicated, smoothing down her skirt. The action served to give her some comfort.

"Miss Harrington," Mr. Glennister said. "We think the time for playing games is well past. I understand you have suffered a recent bereavement."

The lack of any compassion or any show of emotion, however slight and meaningless, raised Vi's anger almost to boiling point. "My brother was killed in a motorcycle accident." Days of grief, frustration and fear threatened to spill over. She fought hard to maintain control, but the power of her feelings gave her strength. These people would not intimidate her any longer. She would have answers. Whatever the cost. "I believe you all know something about that. There are aspects of that accident that don't make sense."

"Oh, really?" Alex said. "And what would those be?"

The man was insufferable. His whole attitude mocked her.

When she spoke, her voice was strong, strident even. Lil's words echoed in her head. "For a start. The weather was perfect, the conditions excellent and the motorbike had recently undergone a complete service. The owner was a good friend of my brother's and is a professional mechanic. He knows what he's doing. There wasn't a screw out of place. Yet somehow, that bike ended up mangled as if it had been in a collision with a much larger vehicle. My brother didn't die instantly. He lived just long enough to tell an ambulance man that a big truck had come out of nowhere and rammed him. It didn't stop. I believe you three were behind that and I demand to know why. I also demand to know what the hell's been going on here and why you have targeted me." Vi pointed at Sandrine and Alex. "I know you two were in Orkney when my brother was stationed there. You, Sandrine, seduced him, before dumping him as a result of your affair with Alex. Pretty poor behavior by any stretch of the imagination. The behavior of a slut, in fact."

"Oh dear," Sandrine said. "We have got our dander up, haven't we? George and I merely had a brief fling. Nothing more. It was a bit of fun. Nice while it lasted. Pleasant even, but that was it."

Vi sprang to her feet and advanced toward the table. She thumped her fist down on it and the water glasses rattled. "And why him? You used him. Not only that but you've been manipulating people around me. People I share a house with. Work with. All except the PM and that's only because you haven't been able to get to him."

"Sit down, Miss Harrington." Mr. Glennister pointed at the chair she had been using.

"Not until I get some answers."

"If you don't sit down, they will not be forthcoming. Now, *sit down*."

Reluctantly, Vi obeyed, crossing her arms defensively.

"You wanted answers and you shall have them," the civil servant said.

A faint buzzing began. It seemed to be coming from inside the wall somehow. Vi looked around but could see no sign of a door. On the far wall, a circle of light began to glow. It pulsed, radiating orange and yellow light and a humming sound. It grew, louder and louder, until her ears were ringing and smarting with the noise.

"What are you doing?" she demanded, clamping her hands over her ears in a futile gesture. Nothing would keep that penetrating sound out. "Make it stop. *Now.*"

"You wanted answers," Sandrine said. "We're providing you with them."

The noise stopped as suddenly as it had begun. Vi realized she had squeezed her eyes shut and forced them open. She lowered her hands from her head as she took in her surroundings. Gone was the office and any sign of the three people who had been there with her. The room was empty, dark, lit only by a single candle in a holder standing in the center of the floor. She was sitting on the same chair as before.

Her legs wobbling, she managed to stand, and bent to pick up the candle, wafting it around so she could get her bearings. As far as she could make out, this wasn't the room she had been in. Although, like this one, the other room had no windows, it did have maps on the walls, the odd picture, and a calendar. This one had bare walls and one door. Vi crossed the room and turned the handle. Locked. It made a hollow echo when she rattled it. She banged on it and called out, but no one responded. She put her ear to it. No sound penetrated from outside.

Still holding the candle, Vi looked around and shivered. It wasn't cold but there were too many shadows and, right now, one was growing. To the right of her in a far corner, it twisted and writhed, like some strange kind of wraith performing an exotic dance.

A deep groan emanated from it. Vi cried out, "Who are you?"

Another groan so desperate, it seemed to have been torn from the depths of hell itself.

"Vi – o – let." It was like no voice she had ever heard. Rasping, uttering her name as if it were a foreign sound it hadn't encountered before.

The floor beneath her feet shifted. She looked down and found she was standing on grass. She looked around. The room had vanished, leaving her outside, on a small hillock. A full moon cast a silver light across the landscape. In the distance she saw the outline of tall standing stones arranged in an arc of a circle. As she stared, a wisp of cloud moved across the moon and away. The moonlight grew brighter. The stones were growing taller. No, *she* was moving closer to *them* even though she was standing perfectly still.

A low hum, like the sound of an electric pylon, surrounded her. It swelled and she realized it was the sound of voices all chanting one note. Ahead of her, moving from the stone circle, hooded figures marched. Vi tried to move but couldn't. Her feet wouldn't obey her. It was like being in a dream, rooted to the spot and unable to escape the nightmare demon. Except, this was no nightmare. She felt the cool night breeze on her skin, raising goose bumps. She hugged herself and prayed for it to be over.

They were only a few yards away now. She couldn't see their faces but there were around twenty of them. Identically robed, head to foot in black, their only mark being a large white stylized Odal's rune adorning their chests.

They said nothing, but in her head, words formed.

You have been chosen. Out of all women, you have been blessed. Our noble lord will take you as his own and you shall bear the fruit of his loins.

"*No!*" Vi scarcely recognized her voice as her own. Invisible hands grabbed her and held her tightly, as pain shot through her shoulders. They gripped her arms so firmly behind her back she felt they would surely dislocate. The hooded figures parted to let her through as her invisible captors dragged her, writhing and screaming, closer to the stones. A fire burned brightly, shooting orange and red flames skyward in a smell of burning wood. The chanting grew ever louder, mingling with Vi's screams. They threw her roughly to the ground and she lay sprawled in front of a figure brandishing a massive gleaming silver sword. The figure spoke and it was Sandrine's voice that rang out over the assembled crowd.

"Tonight, the noble lord's wish shall be fulfilled. Tonight, he will come to this, his servant."

Vi struggled to her feet. "What are you doing? Let me go. Let me go *now*."

Sandrine laughed. She threw back her hood and her normally scarlet lips shone black in the flames. "You wanted answers. Now you have them. Those of us who wear this sign are followers of the one true noble lord, Eligos. This is the dawn of a new and mighty age, and you are truly blessed to be a part of its creation. His kingdom shall reign forever."

Invisible hands pushed Vi to the ground and spread her legs and arms. A roaring sound, like the onset of a mighty wind, tore through the air. The flames shot higher as the chanting grew and merged with the roar. Above her, flaming eyes in a reptilian face bored into hers. A pain scythed through her insides as if it would tear her apart. Her screams grew louder, until blackness and silence claimed her.

★   ★   ★

Vi woke with a start, her stomach reeling. She opened her eyes to find herself in her bed at Quaker Terrace. Across the room, Tilly stirred. Vi grabbed her toilet bag. The cramping was growing worse. Her period must have come early this month. She raced down the corridor to the bathroom, closed the door quietly behind her, and locked it. She pulled up her nightdress and winced at the splash of scarlet staining it. It wasn't her day to have a bath and Mrs. Sinclair was strict about such things, so a good, thorough wash would have to suffice.

Washed and refreshed, with a new pad in place, Vi grabbed her towel from the rail, wrapped it around herself and rolled the stained nightdress into a ball under her arm. She dived back down the corridor and got dressed, wishing her stomach would stop cramping up. Only now did she check her watch. Just after six.

When she was ready, she left Tilly sleeping and tiptoed down the stairs. All quiet. Mrs. Sinclair would be up in around an hour or so. A bit too soon to make a pot of tea. It would be cold by the time the landlady emerged and Mrs. Sinclair wouldn't approve of wasting the tea ration on just one person. Vi decided to make do with water, poured herself a glass, opened the wall cupboard door and reached for the bottle of aspirin. Mrs. Sinclair wouldn't begrudge her a couple, considering the reason.

Vi swallowed them down and wandered into the living room.

She pulled back the blackout and blinked at the bright sunlight. Nauseous dizziness rocked her balance and she eased herself down into a comfortable chair, the pain in her stomach making her gasp.

Only then did it all come flooding back to her.

CHAPTER FOURTEEN

The pain wasn't right. Period pains had a character all of their own. The cramping, gut-clenching ache was something she rarely suffered from, and, in any case, it wasn't like this scything, gnawing, griping agony that made her want to double over and be sick, while draining her body of every ounce of energy.

Draining it, yes, but not out of her body. It was as if all her energy was being concentrated in one area. In her belly. Deep inside. Whatever was orchestrating it seemed to have its own intelligence and was drawing from her for its own ends. Its own survival.

The door opened. Tilly rushed in. "Good grief, Vi, whatever's the matter?"

Vi clutched her stomach tighter and rocked back and forth. "I don't know. Something's wrong. I thought it was my period but...." She shook her head.

"Heavens, girl, you look terrible. You're sweating. Must be a temperature. I'm going to call for an ambulance. You stay there."

For one glorious second, the pain subsided. Vi inhaled, only to be regaled with a double-strength rush of pain that tore through her insides. She had heard trapped wind could make you feel as if your entire body would explode, but what she was feeling now wasn't that, nor was it appendicitis. She was pretty sure it didn't meet the criteria for that. In fact, it wasn't anything she could think of.

Tilly was back within a few minutes. "The ambulance is on its way. Thank goodness Jerry gave us a quiet night last night or I don't know what we'd have done. Where does it hurt, Vi? Can you point to it?"

Vi struggled to breathe over the constant white-hot pain. She pointed vaguely to an area encompassing her entire abdomen. Doing so meant she released her grip on her tummy and Tilly studied her. "You do look rather swollen there, but that could be your period. Do you normally swell up at your time of the month?"

"A little..." Vi gasped. "Not much—" A renewed burst of pain cut her off.

"It's all right. Don't try to speak anymore. We'll see what the doctors say."

Tilly took her hand and Vi clung on to her too tightly, so that she had to concentrate on lessening her viselike grip as she felt Tilly wince.

The distinctive sound of ambulance bells drew closer and the sound of brakes squealing was followed by doors opening and banging shut. Tilly sprang up off her knees beside Vi to let them in. Through her semi-delirium, Vi heard a rapid exchange of voices and then the door flew open and two burly ambulance men entered with a stretcher.

"All right, Violet. Let's get you to hospital where they can have a look at you. Can you stand?"

Vi tried to raise herself, one man holding each arm to steady her. She swayed as everything began to swim around her.

"Best get her on the stretcher, Bert. She isn't too steady on her pins."

Vi was aware of gentle hands lifting her and laying her down on the stretcher. As her world changed from the semi-vertical to the horizontal, her stomach churned and bile swam up into her throat. She swallowed hard and frequently and kept on doing that for the entire short journey to the nearest hospital.

At some stage, she must have passed out because when she opened her eyes, she was lying in a clean bed, tucked in firmly and with a drip in her arm.

She tried to lift herself higher to gauge her surroundings but a sharp twinge from the needle in her arm made her think twice. Mercifully the pain in her stomach had receded to a dull ache.

Vi lay quietly for a few minutes and closed her eyes. It seemed no time had passed before an unfamiliar male voice roused her and she opened her eyes to see a middle-aged man wearing a tartan bow tie and white coat, sporting a stethoscope around his neck.

"Ah, Mrs. Harrington. Back with us at last. You gave us quite a nasty scare there."

"I'm sorry...and it's Miss Harrington. Violet."

The smile vanished from the doctor's face. His voice was curt. "I see."

What had made him change his attitude so drastically? Somewhere nearby a baby cried, then another and another.

A nurse sped past the end of her bed. "One starts and they all join in."

"It's always the way of it," the doctor called after her. "Now, Mrs....*Miss* Harrington, if you're sure that's what you want me to call you."

"It's my name, Doctor. Violet Harrington. Miss."

"And what is your...*profession*, Miss Harrington?"

"I'm a civil servant. Shorthand typist."

"Indeed." The doctor sighed. "Any family living nearby?"

"My parents live temporarily with my sister in Cheltenham. Look, doctor, what's the matter with me? What's causing all the pain?"

"My dear young lady, you mean you don't know?"

"No." Vi's anxiety hit fever pitch. Why wouldn't the man simply come out and tell her?

The doctor leaned closer to her and she could smell tobacco on his breath. "You're pregnant. Around four months I would say."

Vi blinked. Surely she hadn't just heard that. "But it's impossible. I've never. I mean.... I know how women fall pregnant and no one has ever...."

"I can assure you *someone* has. Unless you're going to try and convince me that yours is the first immaculate conception since the Virgin Mary."

"But I'm telling you I haven't been near anyone in that way. I can't be pregnant."

"I would lower your voice if I were you, Violet. You're beginning to attract attention from the other mothers, and we don't want them upset, do we? Stress of any kind can transmit itself to their babies."

Vi made a conscious effort to lower her voice, but her heart beat faster with every second. "There must be another test you can do? And what about the pain? It's not as bad now, but it was awful."

"I can find nothing medically wrong with you. You are definitely pregnant and, so far, everything seems quite normal. Of course, you need regular checkups throughout your pregnancy, and we can organize those with the local midwife. Meanwhile, we'll keep you in for a further twenty-four hours and if there's no recurrence of the pain you experienced earlier, there's no reason why you shouldn't go home. You'll need to inform your employer, naturally. As a pregnant woman, and an unmarried one at that, they may wish to dispense with your services forthwith. In which case, your best course of action would probably be to join your parents at your sister's home."

"This isn't happening. It can't be happening. I cannot be expecting. I haven't even got a boyfriend."

"Nevertheless, the facts speak for themselves." The doctor checked Vi's drip. "The nurse will be along soon to remove that."

The rest of the day passed in a blur, until at six o'clock, Tilly came to visit. She sat in the visitor's chair next to the bed. "How are you now? You still look horribly pale."

"The doctor told me I'm pregnant."

Tilly almost fell off her chair. "*What?* But whose is it? I didn't know you were seeing anybody."

"I'm not and I haven't been in ages. And anyway, I've never.... This can't be happening, but, Tilly, I had a terrible nightmare last night and if this is true, I think the nightmare was more than just a bad dream. I think it actually happened."

Who cared if Tilly denied part of their shared past? At this moment, in her time of crisis, she was the only person Vi could turn to. At least she seemed genuinely concerned and shocked. Vi told her everything. When she had finished, Tilly stared at her.

"You don't believe me, do you?" If Vi's spirits could have tumbled any further, she didn't know how. In that second, loneliness enveloped her, along with a sense of deep dread. She still had to break the news to her parents and sister. This on top of George's death. She had brought disgrace on the whole family.

Tilly laid her cool hand over Vi's, where her fingers were picking at the blanket.

"I do believe you, Vi. I believe you because I think I was there. I had a nightmare too. You were in it and we were in this desolate place, a landscape, empty except for an ancient stone circle. A bit like Stonehenge only, maybe, smaller. I was dressed in a floor-length black robe, with a hood that covered my head and forced me to look downward as I walked, or I would have tripped. Only when we stopped – and we all stopped in unison. I don't know how – only then could I see straight ahead and I recognized you, screaming, being tortured by some creature. It wasn't human, nor was it any animal I've ever seen. Its back was to me and it was scaly, glistening in the moonlight and I watched it tear into you. Then I woke up. Like you, I thought it was a nightmare. I came downstairs and found you in agony, but I still thought I'd had a bad dream. Until now."

"But what does it all mean? And what the hell am I going to do about this?"

Vi pointed at her stomach, the mound visible under the blanket. "And that's another thing. The doctor estimates I'm four months gone, but this only happened yesterday."

Tilly shook her head. "Something else happened. You might as well know now. The MO people have queried a report of mine about that woman you swore we both shared a house with – Sandrine Maupas di Santiago – and that man, Alex. They returned it to me, asking me to swear an affidavit that everything I wrote is true. The problem is, Vi, I don't remember writing it and I still don't remember anything about that woman or her accomplice. But I *do* recognize my handwriting, and when I read it, I got, sort of, goose bumps. Something stirred in my mind but it's as if it's just out of reach and I can't quite grasp it. It looks like the powers that be are on to her and are using my MO report as part of their evidence. I want to help, but how can I when I don't remember anything about it? I need you to help me remember. Help me unlock that part of my brain that's suppressing these memories. I hate to ask right now though. You've got enough on your plate."

"Maybe we can help each other. Perhaps this is a way of finding out the truth. There seem to be so many layers to this, it's like peeling an onion. Now I know why I can't stand the things." Vi managed a smile and Tilly squeezed her hand.

"They're letting you out tomorrow, I believe," Tilly said. "I can come and get you at lunchtime."

"Thanks. I don't know if they will have signed me off by then and I need to know what I do from here on in. I know there are women who—"

Tilly smacked her hand. Her voice was a furious whisper. "Don't say it. Especially not here. It's illegal."

"I know, but who is its father? *What* is its father? I can't bring a monster into this world. There are enough of them here already."

Tilly sighed. "The Aryan superrace. Hitler's dream. It's all in *Mein Kampf*, you know. I read it once. Dull as ditchwater, but you can tell he's in cahoots with all sorts of occult practices and will stop at nothing to achieve his insane ideas. It's all laid out there in black and white for everyone to read. What if this is all connected? People dismissed that book as the ravings of a madman, if they bothered to read it at all. Only our Churchill took him seriously."

Vi was seeing a new side to Tilly. She had thought her mercurial, possessed of a short fuse and given to reading light, frothy novels and film magazines. Now she had revealed a deeper, more serious side and it left Vi wondering if she had ever really known the woman at all.

★   ★   ★

In the event, Tilly had to work late and not only could she not get to Vi at lunchtime, the message she sent said she would have to stay the night in the Dock. Vi left the hospital midafternoon with instructions on how to contact the midwife if she felt unwell and what to do in the coming months to prepare for the birth of whatever was growing in her belly. And it *was* growing, she could feel it. Like some parasite draining all the marrow from her bones and the iron from her blood, it left her tired, aching and feeling like a woman twice her age. She felt its entwining presence insinuating itself into her brain, assimilating and feeding off her knowledge and experience, hungry for whatever she possessed and prepared to take whatever it wanted. This was no symbiotic relationship. It was like being eaten from the inside out.

For the next hour, Vi struggled with endless staircases up and down to the Tube, trudged along dimly lit corridors until she finally emerged into the bright sun. She squinted up at the clear blue sky, swayed and steadied herself on the banister.

"You all right, love?" A sailor touched her arm.

Vi smiled and nodded. "Just a bit tired, that's all. Been overworking."

"You shouldn't ought to be working at all in your condition," he said, concern showing in his warm brown eyes. "Here, let's get you sat down. There's a seat over there." He steered her through the hordes of people, and she sank down gratefully on the hard, wooden bench seat. He perched beside her. "Can I get you some water? There's a café over there. They'll help out a lady in distress."

"No, honestly, you've been very kind. I just need to sit for a few minutes. It's quite hot today. Especially on the Tube."

"Tell me about it. Proper stinks down there as well. I'm Tim, by the way."

"Vi."

"Well, Vi, I have half an hour to spare if you want me to see you home safely."

That was the last thing Vi wanted. As soon as the young man had spoken so kindly to her, it was like a bomb had gone off inside her. Whatever that thing was didn't like the intervention. It wasn't about to let her have any outside help. For its own ends – whatever they were – she was on her own. She even began to wonder whether Tilly really did have to work late or whether the creature had manipulated that somehow. After all, so much else had been engineered. So many false memories, or memories wiped clean. So many lies and so much deception. She no longer knew what – or who – to believe and felt so weary, all the fight had been sucked out of her.

"I only live round the corner," she said. "I can be there in a couple of minutes."

"That's even better. I'll wait until you feel better and then I'll walk with you. Don't want you fainting in the street. My wife, Betty, she's in the family way. She's up in Derby and I don't get to see her much. She's due in a few weeks but I think I'll be overseas. The kid'll probably've started school before he gets to meet his dad. Is your husband...?"

Vi knew at that moment he had caught sight of her ringless finger. She could always lie and say her hands had swelled up so she had to take it off but, right now, the opinion of a total stranger – even a kind and well-meaning one – was the least of her concerns. "I don't have one," she said, her voice almost a whisper. "This is all a huge mistake."

A shard of pain, as agonizing as it was unexpected, shot through her and she cried out. Several passersby stopped and stared before deciding it was none of their business. Tim stood up. "You need to be in a hospital."

"I just came from one. They said there's nothing wrong. Nothing wrong!" Vi broke out in hysterical laughter. Tim backed away, and Vi read fear in his face. A voice spoke. An inhuman, raucous voice.

"That's right, back away. Leave her. *Leave her.*"

"Dear God." The sailor crossed himself repeatedly and retreated, half falling into people hurrying for the Tube. "What's the *matter* with you?" he demanded.

Vi realized no one else could possibly have heard what he had, or they too would have been as scared and white-faced as this good Samaritan was now. She also realized where that terrible, roaring guttural voice had come from.

It had come from her.

Tim dashed away and no one else took any notice of the pregnant woman slumped in the seat. Maybe they thought she was drunk. When Vi looked down at her bulging belly, it was as if three months had elapsed since she was in hospital. Her skirt strained at the waist and, with effort, she managed to undo a couple of buttons to release the pressure. It was then she felt the thing move for the first time. She had remembered touching Lilian's tummy when she was about seven months pregnant and feeling the butterfly-like movements of the baby inside her womb. Now, when she touched her stomach, she felt a kick so strong, it pushed her hand away.

"I have to get this thing out of me." She realized she had said the words out loud. A couple of women exchanged shocked expressions, shook their heads disapprovingly and sped past.

Vi had to get home. She must get to her room and shut the door. What to do about Tilly and Mrs. Sinclair she had no idea. But she couldn't stay out here. Sooner or later someone, alarmed by her strange behavior, would call the police, and they would take her away to God alone knew where.

She struggled to her feet and lurched forward, clutching her bag and gas mask awkwardly over her belly. She lived ten minutes away, but it took her more than twenty to finally make it to the front door. All the while, voices thrummed in her head, chanting in strange languages she had never heard before and couldn't comprehend. But even though she couldn't understand a word of what they were saying, she knew that beneath it all was an evil deadlier than she could ever have imagined. An evil hell-bent on destruction, whatever the cost. Death and suffering were its food and drink, of that she was certain. The entity inside her transmitted it to her. It had only been in her body for such a short time, but already she could sense the demon wrapping her in its filthy, rancid darkness. How long before it possessed her entirely? How long before nothing of *her* remained?

*　　*　　*

At home, Mrs. Sinclair was busying herself in the kitchen preparing the evening meal. She didn't notice Vi's arrival, for which the tortured woman was grateful. Vi made her unsteady way up the stairs, clinging to the banister for dear life.

Once inside her room, she was equally grateful for the coolness afforded by the partially open window. She half fell on the bed and lay there for some minutes, trying to catch her breath, which felt compressed by a great weight she knew to be the burden she carried inside her.

"You are ready for the next stage, Violet. I am here to conduct you."

Vi opened her eyes. Sandrine was sitting, one silk-stockinged leg crossed elegantly over the other, in a chair on the opposite side of the room. The sun framed her black hair in a halo. Ironic, Vi thought, considering she was the antithesis of a saint.

"What do you want from me and why is this…thing inside me? What does it want? It's killing me."

Sandrine spread her hands expansively. "It merely wishes to be born and to be welcomed by its mother."

"Never. I had no part in its conception and I am having no part in its life. I need to get it out of me. Now."

"That won't be possible. Oh, you won't be troubled by it inside you for much longer. A few days maybe. No more. Then we will take it."

At last, a ray of hope. "And that will be an end of it?"

"Naturally. We only needed a host body. The right host body."

"And why is that me? I'm nothing special. Nothing out of the ordinary. If you picked *me,* you could as easily have chosen anyone off the street."

"Possibly, but you were the one we wanted. We took great care in selecting the right one. You have no idea the measures we took."

"I have some idea." Vi shifted position. With the advent of Sandrine, the creature inside her seemed to have calmed down. Soothed perhaps by her voice, recognizing one of its own. But however much the easing of the excruciating pain was welcome, Vi was still far from comfortable and now had a vile taste in her mouth. Part copper, part something that tasted like rotten cabbage mixed with eggs that had gone off. She craved a drink of water. Or, better still, a cup of tea, to take away the horrible taste and assuage a thirst that was fast developing.

"Your friend, Tilly, won't be coming back here. She's going to be working and staying in the Dock for at least a week, maybe more if we need her to."

The implication of Sandrine's words hit her from all directions at once. Fear of being left virtually alone with Sandrine or one of her henchmen – perhaps Alex – piled onto her now-firm conviction that Sandrine's dark forces had infiltrated the government at its highest levels. Was the Prime Minister aware of what was going on? Memories of her encounters with Churchill flashed through her mind. He had been the only one who acknowledged the reality of Sandrine and her cronies when everyone else, from Tilly onward, denied their existence.

Vi became aware that Sandrine was watching her, one eyebrow slightly cocked. Could she read her thoughts? It seemed pretty much anything was possible for that one. Vi swallowed what little saliva remained. "So, what is to happen to me?"

"You will stay here and have the baby. We will know when it is about to be born and someone will come to assist you."

"But, Mrs. Sinclair—"

The door opened.

Sandrine looked over Vi's head at the person who entered. "Amelia. Please come in. I have been explaining to Violet what will happen in a few days' time."

Vi struggled to turn round, inhibited by the bulk which seemed to have grown even larger in the last few minutes.

"Mrs. Sinclair!"

The landlady looked from Sandrine to her, unsmiling. "It was always meant to be. You were always supposed to come to me."

Sandrine stood. "I shall leave you two now. Until we meet again, Violet, here's something to remember me by." She tossed a studio photograph of herself onto the bed. "You have been helpful in ways you couldn't possibly begin to imagine."

"If I have, it's because you've taken everything from me. Even my own brother. You didn't have to take him. He did you no harm."

Sandrine paused at the door. "Didn't he? He didn't tell you he wanted to join us, did he? He didn't say that he would do anything to keep me. Anything I asked of him. And I asked plenty, Violet. Without him you wouldn't have obtained your position at the Treasury or been given that promotion to work in the Cabinet War Rooms. He was involved in far more than merely flying. He was in covert operations. A spy. For your side. He didn't tell you that, did he? He allowed me to enter his mind. He couldn't help himself." She smiled and the sight chilled Vi.

"Poor George. He was so willing, so malleable, so besotted with me, he kept nothing back. He gave me everything. I even saw your entire childhood played out in front of me. I saw you in your mother's womb. I knew then you were the chosen one.

"You have collected and amassed so many memories for us. Your meetings with Churchill, the documents you have typed for him and for his senior officials. All of this and more is stored in your brain and now, in the brain of your soon-to-be-born offspring. There are others like you, Violet. Other young women we have – shall we say, recruited? Some here in Britain, some in the United States, Canada, France. Oh, you would be amazed at what we have learned and what we shall continue to learn."

Vi sat in stunned silence throughout all this. Sandrine moved to leave the room. Vi found her voice. "And you are going to sell these secrets to the enemy?"

Sandrine turned back. "The enemy? Oh, you mean Hitler. Among others, yes. But he is only one of the megalomaniacs currently at work. They come and they go. Our work continues. Our purpose is far greater than the petty ambitions of a tin-pot dictator or two.

They serve us and our ends for a while, but we grow stronger while they weaken and fade into history. It has been like this for all time. Once you have played your part, your obligation to us will end and you will go on with your life. It wasn't the same for your brother. His was to have been a lifetime commitment and he reneged on it. When he realized he could never have me, he tried to escape us." Sandrine and Mrs. Sinclair shook their heads. "So foolish. He could have died a hero's death. That is what was mapped out for him. But instead...." She let her words hang while, once again, the image of a burning aircraft, hurtling downward, flashed into Vi's mind.

Sandrine left with Mrs. Sinclair close behind her. Vi sank back on the bed, exhausted. She closed her eyes and finally, a mercifully dream-free sleep claimed her.

★   ★   ★

Hours passed. Maybe even days. It was night. Or perhaps day, but with the now-permanent blackout in her room, how could she know? She tried to lift herself from the bed and couldn't. Then *they* would come. Mrs. Sinclair and...something. Such an ordinary, respectable name, Sinclair. Not her real identity, of course. Glimpses Vi caught of her made her wonder if she was even human. Sometimes, the landlady would enter her room when she thought Vi was asleep. She wouldn't bother with the lamp, and didn't appear to need one, but a stray shaft of light from the landing revealed a body too tall and thin to be who she purported to be. The neck, long and sinewy. A strange guttural croak emanated from her mouth when she breathed. Vi would clamp her eyes tightly shut. Whatever this was, she didn't want to see it. She didn't even know if she was awake or asleep, and all the while, the thing inside her kept her under its increasingly firm control. Her thoughts were shared with it, her feelings suppressed by it, her emotions spent by it.

Time passed.

They moved her sometimes. They would take her to the

bathroom. There she would use the toilet, on command, except *they* weren't issuing orders to *her*, they were encouraging the thing inside her to perform her bodily functions. She didn't eat for herself. They inserted a tube in her arm and drip-fed her some concoction meant to nourish that creature. At these times, a foul sulfur taste wafted up into her mouth, making her gag. They would hold her down, inject her with something and the nausea would pass over, leaving her ever more exhausted.

All concept of passing time gone, she had no idea whether days, weeks or even months had passed when the first agonizing shard of pain hit her and a warm gush escaped her. Did she cry out? Was that why they came so fast? Or did the thing inside her summon them?

The light was snapped on. Her bleary eyes picked out Sandrine, Alex, Mrs. Sinclair and someone she could not recognize. Others stood out of her vision. A male voice she recognized. Glennister was in the room.

The chanting began. In that strange language she had heard at the stone circle on the night the beast, Eligos, raped her and the creature was conceived.

Sandrine stood over her, robed in a deep red velvet gown that seemed to swim before Vi's eyes. The woman raised something gold in color and Vi could make it out as a chalice like ones she had seen in church. Sandrine's lips were more scarlet than ever, and Vi had a sudden thought they might be stained with blood. But whose?

The chanting grew louder. The air was filled with the iron stench of blood. Vi's legs were pulled apart and secured in stirrups. She tried to struggle but realized they had tied her hands so that she was spread-eagled. Her movements were like those of a frightened, tortured kitten. She could only moan and squirm, and every sound, every movement, struck through her with an agonizing clarity of how sharp pain could be.

The creature wanted her to stop. It wanted her to cease any struggle or protest. It hurt too much to resist. The next wave of pain came at her through a fog. As if it was happening to someone else and she was a witness. She almost fancied she was on the outside of her body, seeing the blood-streaked sheets, her own thighs, dripping with the stuff and with other fluids. Amniotic, maybe worse. The stench in the room was almost unbearable. The stifling heat and the constant chanting. No one spoke to her, no one comforted her. No one even noticed she was anything other than a machine producing their cherished new life.

One almighty wrench threatened to tear out her intestines, bowels, every part of her insides.

Vi let out a long, drawn-out scream, followed by another and another. The thing didn't try to stop her. It was no longer there. She heard it as it was wrapped in a blanket and carried lovingly away by Mrs. Sinclair. No baby cries. This baby produced a raucous caw like that of a crow.

The chanting turned to celebration as the assembled small group congratulated each other, heedless of the suffering woman on the bed. Vi slipped in and out of consciousness.

Finally, when she awoke, she found they had changed her bed, washed and dressed her in a clean-smelling nightdress. Someone had even placed a small vase of violets next to her. She tried to sit up, but her stomach hurt too much.

Scared at what she might find, she pulled back the sheet and blanket and lifted her nightie. Her thighs were bruised, as were her ankles. She opened her legs and peered down, careful not to strain her already tortured muscles.

From what she could see, she wasn't in such bad shape. Certainly nothing like she expected after the terrible pain. That seemed now as if it had happened to someone else. Maybe it had. Her head felt full of cotton wool and she lay back against the cool pillows.

The door opened and her landlady came in, bearing a cup of tea.

"I thought you might appreciate this," she said. "After you've been so poorly. You look a little better today, dear, how are you feeling?"

Vi stared at her. "Feeling?"

The landlady looked perplexed. "Yes, you had a fever. Perhaps you don't remember. Fevers do that sometimes. Goodness alone knows where you got it from, but you've been quite out of it for about a week now. The doctor advised Tilly to stay at work in case she caught it as well. Being as how we've no idea what it is or was."

"I don't believe this. You really are a piece of work, aren't you?" Vi threw back the bedclothes and then wished she hadn't. Dizziness swept over her. Her breasts felt sore and tender, but, surely, she should be lactating? There was no sign of that.

Mrs. Sinclair set down the cup of tea and helped her back into bed. "Come now, it's obviously too soon for you to be getting up. Stay quietly here for another day and then see how you feel. I'll bring up some nice chicken soup later. They say it's good for getting you back on your feet."

Vi felt breathless. "Where is it?"

"Where's what, dear?"

"The…baby."

Mrs. Sinclair's eyes opened wide. "Baby? What baby?"

"The one I had. The one you took out of me."

"I'm sure I don't know what you mean. I think I'd better send for the doctor again. You're delirious."

"No, I'm not. You know perfectly well that you, Sandrine, Alex and that man, Glennister, are all in this together." As she spoke, Vi realized that, to a sane person, she must sound mad, but she knew what she knew. "You're in some black magic sect and you conjured up a devil. I have now had its child and you've taken it away. I don't know what you're feeding it on because it certainly doesn't seem to be coming from me, but then that…thing… isn't even human, is it?"

Mrs. Sinclair stared at her in such disbelief Vi even began to doubt the truth of her own words.

"I'll call the doctor." Mrs. Sinclair left before Vi could protest. Her head swam and she lay back.

The next sound she heard was that of an unfamiliar male calling her name. "Violet, Violet, it's Doctor Logan. Can you hear me?"

Vi opened her eyes. "Yes, I can hear you."

"Mrs. Sinclair tells me you have had a nasty fever."

"Yes, she does, doesn't she? She also said she called you in earlier to see me."

"No, that wasn't me. My colleague probably. I've been away in the country for a couple of weeks."

"Then surely a record of it will be in my notes."

"Probably. I haven't seen them and it's quite possible my colleague may not have had time to write them up. There *is* a war on, you know. I'm afraid some paperwork becomes a little neglected. Now, the good news is I've taken your temperature and it's normal. But I understand from Mrs. Sinclair that you're suffering from some rather odd delusions."

"They're not delusions, doctor, they actually happened. You can tell if I've recently had a baby, can't you? Examine me and you'll see."

The doctor exchanged glances with Mrs. Sinclair, who was standing nearby, arms folded, her lips pursed.

"Very well," he said.

He gently examined her and after less than a minute, pulled the sheet back over her.

"Well?" Vi said. "Do you believe me now?"

The doctor folded his stethoscope and pushed it into his bag. "I can find no evidence that you have had a baby in the recent past. Obviously, I would have to perform a more detailed internal examination to determine whether or not you had ever been pregnant, but as to the question of whether or not you have produced a child within the last few weeks? No, you have not."

"But that's impossible." He was lying. He was in on it. One of them. That was the only explanation.

The doctor fumbled in his bag and produced a sealed hypodermic and a small bottle. "Lie still, please."

"No. I won't. You can't do this."

"It's for your own good, Violet." Mrs. Sinclair grabbed her arms and held her still. Vi was too weak to put up more than a perfunctory struggle. She felt the sharp prick of the needle in her arm and a buzzing cloud descended on her.

*   *   *

The sun was shining and the sound of birds twittering outside the window drifted into Vi's consciousness. She blinked at the unaccustomed bright light pouring into the room. Tilly stood by the window and turned as Vi shifted in bed.

"Hello, old thing," she said. "How are you feeling?"

Vi shielded her eyes with her hand and struggled to sit up. "What time is it? What day is it?"

"Just after ten. Thursday."

"And the date?"

"Gracious, you have been out of it, haven't you? June twenty-third. Oh, and by the way, we no longer appear to have a landlady. I got back late last night, let myself in and came up to find you sleeping soundly. The house was so quiet, and I felt something wasn't right. There were no lights on anywhere and Mrs. Sinclair's door was open. I peered inside and her bed was neatly made up. I checked her wardrobe and cupboards. All empty. She's scarpered and something tells me we won't be seeing her again in a hurry. I mean, she's taken everything with her. All her possessions, clothes, the lot. All that's left is food and household stuff. Really odd."

"No, it makes sense in a way. If anything about this can make any kind of sense."

"What do you mean?"

"You wouldn't believe it."

Tilly came to sit on the edge of the bed. "I bet I would. Try me." She rolled up the sleeve of her cardigan and turned her inner forearm to face Vi. Odal's rune had been tattooed into her skin, leaving sore red welts around it.

Vi gasped. "Did they burn it in?"

"I've no idea. I don't think so. I was in the Dock one night, asleep, and had some really weird dreams. When I woke in the morning, my arm felt sore and…there it was. This was about three days ago. They'd told me you had this fever and asked if I was prepared to put in some extra shifts, staying in the Dock so I wouldn't come home and catch whatever it is you had. Here, let me help you. Can't let a woman in your condition...." Vi was half out of bed and Tilly's gaze was fixed on her midriff. "Where's it gone?"

"Thank God. I began to think I really had imagined it all." Vi told an increasingly befuddled Tilly all that had happened. Including Mrs. Sinclair's involvement.

"And you don't know where they've taken it?"

Vi shook her head. She shifted position on the bed, sitting on the edge with her feet resting on the floor. "Frankly, I'm relieved it's all over. That part anyway. The problem is, I don't know what other plans they have."

Tilly sighed.

"What's the matter? You look as if you want to tell me something, but you don't know how. Just come out with it."

"Very well," Tilly said. "There are more of you. More young women who've been chosen to be the bearers of this evil deity's offspring. It's all part of Hitler's plan for a superrace of Aryan conquerors. At least that's what they're saying in Whitehall."

Sandrine's words came back to Vi. "How do *you* know that?"

"I've been doing your job while you've been away. I've been typing stuff. Of course, I shouldn't have told you any of this and they'll probably shoot me as a traitor if they ever find out I have, but let's face it, if anyone needs to know, you do. And the other poor blighters who're going through what you are."

Vi shifted slightly, trying to make herself more comfortable. "What you've just told me is exactly what Sandrine said. There *are* more of us. According to Sandrine, that sect of hers or whatever it is, is merely using Hitler for their own ends. Unless I imagined it, she told me he was only one of a long line of power-mad dictators they have used down through the ages. But surely what you've been typing should have been encrypted. You shouldn't understand a word of it."

"Don't let this dotty, yet Hollywood-perfect, exterior fool you," Tilly laughed. "I'm quite a dab hand at the old code breaking when I set my mind to it. They weren't exactly using anything a child of six would have had any real problems with. Well, a child of six with any kind of mathematical brain anyway."

"You should be in the secret service," Vi said.

Tilly laughed and tapped the side of her nose.

"You're not...."

"Oh, heavens no, Vi, I'm nowhere near good enough – or brave enough. But I did do some of the basic training and that was enough, I can tell you. They really put you through it. They even try a form of brainwashing the Nazis use. Pretty bloody frightening. You don't know whether you're yourself or someone else half the time."

Now seemed as good a time as any. Vi plunged in. "I have to ask you. Do you really not remember living with Mrs. Harris in her house in Boscawen Walk? Don't you remember the night the plane came down and took half the street with it? Mrs. Harris had a heart attack and died, right there on the street in my arms. You went to get help."

"I've thought long and hard about this because I know you believe it. I even managed to get access to our personnel records – don't ask me how, the fewer people who know about my little ruse the better. Suffice it to say, our records are sketchy to say the least. And what's there has been doctored. Quite expertly but, like I said, I had some basic training in the Special Operations Executive. I know how to spot a forgery, even a clever one. Look, I wouldn't be telling you any of this if I hadn't already checked this place for electronic bugs. I don't remember Boscawen Walk or a Mrs. Harris, but I can quite believe that you, I, or both of us have been targeted. I think you deserve to know what I've found out – especially after what happened to you."

Tilly moved closer. "Vi, you must never, ever tell anyone what I'm about to tell you. Only the PM and a handful of trusted people right at the top know this. I doubt even the King has been told. Some old friends of mine have been doing a bit of digging around and what they've discovered is enough to turn our hair white. I would love to say that we're dealing with mere humans here, and in some cases we are. Living, breathing, evil humans like Hitler and his cronies, but the power they worship is far stronger than they are. It won't be so easily destroyed. Churchill can't bomb it, gas it or neutralize it with chemical weapons. It's been part of this world since time began and all we can do is try to contain it for our generation. As for future generations...." She spread her hands expansively. "All the information we have is kept. Including the reports that come in under the Mass Observation project that don't, well, let's say, that don't fit the normal bill. They call it 'Dark Observation'. In fact, without the MO project we wouldn't have known there were more than one or two examples of impregnation and abduction."

"You mean, women like me?"

"Exactly. There are, at present, probably a couple of dozen, or maybe up to a hundred, scattered about throughout the country. They follow a pattern. Just like yours. The mother is normally released, as you were, and left to get on with her own life. Generally, she has no maternal feelings for the offspring and is only relieved to be rid of its evil influence and presence. Occasionally things don't go according to plan and the mother wants to keep it."

"And does she?" Vi asked.

Tilly shook her head. "Not as far as my friends can tell. Every case like that, so far, has resulted in the mother turning up mysteriously killed. Of course, during wartime, it's easy to dispose of a body. Wait for an air raid. Add to the casualty list. No one asks any questions."

Vi shuddered. "Looks like I had a lucky escape."

"You certainly did the right thing by not deciding that now was the time you wanted to be a mother."

"After this, I don't think I ever will."

Tilly looked at her seriously. "Oh, I think you will. Vi. One day. When the right man comes along and the stars are aligned, as they say. I reckon you'll have a daughter and you will be very proud of her."

Vi laughed and then realized. Her friend was being serious. As if she had somehow peered into the future and seen her friend's life mapped out for her. She nodded. "Right." Would any of this ever make sense? One day, maybe, then Vi and her friend would sit down over a glass of warm beer and reminisce. But, right now, that day was a long way off. If ever.

CHAPTER FIFTEEN

A week went by and one morning, over breakfast, Tilly rolled up her sleeve. "Hey. I've got to show you something." She held up her bare arm and turned it front and back.

"I can't see anything."

"That's the whole point. That tattoo they burned into me. Odal's rune? It's gone. It vanished sometime in the last day or two. I suddenly realized it wasn't there anymore."

"Maybe it was one of those temporary things. Like a transfer."

"Oh no, it was permanent, all right. I reckon it simply didn't take. They marked me out as one of theirs and either the demon rejected me, or I simply wasn't made of their sort of stuff. That could also explain why you haven't got one. Of course, your involvement with them was always meant to be temporary anyway, so perhaps that meant they didn't need to mark you. Or maybe that training I had resisted some of their brainwashing, who knows? Either way, I shan't be scarred for life and neither will you."

Maybe not physically, Vi thought. But as for mentally, would either of them ever be the same again?

★   ★   ★

1941 rumbled on. Mrs. Sinclair never returned to Quaker Terrace. Vi and Tilly fended for themselves, treating the house as their own. They continued to work together, as Ethel had left to join the ATS.

News continued to worsen. The Blitz continued. Liverpool, Belfast, major ports, installations and cities faced nightly bombardment. At work, rumors began to circulate about Hitler's deputy, Rudolf Hess.

"They say he flew over Scotland, ran out of fuel and had to land there," Nancy said to an astonished Vi. "Never tried to cover up who he was. Of course, he was arrested and thrown in prison."

"What on earth do you suppose he was up to?" Vi asked.

"Mentally unstable. They all are," Tilly said.

Nancy nodded. "Or maybe he was planning to overthrow Hitler. *He's* not having it all his own way, you know. And now there's rumors he's going to invade Russia."

Miss Brayshaw came in and clapped her hands. "Nancy. Careless talk!"

"Sorry, Miss Brayshaw. But the men were talking about it openly in the mess."

"Well, they shouldn't have and I will be having words with their superiors, you can rest assured on that. Now, back to work. There's a lot to do. The PM will be coming down before long and I don't want him walking in on a gossipy women's tea party."

Churchill came down about half an hour later. It was extraordinary how his mere presence on the corridor could instill a hush. It was as if everyone sensed his presence almost before he was there, although Vi had to acknowledge that the couple of gentle, warning taps echoing down the air-conditioning pipes did give the game away somewhat.

After a few minutes Miss Brayshaw appeared at the entrance to their office.

"Violet. The PM has asked to see you."

Vi exchanged glances with Tilly, who raised her eyebrows before putting her finger to her lips. Vi gave the briefest of nods and straightened her blouse and skirt before grabbing her pad and pencil and leaving the office.

At the sound of her arrival, the PM laid down his pen. "Close the door, Miss Harrington, and sit down. I wish to talk to you about a matter of some importance."

Vi did as she was bid and sat in the chair indicated.

Churchill lit his cigar and puffed aromatic smoke, which welled up like a cloud around him. Vi knew for as long as she lived, she would never forget the smell of that particular brand – *Romeo y Julieta*, Havana cigars.

Churchill removed his cigar and rested his hand on the desk next to him. "Miss Harrington, for reasons none of us can quite determine, you have become embroiled in a particularly vile Nazi plot, part of Hitler's plan to create some kind of master race. I think that this is probably not entirely news to you, as I am aware you needed some time away from work owing to a sudden, unexpected and, to many, impossible malady."

"Yes, sir."

"Are you quite recovered from your ordeal?"

What an extraordinary question. How could she ever really recover from it? And yet, in some ways, she did feel remarkably calm, as if, incredible though it had been, it was now over, finished, and the time had come to assign it to the past.

"Yes, sir. I am quite recovered, thank you."

"The other…losing your brother so tragically. That is far harder to come to terms with. Especially in those circumstances."

"I believe he was murdered, sir. I believe *they* did it. And I'm certain they've infiltrated here. Mr. Glennister…." The words had spilled out, without any thought or warning. Now they lay there. Churchill barely blinked.

"Quite so, Miss Harrington. I am positive you are correct, and this is the reason I wished to speak with you. There are, it would appear, two possibilities relating to your brother's death. One I am not at liberty to discuss but, as for the other, I can tell you that it is officially being treated as murder as yet by person or persons unknown. If this is indeed the way he met his end, we have our suspicions as to the identities of the murderers and I suspect they mirror your own. As for Glennister…I shouldn't worry about him anymore. He was found dead in his flat. Shot himself. I suspect that news will come as something of a relief. He knew we were on to him."

"Yes, sir."

Churchill puffed at his cigar. "Miss Harrington, you have heard of an entity known as Eligos?"

"Yes. I believe I have actually encountered it."

"The characters you met – the Santiago woman and her accomplice – the man you know as Alex – are followers of it. Disciples. But then you probably know that already. I should tell you, Miss Harrington, my late mother was a lifelong student of the supernatural and passed on her fascination for the subject to me. I have studied many of the cults and beliefs and, among the most interesting, and indeed dangerous, is the cult of Eligos. When I read *Mein Kampf*, I was struck immediately by the inferences and references that mirrored much of the cult's beliefs. I tried to alert those in power around me but, as we have seen, none would listen. Closed minds, Miss Harrington. Closed minds. They have brought us to where we are today." He checked his pocket watch and frowned. "Time has sadly caught up with us, and I must meet with my generals, but I wished to reassure you that all that can be done will be done in this matter. I must, of course, require you to refrain from discussing this with anyone. I trust I can rely on you?"

"Yes, sir."

"We will get them, Miss Harrington, I am determined on it. And we shall put an end to their evil, once and for all."

"Thank you, sir."

★　　★　　★

Vi left the PM's office feeling lighter than she could remember. She longed to share her news with Tilly but, this time, she mustn't. She had promised no less a figure than Churchill himself. The fact that he was interested enough in her brother's case to be dealing with it personally was enough to convince her that nothing must slip out.

She almost skipped down the corridor, so wrapped up in her thoughts, she took a wrong turn and had to double back on herself.

Someone blocked her way. Alex smiled his Clark Gable smile, white teeth flashing as Vi made to skirt around him. He caught her arm.

"What's the hurry, Vi? No time for a quick chat with an old friend?"

"You're no friend of mine. You murdered my brother."

Alex's grip tightened painfully. "Now, hold on, I would be very careful about throwing such accusations around. Someone might believe you."

"What does it matter to you if they do? You'll simply disappear and turn up somewhere else. Maybe as someone else entirely. You're not even human."

"Take care, Violet. You were useful to us but now your usefulness is at an end. We have what we needed from you. You're the one who could disappear. I could make it happen. You know what I'm capable of. Remember dear George."

He brought her up close to him. So close she could see deep into his eyes and the creature within. She had seen it before. It fluttered, deep within the dark iris. It glowed a yellow-red and seemed to grow as she watched it rise, unfurl wings…. He released her and she fell back against the wall.

★   ★   ★

The long process of self-healing led to sleepless nights. Cups of tea in the early hours, by herself or occasionally with Tilly when sleep eluded her as well.

The war dragged on. Rationing got worse. 1942 saw the Americans declare war after the fleet was bombed at Pearl Harbor. Vi and Tilly continued their work, like millions of others. They lost friends, they mourned. They picked themselves up and carried on.

Finally, the war took a turn and the news was of victories. Liberations. France in August 1944. Then, in April 1945, horrifying footage from the concentration camps. Vi and Tilly sat in a packed, silent cinema as scene after scene of appalling barbarity played out on the screen.

And Vi knew. Sandrine. Alex. Glennister. They had all been part of this.

And two of them – along with countless others – were still out there. Somewhere.

CHAPTER SIXTEEN

August 1945

It was so quiet down there. Almost everyone had gone, but Vi could still hear the echoes of voices, some familiar, some she never got to know, others who came and went. Some she lost along the way....

A breeze ruffled through her hair. She caught her breath. Footsteps. Two sets of them.

Long, striding. A man. Behind him, quicker, smaller steps. High heels, she was sure of it. But no one should be down here. Only Vi and a couple of guards along the entire corridor. Maybe someone had forgotten something? Vi crept over to the doorway and peered out. The footsteps had ceased now. She barely breathed, anxious not to miss a single sound. All that wafted toward her were faraway sounds, voices, a man whistling somewhere a long way away.

Vi felt someone close behind her, the touch of fingers ruffling her hair. Out of the corner of her eye, the flash of a smile.

"George?" In her mind, she heard him speak.

Well, cheerio, then, sis. Take care of yourself.

The illusion and the sound vanished. No one would ever believe her, of course. That didn't matter. She knew. Somehow, her brother had reached out from beyond and touched her soul. Whatever Sandrine had said about him no longer mattered to her. He had been under the influence of Eligos. At least now he was free.

Vi wandered down the corridor toward the PM's deserted office. She paused at the entrance. On an impulse, she made her way farther along, her footsteps echoing the empty hallways as she drew closer to the far end where the ethereal Room 338 sometimes appeared.

No guards stood to attention, waiting to challenge her presence. It seemed darker, as if someone had turned the lights down. That would have been possible if there had been dimmer switches, but there weren't.

Vi's mouth ran dry, but she persevered. She must face her demons.

Something grabbed her attention. She stopped, looked to her left and let her eyes travel upward.

Room 338.

Vi turned the handle. It opened. She pushed it and met a slight resistance, shoved a little harder and it opened. A rush of fetid air choked her. She stepped back, coughing to clear the foul odor and taste. By all accounts this door hadn't been opened in months, years even. She reached around the wall just inside and found the switch. When she depressed it, a weak central light revealed something horribly familiar in the darkness. A formless, huddled shape that rapidly uncurled itself until it stood. The demon Eligos rose before her.

Frozen to the spot, barely able to breathe, Vi could only watch as the demon shimmered. It morphed. Scales became skin and hair as it transitioned from beast to human – or what passed for it. In seconds, Alex stood before her, all trace of Eligos gone.

"What do you want from me now?" Vi said. She found she could move. And she no longer feared him.

"From you? Nothing more. You gave us what we needed, and, in return, we gave you your life to live."

"But why did you choose me? And why is it that I still have so many questions but no answers?"

"You were chosen because your line has always been chosen and will be again when the time is right."

A sharp breeze whistled around her, its chill misting her eyes. She wiped them with the back of her hand and when she opened them, she was out on that plain she had last seen the night she had been violated.

The wind swirled and billowed around ancient stones. Clouds sped through the skies like a film on fast speed. Day became night, became day again. Hooded figures offered supplication to their gods. They ignored Vi. She wasn't there. Merely a spectator, caught up in some unholy vortex.

The scene before her melted away and she was standing in the hallway of Mrs. Sinclair's house in Quaker Terrace. The woman herself emerged from the kitchen and Vi felt tangible fear once more. That woman had done her harm.

"Get away from me!"

The woman laughed and, in an instant, Vi saw Sandrine, Alex and Glennister. Each, in turn, took possession of the figure in front of her. Each stared at her before they too threw back their heads, one after the other, and laughed at her.

Finally, Vi understood. And, at that moment of understanding, she found herself once again in Room 338.

Alex stood in front of her. "So, you see, Violet, your brother unwittingly gave us access to you, your thoughts, mind and body."

"And you stole everything from me."

"Oh, not quite everything. You have the rest of your life. That will be yours to do with as you will. As long as you don't try to hurt us, of course. Not that you would be capable of it anyway."

"You're not as powerful as you think you are. You never got to Churchill."

Alex's expression darkened. "He is protected by strong and powerful forces. You, however, are not. Do not ever forget that."

The room swirled, drifted out of focus, and Vi rubbed her eyes. When she dropped her hands, she was out in the corridor and facing Rooms 81 and 82. No sign of the room she had just been in.

Vi ran back to her own corridor. Half of it was in blackness. She must get out now or risk being trapped in here.

She picked up her small suitcase with her few personal belongings and, without a backward glance, made for the stairs to take her back up into the daylight.

★　　★　　★

The blaring horns, the clip-clop of horses' hooves from the brewery drays and all manner of delivery vehicles, did much to restore her equilibrium. Vi made her way through crowds of excited people, celebrating the end of the war in the Far East. With the war in Europe already won, it was truly over at last.

As she was about to turn the corner into Quaker Terrace, Vi stopped and changed her mind. On a whim, she walked back the other way, in the direction of what she had always thought was Boscawen Walk. The streets seemed familiar. Further bombing had destroyed more houses, rubble lay everywhere; ragged, but happy children played with old tires, creating makeshift and ramshackle toys out of bits of unrecognizable debris.

She crossed over, negotiated yet more rubble, turned a corner and prayed she wouldn't see the sign for Bottomley Way. Vi looked down. The house on the corner had been demolished or blown up. There was no street sign. She looked around and then found it, upside down, a rectangular enamel sign, rusting at the edges. Vi picked it up and read it. *Boscawen Walk*. She could have simply left it where she found it, but suddenly its existence seemed the most important thing in her world. Something tangible to hold on to. Whatever else had been a lie, this hadn't. Even though Tilly still could not remember ever having lived there.

Tucking the sign under her arm, Vi pressed on, past the silent shattered houses and fluttering, tattered curtains, until she found what she was looking for. Except....

She checked again. Number Twenty-three. Mrs. Harris's house. There it was, standing there, barely marked. The only one in that part of the street.

But that's impossible. I saw it with my own eyes. Demolished by that plane.

She looked around at the scarred and ruined landscape. Sure enough, there were still bits of twisted aircraft, although the piece of wing emblazoned with its swastika had been pilfered. Last time she had seen it, the entire house had lain in ruins, barely two bricks still attached. Now she stared up at the house that looked as if its owner had left it for a few minutes to go to the corner shop. If there had still been one.

What now? Walk away and get on with her life? *I have to know....*

Vi marched up the path and knocked on the door. A few seconds went by. Should she knock again? She raised her hand and the door opened.

She knew it wasn't possible but there was the woman, standing there.

"Mrs. Harris?"

Instant recognition. The woman beamed. "Violet. Oh, how good to see you. Come in, come in."

It felt comforting to smell the familiar aroma of polish. The hall and living room were exactly as she remembered them. Time had stood still here. Vi had no explanations. She could only play out this scene by its own rules, and that meant forgetting the ruined house, and the dead woman. For now, at least, the normal rules of nature didn't apply. All she could do was see where it led her.

"You were lucky to be left standing here," Vi said as she made herself comfortable in her usual chair. It seemed like the most appropriate thing to say in the circumstances. After all, the neighborhood was all but wiped out.

"What, dear? Oh, yes, the bombing. Yes, very lucky, but tell me, where have you been, what has been happening to you and Tilly?"

"Tilly is fine. She's joined the WRNS. I almost did as well but I decided life in the services wasn't for me. They're sending her off to the Pacific soon, and she's met such a nice sailor. There'll be wedding bells one of these days."

"And what about you, dear? Have you found a nice young man yet?"

"Well, there is someone. But it's early days. We'll see." Despite the incongruity of what was happening to her, Vi felt an excited tingling she always experienced when she thought of Ron Scott and his warm brown eyes. Twice he had taken her to a dance, dressed in his smart army captain's uniform. "How about you, Mrs. Harris?"

Mrs. Harris blinked a couple of times as if she didn't understand the question. "Me? Why nothing, dear. I've just carried on. Like Mr. Churchill told us to. I go out to the shops every day and queue. I come home, dust and polish. Cook a meal. The usual, normal things."

Maybe this version of Mrs. Harris could answer some of her questions. Vi plunged in. "Have you ever heard of a street nearby called Bottomley Way?"

Mrs. Harris looked thoughtful. "The name's familiar…. Oh, yes. I remember. This street used to be called Bottomley Way before it was rechristened back at the turn of the century. The man it had been named after was discredited for something and the local council took it upon themselves to change anything with Bottomley attached to it. Oh, I see you have our street sign." She pointed to the plaque which Vi had leaned up against her leg, hoping no rust or dirt got onto Mrs. Harris's clean carpet. Why on earth hadn't she left it in the hall?

"I'll move it straight away," Vi said.

"Probably best, dear."

Vi stood and carefully picked up the sign, before taking it into the hallway. She went through the living room door.

Out into the street.

Vi spun round. She was standing on a mound of rubble that had comprised the front of the house.

"Oy, you. Miss!"

An ARP warden in uniform and tin helmet was waving wildly at her. "Get off there. It's not safe. The whole lot could come down at any minute."

As if on cue, a low rumbling began, and the earth trembled beneath her feet. Vi clutched her sign and scrambled off the rubble. The ARP warden put out his hand to steady her. The rumbling stopped.

"That was a close call, miss. You shouldn't be wandering around here. The army bomb disposal people haven't had time to check it yet."

"When did this happen?" Vi asked.

"Can't remember exactly. Sometime in '41, I think. It's going to take years to sort London out. And it doesn't help the rest of us when young women who should know better go scrambling about in the ruins as if they're some kind of playground."

"I'm really sorry. I used to live there and...."

"Well, I'm very sorry you lost your home. I lost mine as well, so I know the feeling. At least we got out of this mess in one piece, though. We're the lucky ones."

Vi smiled. "Yes, you're right. We're the lucky ones."

★   ★   ★

Vi wandered back to Quaker Terrace, where she had lived on her own since Tilly had moved out. She unlocked the door and let herself in. There were too many echoes here, in its hall, its rooms and the stairway. Today it seemed emptier than ever.

So many times, alone here with only her thoughts for company, Vi didn't know what had been true and what had been somehow created. Maybe none of the peculiar events had actually happened. Perhaps that creature she had given birth to had all been a nightmare. But George *had* been killed. That wasn't a bad dream, and not a day went by without her missing him and feeling as if a part of her had been ripped apart. No one else might believe her but Vi knew he had finally said goodbye to her today and his spirit had moved on, hopefully to eternal rest, whatever that might be, or wherever. Surely, she should be happy for him? But the truth was her body felt emptier than ever.

Vi made her way upstairs to her room. She opened the door, reached up to the top of her wardrobe, lifted off her suitcase and carefully packed her clothes, books and toiletries.

She emptied the drawer of the bedside table and a photograph fluttered to the floor. Vi bent to retrieve it.

The face of Sandrine Maupas di Santiago stared back her. Vi brought the photograph closer to her eyes. There it was. Difficult to see, especially in black and white, but it was there, in her eyes. The strange light from the extra presence that inhabited the woman's body. Eligos. A voice inside her told her to rip the picture up. Destroy it forever. But Vi stopped herself and slid the photograph into her case before closing and locking it.

She must keep that picture. One day, if she was fortunate enough, she could have children of her own. Real children she would birth, raise and love with all her heart. Alex's warning rang in her ears. Maybe she was alone now, but *they* could always return. Wherever she went, whatever her life turned out to be, they could always find her and if they could find her, they could find her family. After all, they already had, and her brother had paid for it with his life.

With a force like theirs, there was little enough Vi could do to protect herself, but at least if her children knew what to look for, they could protect themselves. A little knowledge could put them on their guard right at the time they needed it most.

Downstairs, she took one last tour of the rooms. In the kitchen, the tap dripped rhythmically. It had done so ever since Vi could remember. For the first time she wondered why she and Tilly had stayed on here after Mrs. Sinclair – or whatever her name was – had disappeared. No mail had ever come for her. They had paid the utility bills, but no one ever asked for rent or questioned their presence in the house. Vi had thought that strange at first but, after a few months, she forgot about it as she and Tilly concentrated on getting through the rest of the war as best they could. Now it was all over, there was no point in staying. With Tilly starting her new life and her own job ending, there was nothing to keep her here. Her parents had finally been rehoused, in a flat near her sister's, and, for the time being, Vi would sleep on Lilian's settee until she found a job and a place of her own.

Vi checked out the photograph of Sandrine once more. The woman's eyes seemed alive. *Did her lips move just then? She seems about to speak.* Vi hurriedly thrust the picture deep into her handbag and closed it with a resounding click.

When she got to Cheltenham, she would buy a small photograph album to house that picture. No other photos would join it. She didn't want them contaminated. But, one day in the future, she would open that album and tell of the evil that had been Sandrine Maupas di Santiago.

PART THREE
HEATHER
PRESENT DAY

CHAPTER SEVENTEEN

I decided to stay in Salisbury and lived with Mum until I found somewhere I liked, and a job to finance it. It took Mum a long time to tell me about Gran's experiences as she had recounted them to her, and it took me far longer to process what she told me. In fact, it's only now, months later, that I think I've finally got a handle on it. One morning, a few weeks ago, a bulky letter arrived which took me aback as it was from Gran. To be accurate, it had been mailed by her solicitor on her instructions. She had clearly written it some years earlier as the paper was slightly yellowed. All thirty-odd sheets of it.

In it she detailed her experiences, covering much the same ground as Mum had but with a few extra touches. She had drawn Odal's rune so that if I should ever see it, I would recognize it and give its owner a wide berth. She wrote of Tilly's Mass Observation diary, urging me to trace it if I could. She wrote about her brother, George, and how he had become mixed up with Sandrine di Santiago and her accomplice, Alex, and she wrote of the strange lapses in perception, of finding herself reduced to miniature and standing on Mrs. Harris's shelf.

I have lived my life not knowing what was true and what was a lie fabricated by some of the most evil beings ever created. They implanted false memories, layer upon layer of them until I didn't even know if certain people ever existed. The visions I experienced were so real and so vivid. For years I believed I must have imagined being violated by their demon and having a baby, but then, before your mother came along, I had to have an internal examination and a doctor told me I had given birth at some stage. Whatever happened to it, I have no idea.

Gran wrote of Churchill. *Our paths crossed only once after the war. He was a very old man by then, and quite frail. He remembered me and said that he deeply regretted not being able to weed out 'that bunch of infidels' as he called them. He had tried to 'beard them in their lair' but they were always one step ahead.*

The existence of a secret society called the Vrill (I think that's how you spell it) came out after the war. It was based on a cluster of old beliefs, many of them pagan. Mr. Churchill explained it a little but I'm afraid I was still too much in awe of him to take it all in. Hitler, Goering, Hess and Himmler were all members, and it all fitted with what Alex and Sandrine had told me. I am forced, however incredible it may sound, to believe them. Mr. Churchill warned me to forever be on my guard against them and to pass that warning on to my children. He said it didn't matter that Hitler and his motley crew were all long dead. They had managed to release the force of Vrill into the world. Sandrine was one of its high priestesses and Alex a high priest – reputed to be immortal and able to shapeshift, although, despite his own beliefs in the power of the black arts, Churchill expressed contempt for those notions. He patted my hand and smiled at me – a warm and genuine smile. Sadly, I never saw him again.

I have learned that all the surviving Mass Observation diaries are in an archive, maintained for posterity. I made enquiries about Tilly's entries and reports but there is no trace of anything. If only I had known enough to ask Tilly about them at Gran's funeral, but it wasn't to be.

My research into the Vrill – or more accurately Vril – resulted in a fair amount of information – much of it disputed, but the name itself seems to have come from a book by Edward Bulwer-Lytton called *The Coming Race*, in which he writes of a superrace who lived under the earth, in huge caverns. Lytton's super-beings had developed a force of energy they called *vril*, which boosted them to the ranks of gods themselves, enabling them to emerge from their underground empire and rule the earth. I concluded that Hitler's evil, and his incredible belief in his own invincibility, could so easily have come from devotion to the beliefs and doctrines of the Vril Society. I read that some of their members believed they had actually made contact with these creatures. When I read more – including some physical descriptions – I looked again at the photograph of Sandrine.

She fitted the type exactly. Not blond, blue-eyed and wide-hipped as the typical ideal Aryan woman was depicted, but tall, slender, almost androgynous of body, with dark hair, olive skin and a hypnotic gaze.

If these beings really did exist, then Sandrine was surely one of them.

As for Uncle George…I think the term 'more sinned against than sinning' applies. He fell in love with the wrong woman and she used him. Plain and simple. She played him and he couldn't get her out of his system. He was obsessed with her and he paid the ultimate price. As to whether he died in a motorcycle accident or was shot down…. I tried to find out, but some records from around that time had been destroyed in a bomb blast toward the end of the war. It seemed that all trace of Flight Lieutenant George Harrington since 1941 had been erased from history, and that in itself is odd.

I find myself opening that album of Gran's quite regularly – the one with the photograph of Sandrine in it. She fascinates and frightens me. There is a horrific amount of power in those eyes of hers. I used a magnifying glass one day and was astonished to see something like a dragon, its wings partially unfurled, lurking in her gaze. It must have been a reflection – or maybe camera flash – but it was strange to say the least.

The rest of my life continues as normal. I have settled into my new apartment – it's small but overlooks the river and I can watch the swans gliding gracefully upstream as I sip a glass of chilled white wine of an evening. I found a job with a financial services company and I go to work, come home, prepare a meal, maybe watch TV or a boxset, go out once or twice a week, and I'm making new friends. Tonight, I shall go to dinner with a new man in my life.

Gavin Jordan. He has the most gorgeous deep brown eyes, black hair and a smile that lights up a room. He is also kind and generous and I would like to think we might have something worth developing. I've known him casually for a couple of years as he works in a law firm on the top floor of the building where my office is. When I'm with him, I can really be myself and relax. It's such a good feeling and I don't want it to end. Losing Gran has been so hard. I could always talk to her. Mum and I are close but it's not the same. Gavin, on the other hand, is easy to be around. He is so interested in everything I do. He must know everything there is to know about my life and, yet, when I think about it, I know next to nothing about his. He told me his parents died when he was still very young, he has no siblings and lives alone in a large apartment to which I haven't yet been invited. He achieved a first in law at Oxford and is working toward being called to the bar. His specialty is criminal law and he has defended some rather dodgy characters. Beyond that, his life is pretty much a closed book. I'm hoping to open it up a little this evening.

★　★　★

I had the oddest experience this evening. I met Gavin in the restaurant as planned. Everything was going really well. Between the starter and entrée, he excused himself and I watched him go off in the direction of the gents'. Then he veered off to the left and spoke to a woman standing by the street entrance. She was tall, slim, elegant-looking, with jet-black hair, swept up in a chignon. She looked so familiar, but I wasn't close enough to be sure. She was also standing partly in profile, which didn't help. Then she turned in my direction and I felt her eyes burn through me. I dropped my fork and it clattered to the floor. A waiter was there in an instant, picking it up, changing it for another one and completely blocking my view of her. When he had finished fussing and moved away, she was gone, and Gavin was going into the gents'.

He emerged a few minutes later and strode back to our table.

"I'm sorry I took so long."

"Is she a friend of yours?" That didn't come out as I wanted it and he looked a bit taken aback. I must have sounded like a jealous girlfriend. Well, maybe I was.

"Who? Oh, you mean…. A friend of my late parents."

"Sorry, I didn't mean to pry, but she looks so familiar. What's her name?"

He hesitated and it bothered me. Why not come straight out with it?

"Hester. Hester Neilsen."

For some reason, I felt sure he was lying. But why would he? I suppressed the feeling and the main courses arrived. Salmon for me. Duck for Gavin.

"You should have brought her over to join us," I said, taking a forkful of delicious poached fish.

"She was on her way to some function or another. She's a very social person. Always going out and about to concerts, parties and country house weekends."

"You're very well-connected," I said, and sipped some perfectly chilled Chablis.

"It all helps in my profession." He smiled and I forgot all about suspecting him of lying as we slipped into our usual comfortable warmth.

We enjoyed the rest of our meal, sipped liqueurs and coffee, and Gavin insisted on paying the bill.

"My turn next time," I said.

The waiter brought our coats and we left, arm in arm, as we strolled back to his car, parked about a hundred yards up the street.

Gavin clicked the key fob and the lights flashed. As he opened the passenger door for me, I had the strongest feeling of being watched and glanced across the street to find I was right. It was dark and a man stood, partially illuminated by a streetlight, smoking. I spoke to Gavin.

"That man across the street is staring over here. Do you know him?"

Gavin looked over. "What man?"

"The one by the streetlight."

Gavin looked over again. "There's no one there."

"I'm looking straight at him. You must be able to see him."

Gavin shrugged. "Honestly, Heather. There's no one there. Now, are you getting into this car?"

He sounded irritated but, just then, I couldn't care less. Although the man was half in shadow, I could see enough of him to register a lopsided grin, followed by a mock salute directed at me, before he disappeared down a narrow alleyway between two shops. Gavin was in the car, seat belt on. He started the engine. I climbed in next to him and shut the door.

"I did see him, Gavin. How could you not?"

"Maybe it was a trick of the light."

I said nothing. He drove me straight home and I didn't invite him in. For some reason Gavin had lied to me twice that evening and I hadn't a clue why.

Our good night kiss was a cursory peck on the lips. As I watched him drive away, I wondered if it would be the last time.

★   ★   ★

He texted me the next day, apologizing and asking if he could make it up to me. I said there was no need for an apology. I would be delighted to go out with him again and we made arrangements for the following evening. 'Hester' had given him two tickets for a showing of the work of an 'exciting new artist' at the Reynolds Gallery. I had never been to an art exhibition before and wondered what on earth you were supposed to wear. In the end I settled for a smart black pants suit teamed with a pair of black patent stilettos and a glittery top. Although I said it myself, I didn't look half bad. A little understated make-up and a pair of simple gold earrings completed the picture.

Gavin picked me up, looking ultra-smart in an expensive-looking navy suit and blue shirt with a gorgeous red silk tie. The law paid well all right.

"Will Hester be there tonight? I should love to meet her," I asked as we drove into town.

"No, she can't make it. That's why I have the tickets. They were originally hers but she's in London for a few days."

"What does she do?"

"Do? Oh, you mean a job. Nothing. Hester doesn't work. She doesn't have to. She has independent means. I doubt she would have the time anyway."

"She leads a busy life, by the sound of things."

"She gets around."

We turned into the narrow street housing the gallery, an upmarket bistro and a couple of shops selling expensive women's clothing. Gavin parked between a new Jaguar and a vintage Rolls. His top of the range Mercedes fitted right in.

I climbed out and he took my arm.

The gallery was already busy with the great and the good of Salisbury milling around. An expensively dressed blonde with a smile that must have set her back a few thousand advanced toward us. She ignored me, placed her hands on Gavin's shoulders and planted air kisses on both sides of his face.

"Gavin darling, so good to see you. It's been ages. Venice, wasn't it? The Biennale?"

"It must have been. Davina, this is Heather. Heather, this is Davina Court-Reynolds. This is her gallery."

Davina touched my hand with the lightest of feathery fingertips without taking her eyes off Gavin. My hackles rose and I wanted to slap her face.

"Let me get you both a drink. Champagne for you, of course, Gavin."

"What else?" I didn't like the way Gavin had changed from the moment she had joined us.

Finally, she deigned to speak to me. "And what will you have?"

"The same," I replied as nonchalantly as I could manage, given how much I was holding back my desire to wipe the smile off her face. I don't usually have such a violently negative reaction to someone I meet for the first time, but in her case, I was prepared to make an exception.

Davina clicked her fingers and a waiter appeared at her elbow. The whole move was so clichéd and stagey, I had to swallow a sudden burst of giggles that threatened to erupt at any second.

She presented us both with a glass of champagne and the waiter moved on.

"Now, let me show you some of Andrea's work." She hooked her arm through Gavin's and led him away. I didn't bother following. I certainly wasn't about to behave like some little lapdog, trailing in her wake, and Gavin seemed to have forgotten my existence anyway.

I sipped my drink and wandered over to the nearest painting. Andrea Learmouth was the featured artist in the exhibition. I had never heard of her, but her pictures were colorful enough, if a bit too abstract for my taste. I was trying to decide where the *Woman with Tiger Lilies* actually was in the enormous canvas in front of me when I became aware of someone standing a little too close to my shoulder. I looked back and a man of indeterminate age smiled at me. He reminded me of someone, but I couldn't place him.

"I see Davina is as charming as ever," he said, nodding over to where Gavin was being introduced by our hostess to the artist who was swathed in silks over a pair of distinctly tatty blue jeans.

"I've never met her before this evening," I replied, wishing I could remember where I had seen this man before. "Is she always like this then?"

"If you mean rude, overbearing and inclined to take whatever – or whoever – she wants, then, yes, most certainly."

"Have we met before?" It was out before I could stop it.

"We have indeed, although you might not remember. The evening before last."

I remembered. "You were the man I saw, and Gavin couldn't."

"Oh, he saw me all right. Just as he can see me now."

I took a quick glance and caught Gavin's eye. He was staring at us, but quickly looked back to the artist when he realized I'd seen him.

It was becoming increasingly hot in there. "But why would he pretend not to?"

"Why, indeed?"

Beads of sweat formed on my forehead. I blinked and it seemed as if the crowd was getting closer. Or maybe the room was growing smaller. My mouth felt like sandpaper and I coughed as the dryness in my throat threatened to close it altogether.

The man touched my hand. "You're shaking. There's no need. Not now. Not ever."

"Who are you?" I asked and into my head, an image of Gran formed. She was weeping and, at the same time, urging me to leave that place.

"My name is Alex and I have come to take you with me."

"I'm not going anywhere with you." It wasn't my imagination. The crowd was pressing in on me. Davina Court-Reynolds's cruel smile bore down on me. She lifted her arms high and the loose sleeves of her dress slipped back over her elbows. On one arm I recognized a tattoo. A stylized Odal's rune, the same Gran had etched in the notes she had left for me.

Gavin – a sad expression on his face – stood, seemingly helpless for a few moments. He raised his glass to me, drained it and threw it against the wall, where it smashed. That seemed to give a signal to the others.

The room pulsated, in and out, in and out. The champagne glass slipped through my fingers and I realized I had been drugged. That woman Davina had slipped something into my drink. Or maybe the waiter had. It didn't matter. The result was the same. I was sinking into a blackness that both welcomed and repelled me. One moment I was in the gallery and the next, out in the open, in a vast, open plain. In the distance, standing stones. We had plenty within easy reach of Salisbury, but I didn't recognize this circle. Gran's account of her demonic rape echoed in my mind. I must get away.

Cool, fresh air blew across my face. I tried to move, struggle, anything, but the drug must still be in my system. It paralyzed me so I couldn't move my arms or legs. I tried to speak. To call out, but my mouth wouldn't work. They had spread-eagled me over some kind of altar, dressed in my pants suit but my shoes were gone and my feet bare.

All around me, hooded figures chanted plainsong, their words unintelligible, some archaic language maybe, or gibberish. This must be the infamous Vril Society twenty-first-century style. Two figures – taller than the others – seemed to dominate. Each had a different symbol on their black robes. I lay helpless on the slab as they advanced toward me. Both removed their hoods as they bent over me. One I recognized as Alex. The other....

Sandrine. She hadn't aged a day since that photograph. Her cheekbones seemed even more chiseled than in the photograph, her lips black, as were her eyes, only the faintest trace of sclera to circle the all-consuming chasms of her irises and pupils.

In the flickering light from the many fiery flashlights that had been stuck in the ground encircling the altar, I had no choice but to look into her eyes. I saw the crouching dragon-like figure stir and unfurl its wings. Its eyes opened and dominated my entire vision.

The vision vanished and Sandrine straightened. Finally, I managed to move my head a fraction. My arms and legs began to tingle as feeling started to move through them. I mustn't let them see I was becoming less paralyzed by the second. If they knew I could move, they would physically restrain me.

Sandrine's voice rang out over the plain. "Your grandmother gave birth to one of our kind and tonight you will provide the womb for another. We are growing in number. Many of our kind now take power in this world. It is fitting that you shall provide for the seed of your grandmother's child."

Sandrine moved away. My whole body throbbed as the feeling returned. My blood rushed through my veins.

"Behold." Sandrine raised her arms skyward and then to the ground. "He comes."

The ground rumbled, trembled, shook. A roaring, like a pride of lions, rent the air.

"The power!" Sandrine cried over the din. "Can you feel it surge?"

The hooded figures staggered against each other, moaning, some chanting. If I was ever going to get away, now was the time. Willing my body to move, I scrambled off the altar and tripped as the ground shook. A few yards ahead, earth started to move. Great geysers of it tore out of the plain. I caught sight of Sandrine. She could have stopped me but didn't. She merely stared, her eyes penetrating me and a strange smile on her face. It unnerved me but, at that moment, the roar reached a shattering crescendo, sending me running as far and fast as I could, still battling against the numbness in my bare feet.

Something raced up behind me, taking me down, winding me. It turned me over and I stared into the physical manifestation of what I had seen in Sandrine's eyes. Now I understood why she hadn't stopped me. She didn't need to.

It wasn't a dragon and it wasn't a man. It was a hybrid of the two. Fierce amber eyes that held humanity and insanity in equal parts, long lean body, more at home on four legs than two. Clawlike hands that pawed and ripped my clothes. The hint of a scaly tail swished back and forth. It spoke my name in guttural tones, as if language was unfamiliar.

"Heather."

It drove away the last of the numbing drug and I gave vent to an almighty scream. I kicked it, hit out at its face. It grabbed my flailing arms and held them down. Its foul breath left a residue on my cheeks so that I retched.

And then the worst pain tore through me.

It was over in seconds, but the mental violation would never be finished. I lay on the soft grass, and the earth settled once more as I bled into it. Gradually the chanting faded into the distance. I must have fallen unconscious because, when I came to, I was alone. Dawn was on the horizon and a smell of sulfur lingered in the air.

I struggled to my feet and clutched what remained of my clothes around me. My hands trembled uncontrollably. The zip had gone on my trousers where the creature had wrenched them down over my thighs. Great slashes in the material meant they barely provided any cover. I tugged my ruined jacket around me as best I could and stared around me. Nothing looked familiar but somewhere there would be a road and I would find it. Somehow, I would find my way home.

★   ★   ★

A police patrol car picked me up and took me to a hospital where they examined me, cleaned me up, and decided I needed to stay in. It turned out I was eighty or more miles from home in a place I had never even heard of. I had no phone or identification on me, and it was at least thirty-six hours before I was sane enough to tell them who I was and where I lived. When they first admitted me, they determined that my injuries were consistent with having been the victim of a severe sexual attack. But when they found evidence of some kind of ritual – in the form of runes that had been painted on my chest and legs – they started to treat me as a potential nutcase. Maybe the sex had been consensual, after all?

Doctors came and went. Their interminable questions droned on. At least one was a psychiatrist.

I insisted I wanted an abortion. They said it was too early to determine if I was pregnant or not. I told them I knew I was. I could feel it. They said that was impossible. I told them if we waited any longer, it would be too late; the creature inside me wouldn't allow itself to be aborted. They looked as if they wanted to section me.

And so it went on for days. Now, finally, they've done the test. It will be positive. I know that. I also know the creature will not allow itself to be aborted. It has transmitted that to me in some fine order. I have no idea what it will do, but it will put up a fight.

But it mustn't be born. There must not be any more of them than already exist. It's only by the chosen ones like me resisting, refusing to be hosts for these creatures, that we can have any hope of stopping them. There is one thing I can say about being a host for one I shall call Vril. Your perception is vastly increased. Oh yes, make no mistake, the Vril exist. They are not human and never have been. They are indeed a race of super-beings and their natural habitat is way underground. They use humans to do their bidding and to extend both their influence and their race, implanting their seed to parasitically live off the human host until they are ready to be born and taken back to their subterranean home.

And there are thousands of them. Some, like Sandrine and Alex, Davina, Glennister and the others Gran and I encountered, assimilate easily into the world. They may act differently than the norm. Perhaps more arrogant and self-opinionated than the rest of us and, if you look deep into their eyes, you will see the strange creature lurking there – the manifestation of their fatherhood. I also learned Mum wasn't chosen because she was too closely related to Gran. These things skip at least one generation before they return to hurt a family.

*　　*　　*

I am scheduled to have the abortion in a few days. The doctors initially seemed inclined to wait longer, to see if I changed my mind. Now though, I notice the furrows in their brows, the look of disbelief that they don't quite manage to hide in time. I have to watch every word I say, even every thought, in so far as the creature inside me will let me. I must remember that I am dealing with practical medical professionals who are unused to handling a woman who has been raped by a super-being. They keep me alone in a side ward, which is a good thing. It stops me from upsetting the normal mothers. And all the while the thing grows inside me, my belly already looking far bigger than it should after the couple of weeks since I was impregnated.

Mum doesn't know about any of this. I have no idea how to tell her. She saw the letter Gran wrote me and went very quiet. Two days later she announced she was going on a cruise with a friend of hers and would be away a month. I hope it does her good. She doesn't deserve all the heartache. By the time she returns, it will be all over. One way or the other. Time enough then for her to deal with it.

*　　*　　*

The day has dawned. They will come for me at any moment, and the thing inside knows it. They did a scan on me yesterday and another one today. They've been doing them daily since they brought the date of the abortion forward from two weeks to just a few days. On each occasion, the specialty nurse checks and rechecks the results, and, at first, she called in the consultant. Now he comes with her automatically. I see the looks on their faces as they try not to show how horrified they are. I pity them having to deal with that thing when they remove it. At this early stage of pregnancy, it should be a simple vacuuming operation. Not in my case.

They don't tell me much, and I don't ask. I probably know more about my condition than they do and that isn't right, is it?

I hear them. Voices in the corridor outside. The door opens. They've brought a trolley. I don't suppose they want to take any chances that I might cut and run. They probably want this thing out of me almost as much as I do. It will put up a fight. Of that I am in no doubt. And it will stop at nothing to live. Even if it kills me. But I have to do it. I must do whatever I can to stop it being born.

They have affixed some restraints to my arms and legs. I question this. Surely this isn't usual? They tell me it's for my own protection, but then they look away and I wonder...

In the distance, but moving closer, I see a light and know only I can see it. Someone is standing there. He is wearing a World War II RAF uniform and I recognize him. Great-Uncle George. He moves to stand next to me and puts his hand on my belly. The creature within me lashes out but only for a second. And I wonder again....

My great-uncle speaks. Am I the only one who hears him? "I will hold it as long as I can," he says. No one reacts. Not even me.

They wheel me down the corridor and we turn a corner, my uncle beside me. They are taking me into an operating theater.

Everyone is wearing masks. No one speaks. The anesthetist inserts a needle into the cannula in my arm.

The creature inside me lurches.

AUTHOR'S NOTE

As Heather discovered, the Vril Society did indeed exist in Germany and was inspired by a novel called *The Coming Race* published in 1875 by British novelist Lord Edward Bulwer-Lytton. He wrote of a race of super-beings, who lived in caverns deep below the earth's surface and were possessed of a force of energy called *vril*, which gave them godlike powers. The beings themselves he called *Vril-ya*. They possessed the ability to communicate with humans by connecting with them through various portals in the earth.

One of the members of this top-secret society – the existence of which was unknown until after the Second World War – was a young Adolf Hitler, whose *Mein Kampf* illustrates just how closely he adhered to the beliefs and principles of the extreme racist Vril Society. Over the next few years, other members came to include those in his closest circle, people such as Hess, Himmler and Goering.

This is a work of fiction so, naturally, I have taken liberties with the truth of this vile society. As far as I am aware, no *Vril-ya* or similar super-being has yet sown its seed in the corridors of power, even though it may, at times, seem like it. Anyone wishing to know more about its actual practices and objectives can have their curiosity satisfied by a quick search on the internet.

Inspired by his mother – Jennie, Lady Randolph Churchill – Winston Churchill was known to have had more than a passing interest in the occult, and, during the war, the British Special Operations Executive conducted a campaign of 'occult propaganda' stunts to mislead the Nazis, whose much feared SS, in particular, employed symbolism and practices associated with black magic.

The Mass Observation project was real and was revived in the

1980s, persisting to this day. It all began as the brainchild of two young men in 1937. Ordinary people from all walks of life documented their daily lives and wrote reports on specific topics designated by the archivists. The result was an amazing collection of diaries and daily observations – a number of which have been collated and published in book form. Of these, probably the most famous was written by their most prolific contributor – Nella Last – an ordinary housewife from Barrow in Furness, Cumbria. Her diaries – *Nella Last's War*, *Nella Last's Peace* and *Nella Last in the 1950s* – make fascinating reading. Victoria Wood wrote and starred as Nella in a film based on those diaries called *Housewife, 49* – the pseudonym the real Nella used.

The Mass Observation Archive is stored in the University of Sussex and is open to the public. Further information can be found on their website, massobs.org.uk.

Finally, that old Gracie Fields song – *The Thing-Ummy-Bob*, written by Gordon Thompson and David Heneker – was actually released in 1942, but I couldn't resist quoting from it here – a few months early! A quick internet search will take you to your favorite music and/or video sharing site where you can hear the 'Lancashire lass' herself performing it.

Catherine Cavendish
Southport, 2022

ACKNOWLEDGMENTS

As always, massive thanks to Don D'Auria, Nick Wells, Zoë Seabourne, Sarah Miniaci and everyone at Flame Tree Press who make working with them such a privilege and a delight. I must also single out copy editor Imogen Howson, with whom I discovered I share a mutual experience of being given Gripe Water as an infant!

My deepest thanks to my long-suffering husband, Colin, for his support and help in so many ways.

As always, my trusted friend and reader, Julia Kavan – herself a highly talented horror writer – provided much-appreciated help and guidance and prevented me from falling down some serious precipices where suspending disbelief would have been carried way too far. Every writer needs a Julia!

Thanks to Liverpool Horror Club and the horror community in general for being such an amazing, talented and diverse range of people. I wish I could name you all, but, at the risk of making serious omissions, consider yourselves well and truly thanked.

And then there's you – yes *you* – my deepest thanks for reading my story. If it's your first Catherine Cavendish, I sincerely hope it won't be your last, and if our paths have crossed before, welcome back. I hope I continue to entertain you with my own brand of weirdness for many years to come.

Here's to the next time…

Cat

FLAME TREE PRESS
FICTION WITHOUT FRONTIERS
Award-Winning Authors & Original Voices

Flame Tree Press is the trade fiction imprint of Flame Tree Publishing, focusing on excellent writing in horror and the supernatural, crime and mystery, science fiction and fantasy. Our aim is to explore beyond the boundaries of the everyday, with tales from both award-winning authors and original voices.

•

•

Join our mailing list for free short stories, new release details, news about our authors and special promotions:

flametreepress.com